The Eyes of Buddha

JOHN BALL

The Eyes of Buddha

JOHN BALL

PERENNIAL LIBRARY
Harper & Row, Publishers
New York, Cambridge, Philadelphia, San Francisco
London, Mexico City, São Paulo, Singapore, Sydney

A hardcover edition of this book was published by Little, Brown & Company. It is here reprinted by arrangement with the author.

THE EYES OF BUDDHA. Copyright © 1976 by John Ball. All rights reserved. Printed in the United States of America. No part of this book may be used or reproduced in any manner whatsoever without written permission except in the case of brief quotations embodied in critical articles and reviews. For information address Dominick Abel Literary Agency, Inc., 498 West End Avenue, New York, N.Y. 10024. Published simultaneously in Canada by Fitzhenry & Whiteside Limited, Toronto.

First PERENNIAL LIBRARY edition published 1985.

Library of Congress Cataloging in Publication Data

Ball, John Dudley, 1911–
   The eyes of Buddha.

   Reprint. Originally published: 1st ed. Boston : Little, Brown, c1976.
   I. Title.
[PS3552.A455E9   1985]   813'.54   84-48577
ISBN 0-06-080751-2 (pbk.)

85   86   87   88   89   10   9   8   7   6   5   4   3   2   1

*For Yoichi Hiraoka, in appreciation of
his magnificent music, and enduring friendship*

Author's Note

The preparation of this book was greatly helped by the unstinting cooperation of the Pasadena, California, Police Department, of which Mr. Virgil Tibbs is a member. From Chief Robert H. McGowan on down, major assistance was given by dozens of members of the Pasadena department. I hereby extend my warmest thanks and appreciation to them all, in particular to those officers with whom I was privileged to work in the field.

Technical assistance of a high order was generously given by the forensic dentist Dr. Philip Peck, D.D.S.

Contant advice and guidance was provided by Captains William Wilson, John Marshall, Ray Cockel, and William Lewis of Pasadena, and by the Los Angeles County Coroner's office.

My thanks are also extended to Mr. Tyler Tanaka, President of Japan-Orient Tours, whose unsurpassed knowledge and abilities have made it possible for me to reach certain very remote destinations in the Far East.

Lastly, I must note the unending patience of Sergeant

Chris Hagerty, Sergeant Jerry Ferguson, and Agent Gary Bennett of the Public Affairs Division of the Pasadena Police. No problem was ever too difficult for them, no question too trivial to merit less than their full attention. Gentlemen, thank you one and all.

JOHN BALL

The Eyes of Buddha

1

FROM TIME TO TIME, even during the month of February, the city of Pasadena can turn up a gem of a day. When that happens the fabled beauty of California emerges once again and not even the ugly freeway scars gashed across the landscape detract from the stark grandeur of the San Gabriel Mountains that thrust upward a few miles north of the civic center. On such days the air is sharply clear and infused with the tonic of spring, enough to send wanderlust soaring and to fire latent ambitions with new life.

Scoutmaster Bob Larson felt it fully as he led his troop northward through Oak Grove Park toward the Jet Propulsion Laboratory. True woods were almost impossible to find within a reasonable distance, but the area north of the developed section of the park was a very satisfactory place for basic scouting activities; it showed little evidence of ever having been molested by either the shovel or the bulldozer, and quite frequently exciting discoveries concerning the presence of wild life could be made.

The occasional few rusting cans or other forms of civilization's debris were, by the unspoken rules of the game,

3

bravely ignored. If some of the younger members of the troop noticed them at all, they assumed that they had been left behind by the earliest pioneers whose wagon trains had crossed that very terrain.

As he led the line of boys who were his temporary responsibility, Bob kept a sharp eye watching for any rusting pieces of metal that might catch an ankle, or brambles uncomfortably close to the trail. His work as an electronics salesman gave him little exposure to the out-of-doors and he was at times acutely aware that his rotund figure did not fit the image of the lean and powerful woodsman. But he was still one of the most respected scoutmasters in the Pasadena area because he was well-versed in camping techniques and in leading hikes through various types of country. He had once had dreams of becoming a member of the sheriff's Mountain Rescue Team, but his age and lack of athletic agility had defeated that ambition. As a scoutmaster he was a definite success, and the walls of his modest den displayed several plaques that he had been awarded at various times for his work in scouting.

When he reached the base of a small rise, he held up his hand. "Wait here," he directed. "I want to check what's ahead." There was only a very remote chance of finding a rattlesnake at that time of year, but he had killed one close to the same spot two years before. That incident had made him extra cautious for the sake of the boys.

It took him only a few seconds to top the rise and to begin his inspection. It was careful and detailed, which was why he saw something a short distance away that otherwise might have escaped his notice. Signaling with his arms once more to be sure that the boys stayed back, he went down the other side to make certain that he had not been mistaken.

As he approached his discovery he wished to heaven that he had been. He pulled a handkerchief from his pocket and held it wadded in front of his nose as he forced himself to walk up to a position not more than ten feet from the body that was lying on the ground.

It was a horrible sight. At one time the thing that lay there had been a young woman; there was enough of the face left, as he looked at the exposed profile view, to suggest that she might have been personable and pretty. Now there was a swarm of flies and a very distinct odor. Quite suddenly Bob had no further interest whatever in becoming a mountain rescue man: too much of the time the work consisted in the recovery of human remains, and he would not have touched what was on the ground before him for any consideration whatever.

He turned his back and silently thanked the Lord that the boys had been spared what he had just seen. When he rejoined his troop he once more assumed command and tried not to let anything show. "We are going to turn around here," he said. "I have to go back for an important reason. Then we will continue our hike."

It was a disappointment and the boys clearly did not understand. Bob nodded toward his seventeen-year-old patrol leader and tried to convey the idea that he was serious. In that he succeeded; the patrol leader, who was only two steps away from eagle scout status, and who remained active for that reason, gave a commanding gesture with his left arm. "Let's go," he directed. There was a little grumbling as the line reversed, but the boys obeyed. Within a minute they were far enough away for Bob to pull out the small walkie-talkie he always carried whenever he took his troop out. He raised the antenna and established communications.

"Call the Pasadena Police and have someone meet me out here," he said. "I've just discovered a body close to the trail and judging by a first look, it's been here for some time."

Officer "Buzz" Ostrom was on patrol in his white Matador when the call came in; he picked up his mike and notified the dispatcher that he would respond. Within five minutes he pulled into a parking slot, passed the word that he was leaving his car, and set out to find his contact. He started up the most likely trail at a good pace; two girls who were coming down took due note of his blond good looks and said, "Hi!"

"Hi," Ostrom returned, and continued on his way. Some minutes later he saw a line of scouts coming down toward him, obviously unaware of the discovery that had been made. He passed them with a friendly greeting and then looked toward Bob Larson, who gave him an answering nod.

The patrol leader had no further doubts that something was up as soon as he saw Ostrom's uniform. He hung behind as the rest of the troop filed past, hoping to get in on what he knew would be a highly interesting conversation. Larson settled that in a hurry. "I won't need you, Jack," he said. "Please take charge of the troop until I get back."

Reluctantly the patrol leader moved to obey. As soon as he was gone Larson nodded toward the upper end of the trail. "I can show you where it is," he offered.

"Good. Lead the way, please."

Ostram had received the first Medal of Valor that the department had awarded, but the sight of the thing that Larson had found forced him to tighten the muscles of his abdomen in order to keep his stomach under control. He unslung his own walkie-talkie and reported. "I have a female body, now partially decomposed. The deceased was a Caucasian, age eighteen to thirty I would guess, dark hair. Slender figure. The features are partly gone and the body is about half buried, from the waist on down."

He stopped for a moment to think. He remembered clearly the poster that had been on the bulletin board for more than a year and some of the details of the case that had entailed one of the most exhaustive investigations the department had ever made. It was just possible that the solution that had eluded so many highly competent people for so long might be at hand. He switched on his set once more. "Ostrom," he said.

"Go ahead."

"On the body here in Oak Grove Park. It's in a desolate area, but quite close to the trail. Possibly it was concealed and some of the cover has now blown away."

"There were strong winds reported in that area last night."

"I know." Ostrom took a deep breath before he dropped his bomb. "From what I can see, it could be Doris Friedkin."

The dispatcher lost no time in relaying that information to the homicide personnel on duty. Lieutenant Dick Smith, who took the call, in turn notified the office of the Los Angeles County Coroner who would have the responsibility for picking up the body after the preliminary on-the-scene investigation had been completed.

A sergeant and three agents left for the park in a specially equipped car. Two more white patrol units were diverted to the area to keep away the curious who, at such a time, seemed to rise out of the ground. When that had been done, Smith phoned Captain Ray Cockel at his home.

"We have a body in Oak Grove Park," he advised. "Up toward the northern end. The officer on the scene reports it a female Caucasian, possibly in her early twenties, apparently dead for some time. Dark hair."

"Slender figure?"

"Yes, I checked on that."

Cockel drew a deep breath over the line. "It could be the Friedkin girl."

"Yes; Ostrom, who's there, suggested that. He reports that the features are partly gone, but as of now, it's a definite possibility."

That was enough to trigger a full response from the captain. "Call Virgil and get him on it," he directed. "I know it's Sunday, but locate him if you can. Keep me informed. If it is Friedkin's daughter, I'll come in immediately. And notify Chief McGowan."

"Yes, sir."

The possibility that the long-missing Doris Friedkin might have been found was electric; the entire duty staff knew of it within a matter of minutes. One of the female officers on the desk phoned Agent Jerry Ferguson at his home to give him the news. Ferguson, who headed the public information unit, left almost immediately for his office. If indeed the body proved to be that of the Friedkin girl, then he would have a major story on his hands and he would have to be ready to deal with it.

At Oak Grove Park Sergeant Bill Orr was in command. He helped to unload the necessary cameras and other equipment while he instructed the men who had come in the white Matadors concerning the area he wanted kept clear. Children were already beginning to gather and Orr had to chase them politely away.

When everything was ready, he picked up his own load and started up the trail to where he knew Ostrom would be waiting for him. The task he had before him would be far from pleasant, but he kept that thought out of his mind. He was a dedicated police officer, but that fact did not alter his natural feelings and there was nothing that he disliked more than having to deal with cadavers that had been too long in the water or were otherwise deteriorated. But he went steadily on.

It took a few minutes to reach the point where Ostrom was waiting just before the crest of the rise. "You'd better prepare yourself for this one," Buzz warned.

Orr was noted for being businesslike. "How bad is it?" he asked.

"Bad enough. There's some decomposition, and an odor. She was a pretty girl when she was alive, I would guess, but she isn't anymore. I can't understand why she wasn't found before now, or why no animals have disturbed her."

Ostrom's handset came alive. "Is Orr there?"

"Just arrived."

"Anything yet on an I.D.?"

"Negative."

Orr reached out and took the walkie-talkie. "What's the word on Virgil?" he asked.

"The watch commander located him. ETA about half an hour."

"Good," Orr said, and ended the transmission.

As soon as the sergeant reached the top of the rise and

took in the scene before him, he realized that any footprint evidence would be long gone. There had been rain within the past two days; after that a strong Santa Ana wind had swept the surface of the ground and drifted loose soil against the base of the few hardy shrubs. It occurred to Orr that not even Inspector Napoleon Bonaparte of Australia, the supreme tracker, would have been able to read anything there.

The preliminary work was carefully and thoroughly done. Pictures were taken from almost every available angle while the whole nearby area was scoured for such possible clues as a shred of cloth caught on a bramble or a small object of any kind that might have been dropped. Even a cigarette butt would have been carefully preserved, but none were found.

"We'll have to go over all of this with rakes," Orr said. "There's been enough wind to bury things two or three inches deep."

Ostrom used his radio to send for the necessary additional equipment. As he finished speaking, another man came over the rise and started down toward the scene of the investigation.

He was unexpectedly well dressed in coat and tie; his shoes, despite the trail dust, still gave evidence of careful polishing. His slacks were of the best quality and the subdued dark blazer he wore was perfectly cut to fit his somewhat slender figure. On Colorado Boulevard he would have been ideally attired; in the semiwild northern section of Oak Grove Park he was slightly incongruous.

Orr went over to greet him. "A pleasant Sunday morning to you, Virgil. We have the partially decomposed corpse of a young woman and so far not a damn thing else to go on. How much have you been given?"

"Very little. Just that a scoutmaster found the body and that the deceased superficially answers the description of Doris Friedkin. Anything new on that?"

"No, the table is still open for bets. You quote the odds."

Virgil Tibbs did not respond to that. He nodded an informal greeting to the others, then he walked over and stood quite still while he studied the body that lay partly uncovered on the ground. There had been no visible attempt to dig a grave; it appeared rather that the body had been simply put down on the ground and then partially covered with debris and loose soil. Why the head and arms had been left exposed was not quite clear. The features had deteriorated and the hair was partially gone, but it might still be possible to produce a retouched photograph that would give some idea of how she had looked in life.

Orr noted the time and made an accurate deduction. "Sorry to have pulled you out of church like this," he said.

Tibbs relaxed for a moment. "Fortunately, it was just before they passed the plate. Have you got all of the shots you need?"

"More than fifty — both black and white and color."

"Then I'll take a look. I'd appreciate some gloves."

While a pair was being produced Virgil took off his coat and tie, hung them on a convenient bush, and tied a clean handkerchief over his face. These things done, he pulled a pair of rubber gloves over his dark hands and got down on his knees beside the body.

It was not agreeable work, but the job of a homicide specialist seldom is. The normal first consideration, whether or not life was extinct, did not even arise. With a thin steel tape Tibbs took measurements of the exposed portions of the body and then with his gloved hands pulled back the remaining flesh to examine the teeth. He gave close attention to the ears and collected some of the loose strands of hair in a clear plastic envelope. After that he set to work with his hand to exhume the still covered part of the corpse. He was busy doing that when two men arrived from the coroner's office carrying a wicker container and a thin rubber sheet.

Virgil got to his feet and nodded that the body could be removed. "I'd like a complete work-up on this one," he said. "Cause of death, the likelihood of sexual assault, anything about the time of death — everything you can get."

The coroner's man was confident. "Whatever there is to find, they'll find it," he promised. With the help of his partner he carefully wrapped the body in the rubber sheet and lifted it into the carrier.

It was early twilight before the homicide investigation team finally left the scene. A great deal of careful raking had turned up nothing and a widespread detailed examination of the surrounding terrain for any kind of a clue at all had proven sterile. Also, unfortunately, there had not been anything on or near to the body that gave any immediate information as to the identity of the dead girl. The possibility that she had been the long-missing Doris Friedkin was still open.

When Virgil Tibbs returned to the Pasadena Police Headquarters, he was given a message to call Chief Robert McGowan at his home. It came as no surprise, in fact Virgil had been expecting it. He dialed through to the unlisted number and the chief himself was on the line in a matter of seconds. "How do you see things at this point?" McGowan asked.

Tibbs knew what he meant. "Superficially, there is a

resemblance to Doris Friedkin: the height, color of hair, and figure all fit. The features were far enough gone, I wouldn't care to make a guess one way or the other based on the pictures we have. And I wouldn't advise letting any of the family see the body."

"Anything else?"

"Yes, but very preliminary. On my way to the park I stopped in here for a moment to pick up the Friedkin girl's dental chart. There were two fillings that could correspond and two that don't, but they could have been done during the past year. The big thing against it is the odds: having Doris Friedkin turn up again, here in Pasadena, under such circumstances, and after more than a year, is a helluva long shot."

"Yes," the chief agreed, "it certainly is. But I'm going to alert the Friedkin family anyway before they hear anything on the newscasts. How did she die, by the way?"

"She was murdered," Tibbs reported. "I'd say that's pretty close to certain. But if she was killed as I suspect that she was, then we have a very strange one going here. You can take my word for that."

2

A T EIGHT FIFTEEN THE FOLLOWING MORNING a chauffeur-driven limousine deposited Herbert Friedkin in front of the Pasadena Police Station. He entered the lobby and turned toward the counter where two uniformed female officers were posted to assist the public. "Yes, sir?" one of them asked.

"Chief McGowan's office?"

"Through the double doors to your left, sir. Halfway down the corridor there's an elevator: take it to the fourth floor."

"Thank you."

Friedkin turned and did as directed. The vinyl-tiled corridor was strictly utilitarian and heavily used; halfway to the elevator he encountered a motorcycle officer impressively big in his uniform and helmet, his sunglasses in his hand.

"Morning," the policeman said, with the suggestion of a nod.

"Good morning," Friedkin answered. The words were empty; his mind was elsewhere.

When he stepped off the elevator on the fourth floor, he

14

found the kind of built-in quiet that goes with most executive areas. He recognized it immediately; he had spent much of his life in similar surroundings. Without hesitation he pushed through another set of double doors and found himself in a fairly long area divided into a row of offices on his right, each with a secretary out front, and with two larger offices on his left. He turned that way automatically since he was long accustomed to dealing with only the top people wherever he went.

Mrs. Diane Stone, the chief's secretary, had been forewarned by the desk downstairs and was waiting. "Can I help you, sir?" she asked.

"I'm Herbert Friedkin. Is Chief McGowan in?"

The first three words told her everything she needed to know. "Please come in, Mr. Friedkin. The chief is in the building and he'll be up shortly." She showed her guest into the office and indicated a comfortable seating arrangement in the corner. "How do you take your coffee?" she asked.

While she was speaking, McGowan came in behind her. Since he was six feet five he was impressive, but he knew how to put people at their ease. He shook hands and then sat down where he could face his visitor. Since he had already read Friedkin's mood, he came directly to the point. "You want to know if we have anything more definite concerning the body that was recovered yesterday in Oak Grove Park," he said.

Herbert Friedkin was not a man who commonly showed his emotions, but he was under an exceptional strain. "Mrs. Friedkin and I haven't had a moment's sleep all night," he admitted. "The doctor is seeing her now. Perhaps you can understand . . ."

McGowan cut him mercifully short with a nod. "I most

certainly can — and I do. As of this minute, I haven't anything you don't already know, but your daughter's dental charts have been delivered to the coroner's office. I spoke to Dr. Noguchi personally less than ten minutes ago and asked that the examination be expedited as much as possible."

"That was extremely kind of you, and I appreciate it, but if I may view the body . . ."

He was interrupted by Mrs. Stone who came in with a coffee service. As she put it down, McGowan gently shook his head. "The body is in Los Angeles," he said. He carefully refrained from adding that it was in no condition to be viewed if it could possibly be avoided.

"Then may I wait here?" Friedkin asked.

"I was just going to suggest that — it should only be a matter of minutes."

Friedkin relaxed a little. "I believe that we've met before on one or two occasions."

"Yes, sir — that's correct. At a meeting of the Tournament of Roses Committee, as I recall, and at the hospital when your new wing was dedicated."

Friedkin picked up his coffee cup. "This is a good moment, Chief McGowan, to express again my profound thanks for the exhaustive investigation your people made of Doris's disappearance. I know it was an all-out effort."

"They ran down every lead, no matter how doubtful, to its absolute end," McGowan told him. "They even interviewed the crystal gazers and clairvoyants who claimed to have something to tell. Sometimes those people pick up bits of information on the street."

Mrs. Stone appeared once more. "Chief Winders is in," she advised.

"Ask him to join us. And see if Captain Cockel is free."

Deputy Chief Tom Winders appeared on crutches with one leg in a cast. Friedkin stood up to greet him and asked, "What happened?"

"A motorcycle accident — unfortunately not in the line of duty." Winders shook hands as he was introduced.

A few seconds later Captain Cockel came into the large office. Relatively slender, he appeared somewhere in his mid-forties and despite a controlled manner, his eyes had a snap to them that suggested considerable inner fire. The thick file on the chief's desk he recognized at once from its size; as head of the Investigative Division he had been closely acquainted with almost every aspect of the Friedkin case. He shook hands briefly and then drew up a chair to participate in the discussion.

Friedkin began it. "Gentlemen, you know, of course, why I'm here. I've just told Chief McGowan how much I'm aware of, and appreciate, the hundreds of man-hours you put into trying to trace my daughter. It was more than anyone could reasonably expect or ask."

"That's our job," Winders responded. "We only regret that up to now we haven't been successful."

"You could have something definite within the next few minutes."

"Yes, it's possible, but after more than a year, the odds are all against it."

Friedkin looked at the telephone on the chief's desk as though by doing so he could make it ring. When it remained still, he switched to another topic. "You have a man I've read about," he said. "A Negro detective."

There were several members of the Pasadena police who answered that description, but the chief didn't attempt to be coy. "You mean Virgil Tibbs," he suggested. "Our best homicide man."

Friedkin finished his coffee. "If what I've heard is true, he must be quite extraordinary."

"He is," McGowan agreed. "We're rather proud of him."

Friedkin clasped his hands and the multiple tensions that he had been so carefully holding within himself came to the surface. "Since Doris vanished," he said, "neither my wife nor I have had one comfortable night's sleep. Every time the phone rings we jump, and we have listed our number — just in case someone might wish to reach us with some information."

He stopped and reshaped his thoughts. "I realize that we may get the answer this morning, but I agree that the odds are against it. If the girl found in the park isn't Doris, I wonder if you would consider something. Granted that the investigation you have already made was professional and exhaustive, would it be possible to have this Mr. Tibbs take one more look?"

There was an awkward silence, spawned by the fact that no one was anxious to respond to that. Friedkin sensed it, and went on. "I'm not proposing anything further at public expense, but if you could possibly spare Mr. Tibbs for the purpose, I'll underwrite his time and expenses completely. Without limit."

Bob McGowan realized that the financier was reaching for straws but he did not blame him — the man had been through hell. And being a multimillionaire didn't make him any less sensitive to intense emotional pressure. He framed a diplomatic answer. "Before I could respond to that, Mr. Friedkin, I would have to consult the mayor and then the city manager."

Friedkin looked again at the telephone and waited several seconds. Then he chose his own words carefully. "I know both of those gentlemen very well," he said. "Therefore I took the liberty of asking them if I might approach you on the matter. I got identical answers: you are running the Police Department and they will stand behind any decision you choose to make."

Bob McGowan was slightly irritated by that, but he was careful not to let it show. He glanced at Winders and saw that his deputy shared his feeling. Then he forced himself to remember all that Herbert Friedkin had done for the City of Pasadena, even if not directly for his own department. That entitled him, perhaps, to throw his weight around a little. And his only child had vanished just before a climactic moment in her relatively young life.

When he drew breath to speak, he saw that Friedkin had something more to say.

"I'm fully aware that Virgil Tibbs is a full time professional police officer committed to your department, but I believe that you once did make him available to the Wells Police Department in South Carolina. I have already tried private investigative agencies — unsuccessfully. Let me make it clear that if you can grant me this extraordinary favor, I will sign a blank check for it — literally. Not only for Mr. Tibbs's salary and expenses — he is welcome to employ whatever help he needs to assist him. Whatever the tab is I'll pay it gladly even if not one shred of new evidence turns up. At least Mrs. Friedkin and I will know that the additional effort has been made. He will have full authority to make use of all of the resources that I have available: any of the aircraft: my yacht if he needs it. Literally everything that I possess."

Mrs. Stone appeared quietly in the doorway. When the chief nodded, she came in and handed him a slip of paper. He read it and then looked into Friedkin's anxious, questioning face. "It wasn't Doris," he said.

"That's absolutely definite?"

"Yes. We don't know yet who she was, but positively she was not your missing daughter."

Friedkin shook his head in an attempt to clear his thoughts. "She was someone's," he said.

McGowan nodded his agreement. "I'm afraid that this new case may keep Mr. Tibbs fully occupied for a while."

He saw the look of stabbing defeat on Friedkin's face and made a decision. "However, since the case of your daughter is still open, and since this new situation is sure to reawaken it, I will suggest to Virgil that he drop by to see you. It is possible that he may think of something that all the rest of us have missed so far."

3

I T WAS THE CUSTOM in the Friedkin home to take after-
dinner coffee in the living room in front of the fireplace.
By tradition this was a time of relaxation and despite
the heavy shadow that had hung over them for so long,
both Herbert Friedkin and his wife were careful to continue
this genteel practice. It was a small anchor that helped in
some measure to keep their lives from going completely
adrift.

Over the years it had also developed into a time of confidences; a time for saying the things that might be awkward
or difficult to reveal. Grace Friedkin was particularly sensitive to this facet of the coffee hour and feared what it might
bring. Someday, she was certain, there would be news of
Doris. She had already reconciled herself to the fact that it
would be bad news; each day that went by meant that the
chances of hearing from her daughter were lessened. If her
husband had learned anything during the day that would
erase their last hopes, it would be while they were having
coffee that he would tell her.

As she sat down and composed herself, she knew that her
husband had something on his mind, but she did not sense
disaster. With a sure instinct for the right thing to do she

chose to remain silent in order to let him open the conversation.

He did. "I had a meeting this morning with Chief McGowan of the police department and some of his top people. They were most cooperative. You know why I went there."

His wife nodded. "The young woman who was found in the park."

"Yes, and let me put your mind at rest immediately, dear — it wasn't Doris."

Grace Friedkin began to breathe normally once more. "I didn't think that it would be," she said, "but I'm very glad that you made sure."

"While I was there, I discussed something else with them. Perhaps you've heard that they have a detective on their staff who has an unusual reputation. His name is Tibbs — Virgil Tibbs. I asked the chief if it might be possible for this man to ... re-examine the evidence. Since the private agencies haven't produced a thing, I naturally thought of this expert that they have. He's their homicide specialist."

"Do you think then ..."

Friedkin quickly shook his head. "No, I don't think that Doris is dead. But unless another murder crops up somewhere...."

"Another murder?"

"It wasn't said so directly, but I'm sure the young woman who was found in the park was a murder victim."

Grace Friedkin sat forward. "How awful. And it will take all of his time, won't it, until it's cleared up?"

The sound of the front doorbell penetrated into the room.

"Apparently not," Friedkin answered, "because Chief

McGowan told me that he would ask him to stop by. I believe that may be him now."

Something less than a minute later Virgil Tibbs was shown into the room. As he came forward with quiet assurance, certain things about him struck Grace Friedkin immediately: the excellent quality and fit of the suit he had on, the good taste of his tie, and the manner in which he was conducting himself. She guessed that he was somewhere in his mid-thirties. It surprised her somewhat that he was a Negro — or was she supposed to say now that he was black? She didn't know, but Negro was a dignified word and she preferred it.

Friedkin rose and went forward to greet his guest. "Mr. Tibbs?" he said, making the implied question a statement. He shook hands and then presented Tibbs to his wife. "Do sit down," he invited. "We're just having coffee — please join us."

As he spoke a maid came in with an additional coffee service. During the next five minutes the social amenities were observed and all of the proper things were said. When the ritual had been concluded, and Tibbs was comfortably seated with a cup of coffee beside him, his host brought up the subject that was in the forefront of his mind.

"Mr. Tibbs," he began, "as you undoubtedly already know, something over a year ago our daughter Doris disappeared under rather striking circumstances. From then until now we have not received one crumb of real evidence concerning what happened to her."

"I'm quite familiar with the case," Tibbs told him.

"Then you're aware that your department made an exhaustive investigation at the time that she vanished."

Virgil nodded. "That's correct, sir. And I might add that the people who worked on the case were highly competent — I don't believe that they missed anything."

"I'm completely convinced of that, Mr. Tibbs, and I told Chief McGowan so. I asked to meet with you because I know something of your reputation and past achievements."

For a moment Tibbs seemed almost embarrassed; then he deliberately changed the topic. "I understand that you've asked to have me assigned to review the case once more."

"If you have no serious objection."

Tibbs locked his fingers together and pressed them tightly. "Mr. Friedkin, I spent most of last night and much of today going through the case file once more. I could not find any loose ends whatever; everything available at the time was followed up literally to the limit."

Friedkin turned businesslike. "I believe the key phrase there is 'at the time.' Something may have surfaced since. Understand that I'm not asking for this at public expense; I'll foot the bill. I absolutely don't care how much you may find it necessary to spend and I don't wish an itemized accounting — there is no need for one. You will have carte blanche to make use of any and all of the resources I can put at your disposal. If you want to engage people to help you, I'll have them put on my payroll immediately."

He stopped and changed his tone. "Mr. Tibbs, I'm completely aware of the fact that you are a professional police officer, and one with special responsibilities. To put it plainly. I've asked to borrow you, somewhat in the same way that you were once made available to that southern police chief. What was his name?"

"Gillespie."

"I remember now. I, too, am asking for your help as a

24

policeman. My role is simply to underwrite the additional cost."

For a few seconds it was quiet. Virgil Tibbs drank his coffee and let the atmosphere settle in. When he was fully ready, he responded. "Mr. Friedkin, and Mrs. Friedkin, I can appreciate very keenly the anguish that you have both been going through for so long. And also the terrible uncertainty."

"It's with us every hour of every day," his hostess said. She bent over and refilled his coffee cup.

"Thank you." Virgil drank a little of the fresh coffee and then came to the point. "If I am to undertake a new investigation, especially after so long a time, then there is only one approach I can use — I will have to dig deeper than anyone has before in the hope that by so doing, something new may come to light. This means, among other things, that I will have to invade your privacy, perhaps to an intolerable degree. Have you ever gone through an audit of your personal income tax?"

"Yes," Freidkin answered, "and some parts of it approached an outrage."

"I know, sir, but what I may have to do could be worse still. I may require information that you would greatly prefer to keep to yourself, such as minutiae of a very intimate nature concerning your daughter. It's a little like exploring for oil: the easy finds have all been made. To get anywhere now, I will have to dig down very deep into the shale."

Friedkin listened carefully and then spoke. "If you can find our daughter, or establish definitely what has happened to her, we will cheerfully endure whatever may be necessary. Please credit me with enough intelligence to understand your purpose, and to support it as fully as I am able."

"Then, sir, there are certain things I will require to get started. I have a homicide on my hands, but I will also try to do what I can for you."

Friedkin reached behind him and picked up paper and a pen. "Yes?" he asked.

"A letter from you, on your personal letterhead, authorizing me complete access to your daughter's medical records. This is to be addressed to her doctor. Another letter to her dentist and individual letters addressed by name to any other medical people she may have consulted, including gynecologists, psychiatrists, and her orthodontist if she used one."

"I can assure you," Friedkin said, "that she had no need of a psychiatrist; she is, or was, a very healthy, normal young woman."

"Some people who fit that description have been known to seek help to stay that way," Tibbs told him. "I will also want authorization to obtain full disclosure from her minister or rabbi, her optometrist, and everyone else who ever assisted her professionally in any way."

"She never had to wear glasses at any time," Mrs. Friedkin volunteered.

"We did give full statements to the police when they interviewed us," Friedkin added. "And they came many times."

"Thank you." Tibbs seemed unmoved by the comments. "I will also need written permission to have access to your incoming mail. How did you provide financially for your daughter?"

"She had some money of her own. Then, when she was old enough, I gave her the authority to write checks on our household accounts. She never abused that privilege."

"I would assume that, sir, but I will need to have access to all of your financial records that in any way concern her. Also, I would like to have you authorize your attorney, in writing on your letterhead, to discuss with me, fully and openly, whatever information I may require. These are my initial requests: as my investigation develops, I will probably have to make many more."

Friedkin sat quietly, thinking. He looked over at his wife and then spoke with some caution. "You certainly appear to be most thorough, Mr. Tibbs, but I realize that that is what I asked for."

Virgil remained constrained, but he did not soften his attitude. "I haven't even begun as yet, Mr. Friedkin. I have no desire to make a nuisance of myself, or worse, but I will have to know every possible thing about your daughter: what her favorite colors were, what kind of clothes she preferred, what type of underwear she normally chose."

For the first time Herbert Friedkin looked momentarily a little weary. "Isn't much of that already in the file, Mr. Tibbs?" he asked. "We answered thousands of questions — or so it seemed to us."

Virgil's voice remained even and controlled. "No, sir, unfortunately the file does not give as full a portrait of Doris as possible. For example: there is not one word about her tastes in music, and that could be quite important. Can she play any instrument? Does she have a good ear, or is she one of those people who enjoy music immensely but who cannot sing a note themselves?"

Grace Friedkin spoke up. "I can see one thing very clearly, Mr. Tibbs, you are planning to open doors that were never looked behind before. No one did ask about her tastes in music, and I can understand that they might be important."

"You're very right about that, Mrs. Friedkin. I handled a case not long ago of a boy who ran away from home with his father's loaded gun and with a grudge against a playmate. We learned that he was a great fan of the California Angels baseball team and eventually caught up with him at the ball park. Knowing his tastes made things much easier."

The conversation stopped for several seconds. Virgil was careful to remain quiet, drinking his coffee, while his host was obviously doing some thinking. He had deliberately been firm in his requirements in order to measure the amount of genuine cooperation he could expect. The Friedkins were not people who were accustomed to being dominated.

At last Herbert Friedkin declared himself. "Mr. Tibbs, I understand your position and I subscribe to it. Therefore, I will do anything whatever that I can to assist you — that includes accepting personal inconvenience and a considerable surrender of our privacy. You can have anything that you need that I can provide — anything at all — just as long as it has a bearing on your search for Doris. And you will be the judge of that."

"Thank you," Virgil responded. "I appreciate your implied confidence very much."

He stopped speaking for a moment, but it was clear that he had something more to say. When he did resume, his voice remained even and quiet. "In view of the statement that you have just made, Mr. Friedkin, I would like to ask you an important question. Why are both you and Mrs. Friedkin so carefully withholding what could be a very vital piece of information as of right now?"

4

ERBERT FRIEDKIN GLANCED once very quickly at his wife who was lowering her head over her coffee cup; then he returned his attention to Tibbs. "I was quite unaware we were doing that," he said.

As soon as the words were out he wished fervently that he had thought more carefully before speaking; he had unwittingly told a lie and what was more, it was one that was almost certain to be found out. He tried desperately to think of something he might add that would mitigate what he had done and erase the insult to Tibbs, but his brain balked and refused to help him.

He was quite prepared to have the man whose help he so desperately wanted make his excuses and leave; but it was his good fortune that the detective was far too intelligent for that.

Instead Tibbs picked up his own coffee cup, balanced it on his knee, and then began to speak in a quiet, conversational manner. "Mr. Friedkin, in any investigation there are two basic kinds of evidence that are of great value in discovering the truth. The first is obvious: direct facts that can be fitted together to reveal significant patterns. The other, while negative, can be equally as useful. Allow me to give you an example."

He paused long enough to sip some of the coffee and to give his host time to readjust his thinking. Then he continued. "Some weeks ago a man in this city came under suspicion of a certain crime. The reasons are confidential and have no present bearing. He had a loose alibi for the time of the offense, but that meant little because perfectly good citizens are constantly in that position — out of sight of witnesses who could vouch for them if need be.

"The man in question told us that he had left his work later than usual and had hurried home to see the Monday night football game on TV. He stated that he was an enthusiastic fan and never missed a game if he could avoid it. According to his story, he arrived at his house five minutes before the opening kick-off. His wife was out for the evening, so he made himself a hasty sandwich, poured a glass of milk, and then sat down to watch the game. As it happened, the opening kick-off was returned sixty-five yards.

"Just before the half we called on him to ask him some questions. When we checked we learned that he had indeed left his work later than usual and his avid interest in football was confirmed. Also, he was able to describe the opening of the game and the long kick-off return with complete accuracy."

"That would seem solid enough," Friedkin said.

"We booked him for criminal assault, sir, and obtained a confession when one small point was brought out: there were no soiled dishes in his home. His wife had left everything immaculate and it was still that way. It was possible that he could have made a sandwich and held it in his hand, but there was no milk glass. He could not explain that simple fact, or the absence of any crumbs where he had presumably made his sandwich."

"But how was he able to describe the opening of the game?" Grace Friedkin asked.

"I mentioned that it was spectacular; it was replayed at the quarter and he saw it then."

"I grasp your point fully, Mr. Tibbs," Friedkin said. "Now what leads you to believe that we were not entirely candid with you?"

"Specifically, sir, when I stated that I would need to have access to all of your daughter's medical records, I mentioned a gynecologist and a psychiatrist in that order. You very promptly told me that she had had no need of a psychiatrist. Since I assume that she is a young woman of unquestioned character and unmarried, it would be much more likely that you would deny her need for a gynecologist first. Later, when I mentioned an optometrist, Mrs. Friedkin was very quick to state that Doris had never had any need to wear glasses."

"It is quite possible, Mr. Tibbs, for a young woman to require a gynecologist without her character being at fault."

"Granted, sir, but unfortunately our existing file, which is exhaustive, has nothing on that point at all. And health records, in cases of this kind, are of the first importance."

Once more Herbert Friedkin tried hard to think. He did not want to make a second serious mistake, but he was suddenly in a corner which he had been at great pains to avoid for more than a year.

"Mr. Tibbs," he began very carefully, "in talking with your fellow officers, I supplied every bit of information concerning Doris that seemed to me to be in any way pertinent."

Virgil did not turn a hair. "I accept that, sir, but if you will excuse my pointing it out, the data we have, while very extensive, are still inadequate — because we have yet to find her. What we have had to work with has been totally exhausted, and, as I said, by very competent people."

"Therefore you need more data."

"Yes, sir — I do."

Grace Friedkin had been listening intently. Very calmly, she entered the discussion. "Mr. Tibbs, you are obviously a most sensitive man, therefore you will appreciate that there are some things so essentially intimate and private that they are automatically . . ." She found herself at a momentary loss and she was unable to finish her sentence.

Tibbs answered her. "Mrs. Friedkin, during the time that you were carrying Doris, and while she was being delivered, you surrendered certain privileges of privacy — it was unavoidable. In exchange you and your husband received your child. I have seen many pictures of her in our files and she is beautiful. Was it worth it?"

"Indeed it was."

"Then, perhaps by once again setting aside normal considerations of restraint, with which I am certainly in sympathy, I may be able to help in restoring her to you. If that is possible."

It was still — deadly still — for some moments. Then Herbert Friedkin looked toward his wife. Between the two of them an invisible communication passed; Virgil did not see it because he was making a point of quietly finishing his coffee as he looked around the large, perfectly appointed room.

When he looked back at Friedkin, the financier had reached a decision. Having made up his mind, he did not mince words. "Mr. Tibbs, your perception has forced me into something I was determined to avoid. I won't insult you by asking that you keep this conversation as close to totally confidential as humanly possible. I assume that you will do that."

"As far as possible, sir, absolutely."

"Very well. Some weeks before her disappearance, our daughter was the innocent victim of a sexual attack. We did not report it for several very well-considered reasons."

Virgil carefully lifted part of the burden that Friedkin was carrying. "I believe that I already know them, sir," he said. "First, she is the only daughter of a very prominent family, therefore her embarrassment, and yours, would be multiplied many times over. Also, many people are led to believe that all police authorities are highly unsympathetic in rape cases. Had the crime been reported, then we would have had to have asked Doris to submit to an examination by a police physician. Subsequently, assuming that we caught the man responsible, she might have to relate the very painful details on the witness stand. Even if the case were being heard in chambers, it would still be a severe ordeal for her."

Friedkin actually seemed relieved; he nodded his head in agreement and his manner almost visibly eased. "All of that is correct, of course. I'm sorry about the police part, but it is true, nonetheless. However, that was not our principal problem."

"One that I didn't mention?"

"Yes."

"Then, sir, it seems quite possible that you may know who was responsible for the outrage."

Friedkin laid his arms carefully on the sides of his chair

and looked straight ahead as he spoke. "You are right, I do know. I am also quite aware of the frequent statement that it takes two to tango, but I would stake my life, if I'm not being overdramatic, that Doris did not give her willing consent to . . . what occurred."

He turned his head and looked Tibbs in the eye. "The man who violated her isn't worthy of the name. He is still very immature, but apparently uncontrollably passionate. He happens to be the son of one of my best and closest friends."

"Is his father aware of the circumstances?"

"No, and I have no intention of letting him find out. I think that if he knew he would cut his throat, because his son means everything to him. Why in hell the Lord gave him one like that, I don't know. The boy is intelligent, he's exceptionally handsome, and the young women throw themselves at him in droves. But he wanted the unattainable, and when he could not have it any other way . . ."

Virgil stopped him with a gesture. "I am going to interview him," he said, "but I will do my utmost to prevent his father from getting any intimation of the truth."

"I'll settle for that," Friedkin declared.

"So that this topic need not come up again, if it can be avoided, one more question: did a pregnancy result?"

"No, thank the Lord."

"At the time of her disappearance, in your opinion had Doris substantially recovered from the shock of her experience?"

"No." It was Grace Friedkin who supplied that.

Tibbs rose to his feet. "Thank you for your time and your hospitality. I'm afraid that I'll have to impose myself on you quite a bit during the next several days, but it should be considerably less painful."

Friedkin got up as well. "I realize that I should have spoken about this sooner, but at the time I couldn't see how it could possibly pertain. I do now."

Tibbs did not comment on that; there was no need. Instead he followed his host out into the main hallway of the mansion. Virgil noted again the exquisite decor that characterized the Friedkin home. It spoke of a great deal of money, but also of highly refined taste unmarred by ostentation. Most of the objects were Oriental antiques that had been selected with unusual care. A large silk needle painting hung against a grasscloth background gave character to one wall; opposite it an immaculate suit of Japanese armor added richness and depth.

The most striking feature was an obviously rare and beautiful Buddha which sat, in serene dignity, in a niche that had obviously been built to hold it. A soft spotlight concealed in the ceiling illuminated it enough to bring out the extraordinary fluidity of its design. The features were notably well-done, but instead of the conventional downcast eyes, this Buddha looked straight ahead — seemingly directly at whoever might be standing before it. The eyes of the statue had a strange quality of inner life; despite their narrowness, they had a penetrating characteristic that was close to hypnotic.

Tibbs paused for a moment to study the remarkable work of art. Friedkin gladly waited, allowing him time to enjoy the great talent and skill of the artist who had created it.

"It is a very striking piece," Virgil said. "I have never seen such eyes in a Buddha image before."

"It is quite unusual. I will probably give it to the museum one day so that everyone can enjoy it, but in the meantime I admit that it fascinates me."

"I can certainly understand that. It almost seems able to see right inside of anyone facing it."

Friedkin studied his possession from the side for a few moments, then he spoke. "Mr. Tibbs, it occurs to me that if you can produce the same depth of insight in searching for my daughter that this statue appears to possess, then despite all obstacles, very possibly you may succeed."

Virgil turned toward him. "You have my assurance, Mr. Friedkin, that I am certainly going to try."

It was cool when Virgil stepped outside and the night sky blanketed the city, but he was not yet mentally ready to return to the apartment he called home. Despite his choice of profession, he did not enjoy penetrating into the privacy of respectable people. He valued his own too much for that, and like everyone else, there were isolated incidents in his background he hoped would never be made public. He got into his car, fitted the ignition key, and headed toward the Pasadena Hilton.

He was not anxious for a drink, but he felt the need for contact with other human beings on a dispassionate basis. He wanted to be where people were, unconsciously still savoring the fact that he could walk into any place of public entertainment and receive the same courtesy and consideration as everyone else. It had not been that way in his father's day. Most of the change in public attitude had come during his own lifetime, so that to him the new emancipation was still to some extent fringed with illusion: a roseate dream that could vanish into hard, hostile reality at any unexpected moment.

He rode up to the thirteenth floor, got off, and turned down the brick tunnel that led to the cocktail lounge. A few steps took him into a pseudo-Spanish world of subtle soft lights and sophisticated modern music, far more enjoyable to him than the screaming rock of the discotheques.

The manager welcomed him personally and saw that he was provided with a solo table not too far from the bandstand. "We're glad to have you with us again, Mr. Tibbs," he said.

"Thank you, Mr. Gonzalez." He ordered and then deliberately relaxed; putting the day behind him and letting the dream flow on. He looked down once more at his dark-skinned hands and found a fresh strength that he needed.

On the bandstand a girl stepped into an amber cone of light, adjusted the microphone for a few seconds so that the patrons could become aware of her presence, and then took a few moments more to look over her audience. The pale green gown she had on went well with her own dark complexion — and she wore it with the innate grace of a woman in command of her own body. Her hairdo was simple, but very effective in the way that it set off her natural good looks.

When she spoke into the live microphone, her voice was artificially low-pitched, her diction perfect. "Good evening, ladies and gentlemen. Since nostalgia is so big right now, I'd like to take you back — way back — to the old Isham Jones days to revive a tune that had real feeling, and it still does."

The piano gave her a lead, then a muted trumpet set the mood in the style of the well-remembered big band era. The first few bars that the girl sang told Tibbs that she was good, very good indeed. As he listened to *Blue Prelude* he wondered how a song that effective had ever slipped out of the repertoire. The singer's voice was perfectly suited to its lonesome, alone-in-the-heart-of-the-city mood and every note had its own quiet vibrancy that penetrated deep inside.

Virgil finished his drink and was served another while the singer put her special talents to work on Gershwin's *The Man I Love*. By formula she should have offered an upbeat number after that, but instead she chose *Bali Hai* and made it memorable.

When she had finished and stepped down off the low stage, as far as Tibbs was concerned she was due a debt of gratitude; the burden of reality was off his back. Down in the morgue the body of another young woman had already been mercilessly explored on the autopsy table. He had yet to identify her and establish the facts of her death, but that would wait until tomorrow. Tonight was a different and better world.

He finished his second drink and firmly declined another. As he stood up to go, he saw that the singer was coming down between the tables, walking with the easy poise that he would have expected of her. He stepped aside to let her pass and received a polite nod in return. "Thank you," he said.

She paused and smiled professionally at him. "Did you enjoy it?"

"Very much. I want to hear you again. Will you be here for a while?"

"A few weeks."

"Then I'll be coming back." He put a little something extra into that, something to tell her that it was just not an empty compliment given because it would be expected.

She smiled again, this time without the careful patina

that was one of her defenses. "That's nice." She offered him a slim hand, raised just a little.

"I don't know your name."

"Marsha Briggs."

It could have been a stage name, but it didn't matter. "Hello, Marsha. Where from?"

"Chicago. And you?"

"I live in Pasadena. Virgil Tibbs." He gestured toward the table, inviting her to sit down if she chose.

She did so easily, but in a manner that suggested she would not remain for long. He noted at once that her eyes, that had been warm, were distant and the professional veneer was back in place. "How remarkable," she said. "Virgil Tibbs himself. I'm quite honored."

That touched the edge of a nerve and he reacted to it. "Does a policeman bother you that much?" he asked.

She studied him. "No, not a policeman. But you must admit that you don't look very much like Sidney Poitier."

Virgil looked at her evenly for a moment, savoring her beauty and her proximity. Then, without display, he took out his card case and handed her a thin pasteboard that bore the red and blue seal of the Pasadena Police.

She accepted it, read it, and then looked at him again. This time her dark eyes had almost a soft glow and in them he read a request for understanding. "May a lady apologize?" she asked.

"No need."

"Are you always out to bust someone?" He knew that she didn't mean it seriously.

"Usually not. Unless they're murderers."

"I never killed anyone."

"Good."

On the stand the band began another number. "I'd like to dance with you," he said. "May I?"

"I'd like that."

He took her to the open dance floor where the sky overhead substituted for a room. The air had an evening coolness, but there was no wind and very little chill. They danced one number together in the style of the music she had sung, he holding her close enough to know that she was very feminine and very human despite her carefully sophisticated deportment.

When the music ended she lingered just a moment before she broke away. "When I'm through," she said, "I like to have a quiet cup of coffee. I'm off at one."

His apartment was only a short distance away and it would be a simple thing to come back. And he had planned to be up for some time, working. "Where can I meet you?" he asked.

"In the lobby."

"For a little while, then?"

She appreciated that. "For a little while," she repeated.

Then, minutes later, Virgil rode down the elevator and went out again into the night.

5

ALTHOUGH BOB NAKAMURA LIKED to describe himself as a Buddhahead, no one familiar with the West Coast of the United States would ever mistake him for a Japanese. He was as American as the Civitan Club and what was more, despite the Oriental cast of his features, he looked the typical member. His open, friendly manner made him an ideal mixer and he had a flair for leading community singing. He looked so little like a detective, many people had a tendency to discount his abilities in that direction. That was their mistake: he was a thorough professional specializing in robbery and various forms of confidence games.

He was also Virgil Tibbs's partner, a role that imposed some very specialized requirements, ranging all of the way from executive officer to Greek chorus. As is so often the case with brilliant men, Virgil was not always the ideal companion despite the fact that he seldom let himself go on a real tear; he had disciplined himself too determinedly for that. In Bob's opinion, it would be better for him if he did let loose once in a while.

A few minutes after eight thirty Agent Jerry Ferguson came into the office looking for Virgil. "He's over in records checking on some aspects of the Friedkin case," Bob told him. "Can I help?"

"Maybe." Ferguson sat on the edge of the desk. "I'm considering putting out a release on the reheat of the case. The fact that Virgil is taking over and all that."

Ferguson was a man of many hats. He was a first class policeman, as his status indicated. His duty assignment was the Public Affairs Section, which was far from a sinecure. That had been demonstrated when a huge freeway bridge under construction had collapsed without warning. The sudden disaster had brought death to several workmen and, later, citations for heroism to two Pasadena police officers who had laid their lives on the line directly under hundreds of tons of crumbling wet concrete in order to rescue two of the victims who were still alive. Jerry had handled that whole situation under trying circumstances. He had the temperament for it, because in addition to everything else he was the department's chaplain: the only sworn member of the force qualified both to capture a red hot suspect on one day and conduct a marriage ceremony for a fellow officer on the next.

Bob knew Jerry well enough to know that he didn't propose to put out a release just for the sake of a few lines of type. "Give me the reason," he invited.

"All right. The case is more than a year old and it was run all the way into the ground the first time around. Nothing whatever was left undone."

"True."

"By now the public has largely forgotten about it."

"Also true."

"Then if Virgil is going to dig up anything new, some public response might help."

Bob jumped onto that. "Especially if there is someone who had been keeping still, but who now, after a passage of time, might feel more like talking."

"Exactly. Of course we'd stir up the weirdos, but that can be endured."

"Jerry, I'd do it. There's nothing secret about the operation, and some publicity might help. I suggest that you run it past Captain Cockel first."

"Naturally." Jerry got up and left.

A little after ten Tibbs came back to say that he had scheduled an interview and wouldn't be back until after lunch. Was there any news?

Bob reported that all was quiet, as indeed it was at that moment. He made it a point not to remember the proposed press release until after Virgil was out of the room.

The fine weather was still holding as Virgil Tibbs walked across the campus of Pasadena City College from the point where he had parked his unmarked car at the curb. As he approached the large reflecting pool that broke the wide expanse of grass, he wished that it could always be this way —that the annual nightmare of New Year's Eve and its frequent violence could somehow be eradicated. It had only been a few weeks since a charged scene at this same place had come dangerously close to a riot.

Now things were calm and peaceful as he sat down on the edge of the pool and awaited the appearance of a rapist.

As the young man with whom he had an appointment came closer, Tibbs stood up to meet him. He looked the typical college student, but probably with a better wardrobe than most. His face was open, frank, and gave reason for him to be called handsome. His hair was moderately long, but definitely not extreme. He wore a pair of narrow-cut slacks, a tinted shirt open at the neck, and an unbuttoned sweater that obviously had come from an expensive shop.

"Mr. Tibbs?" the student asked. "I'm Randy Joplin. I was told that you wanted to see me."

He held out his hand and Tibbs took it briefly as courtesy demanded. It was easy to see that the campus women would find this young man attractive; he probably had a wide choice and made the most of it. Doris Friedkin could well have been one of the many.

"Yes, that's right." Virgil had already noted his over-careful use of correct English. It was a little out of character. "I'd like to talk with you for a little while — very privately. And confidentially."

"Then we'd better go somewhere; I've got a lot of friends who might horn in if we stay here."

Virgil gestured toward his car. When they were both aboard, he headed toward the Arroyo Seco and the world-famous Rose Bowl. He could feel the concealed tension in the young man beside him, but that was all too common in people who were unexpectedly asked for official police interviews. He kept quiet, concentrating on his driving, and deliberately letting his passenger stew. When the time came to talk, the relief from the silence might impel him to be a little freer in what he said.

When they reached the bowl, Tibbs parked and got out of the car. With Randy following he led the way into the huge stadium and then sat on one of the long concrete benches, hardly more than a pinpoint of life in a vast symmetrical emptiness.

When Randy settled down reasonably close to him, the tension was still strong. It was too tight; Virgil loosened it a little by saying, "We're entirely safe here; there's no chance at all of our being overheard."

"No, this is all right."

Tibbs clasped his hands together, his fingers intermeshed, and began the real conversation. "We are reopening the Doris Friedkin case and I've been assigned to it. There's already been a very thorough investigation, but now we are going to go over everything once more, all the way, to see if there is any chance of turning up a new lead."

He put it very calmly, with no stress in his voice and no hint of the reason why he had set up this particular interview so promptly. He got the result that he wanted — the tension in his subject eased almost visibly.

"Then I wish you the best of luck," Randy declared. "She's a swell girl — if she's still alive."

"Have you any reason to think that she isn't?"

"Well — just logic, I guess. If she were all right, then in more than a year she would certainly have called her folks, or written to them. They were always very close. She would know how tough they would be taking everything."

"That's very reasonable," Tibbs agreed as he looked out across the vastness of the great empty stadium.

After a few moments Randy broke the silence, as he was supposed to do. "Listen, I've been over everything that I know about a dozen times. You know Sergeant Perkins?"

"Yes, very well. It's Lieutenant Perkins now."

"He and I went over it all together and he didn't miss a damn thing. He had me remembering details I had completely forgotten — or thought that I had. Honestly, I haven't got a thing new to give you."

Virgil continued to look across the football field, a device that made his words seem more impersonal. "Let me set the

45

ground rules," he said. "I'm not out to bust you, or anyone else, at the moment. My job is to find Doris — or to learn definitely what happened to her."

Randy seemed genuinely shocked. "Why would you want to bust me? I was pretty close to her, but so what? I'm proud of it. And I dated her a lot, despite the fact that her family never liked me. I told Sergeant Perkins that."

"Why didn't they like you?" Tibbs asked. His voice was very calm and detached as he spoke.

"Bigotry."

"What about — social status?"

"No, not that. Our family isn't in such tough shape, you know; Dad's a millionaire and he's on the Tournament of Roses Committee too. We don't have the Friedkins' kind of money, but who the hell does — around here."

"Let's have it," Tibbs said.

"Off the record?"

"If you want it that way."

"I do. All right: the Friedkins are Jewish. They always threw a lot of stuff at me about tradition and all that."

"Did you explain that to Dallas Perkins?"

"No, not right out in so many words, but he got the idea. And I've had a lot of time to think about it this past year. Doris and I never talked about getting married or anything like that, but we got along together a lot better than most, so who knows?"

"Since you knew Doris so well, how sincere do you think she was in her faith?"

Randy was obviously more comfortable with that question. "I don't think she gave a damn one way or the other. I know that part about Jewishness being handed down

46

through the mother, not the father, but that never bothered her a bit."

Virgil let silence take over once more for a few seconds while he thought. If Randy's story as he told it now checked out, then a charge of rape would be harder to support. He picked the tack he wanted to take. "We didn't find Doris the first time around, one reason being that we didn't know enough about her. Now I need everything possible; some very small thing may be the key."

Randy nodded. "I understand."

"All right, then — since you do, give it to me straight: how much did Doris enjoy sex?"

"What?"

"Did she like it or didn't she? That's simple enough, but it could be important."

"How?"

"Never mind that — just tell me. And don't hold back; this is still off the record."

"Absolutely?"

"Yes."

Randy rubbed his leg with his hands as he sat, trying to find the words that would not commit him too deeply. "I'll give it to you then, if it will help Doris. I'm a damn fool, probably, to trust a cop — but what the hell. I screw around a lot; the girls go for me and I've been doing it regularly since I was fourteen. I don't look too bad, I've got the money to spend, the right kind of a car, and where that kind of thing is concerned, I can have almost anything I want. You know damn well that PCC isn't made up of several hundred virgins running around the campus. Male or female."

"You're lucky." That was a prod, a feeding for Randy's ego.

"Yes, I guess so. But it was different with Doris because she wasn't sexy, if you know what I mean. She was damn good-looking and all that, but she was up tight because her family watched her like their bank account. It held her back, even when we were alone. Her old man used to hire detectives to be sure that she stayed out of the bushes."

"Did she know that?"

"Yes, and she hated it. When we did manage to get off someplace together, she wanted all the loving she could get — short of being laid. I told her she was missing all the real fun, but she was scared stiff of that."

"Did you ever try?"

"Of course, naturally, but she was just too scared of her family." Randy shifted his position. "Besides, I told you, it was different with her. I can get laid anytime I want, and I do a lot with different girls, but I still went a lot with Doris because — well, I loved her, I guess."

He sat up again. "At least she's the only girl I ever thought about marrying. And not because of the family bread either. If she married out of what he called 'the faith,' I think her old man would have cut her off."

"What do you think that the chances were that Doris was a virgin when she disappeared? Don't be gallant; give me a straight answer."

Randy had no hesitation in responding to that. "I'll cover all bets that she was. Because if she wouldn't lay me, she wouldn't lay anybody. I know that, and I never made it with her. We never even came close."

By mid-afternoon it was clear that the missing persons reports were not going to provide an easy identification of the body that had been recovered in Oak Grove Park. No young woman of the proper age and description had been reported missing throughout the entire state for as long as six months back. That called for a national check, a fact that did not improve Virgil Tibbs's mood in the least.

By the time he had digested that information, the coroner's office called with some further news. Due to the condition of the body, a good set of fingerprints could not be obtained. Dental data were available, but unfortunately only a limited amount of work had been done and all of it was of a very usual nature. There had been no extractions, the subject had retained all of her wisdom teeth, and her bite had been normal. Preliminary examination had not revealed any indications of key evidence from that source.

Virgil listened carefully to what he was being told, hoping at every moment for more. He was aware that certain regions, such as the Rocky Mountains, often produced some slight, but detectable, variations in the teeth. But no such clues were forthcoming. "Has a forensic dentist made an examination?" he asked.

"No, but the usual molds were taken and the jaw proper was removed."

"Is there any gold work: a crown, even an inlay?"

It took a minute or two to get the answer to that. When it came through, it held a thread of hope. "Yes, there is a small gold inlay, on the upper right first molar."

Virgil pounced on that. "I'd like to request that a full examination be made as soon as possible by a forensic dentist. After he has, please ask him to call me; I want to speak with him personally."

"Right." The man at the morgue did not entirely see the

point, but the request was completely in order and the specialist would have to be called in.

Virgil made a careful note on a four-by-six slip of paper and then placed it in the front of his center desk drawer. That done, he put through a call to the office of Dr. Arthur Simon, the personal physician to the Friedkin family, who had seen Doris professionally a number of times.

Dr. Simon's receptionist had already received her instructions. She therefore informed Tibbs that the doctor would be glad to see him at the end of his regular office hours. She suggested four thirty. Virgil confirmed the appointment and hung up.

For a few minutes after that he leaned back in his chair with his eyes closed, and thought. Some very wild and undisciplined ideas were beginning to tantalize him, but he was not yet ready to give any of them serious consideration. After he had seen Dr. Simon he might have a little more data. Also, he was most anxious to talk with the forensic dentist as soon as he had made an expert examination of the dead girl's teeth. He did not question the finding that she was not Doris Friedkin — the coroner's people were far too well qualified to make an error on that — but until the whole matter of the unidentified, murdered girl was cleared up, he was not going to have too much time for other matters.

Dr. Simon had a suite of offices that testified to a highly successful practice. But it was not a mass production shop; even the furniture in the waiting room indicated that. There were only a few chairs, comfortable and well-spaced. An experienced glance told Virgil that the room was not used to overcrowding; the wide arms of the upholstered chairs retained their roundness, proof that they had not frequently been sat on. The reading material was current and well selected; there were no patronizing medical pamphlets or six months' old copies of *Newsweek*.

The receptionist's panel slid open for the second time after his arrival. "Will you please come in, Mr. Tibbs," she said. "Dr. Simon is waiting for you in his office."

Arthur Simon, M.D., was a tall man, perhaps in his early sixties, with a deliberate manner which suggested a European background. He wore a moderately heavy mustache that went well with the Herr Doktor image, but when he spoke there was no hint of accent in his voice. He shook hands with a measure of gravity and then closed the door to emphasize the confidential nature of the conversation to follow. He was old school, Virgil defined in his mind, but his steady, careful manner suggested that he was in all probability exceptionally competent. The diploma of the American Board of Internal Medicine framed on his wall confirmed that deduction.

"Mr. Tibbs," the doctor began, "I have received a rather unusual letter from Mr. Friedkin. It was hand delivered to me by his chauffeur. After reading it, I called him and confirmed its contents by phone."

Virgil nodded. The fact that the doctor had been so careful meant that any statement he might make would be well-considered and probably reliable.

"Mr. Friedkin has instructed me," Dr. Simon continued, "to discuss with you, fully and without reservation, whatever medical questions you may wish to raise concerning his daughter. You understand that this would represent a direct violation of the doctor-patient relationship. Despite her father's letter, Miss Friedkin herself, being an adult, would be the final authority concerning any discussion I might have with you on the subject of her medical history."

"I fully appreciate that, sir," Tibbs agreed. "And being aware of the ethics involved, I have taken the liberty of obtaining a court order directing you to make a full disclosure of Miss Friedkin's medical background, in order to assist the further investigation of her disappearance."

He removed a document from his inner pocket and handed it across the desk. "Mr. Friedkin's letter, Doctor, is to assure you that I have also obtained her family's approval in approaching you."

Dr. Simon carefully examined the legal paper he had been handed. "Very well, Mr. Tibbs, I will naturally comply. I appreciate the fact that you also obtained Mr. Friedkin's approval; it puts my mind somewhat more at rest."

"Doctor," Tibbs continued, "I have read very carefully the confidential report of your conversation with Sergeant Perkins a year ago. I understand that it was regulated by the usual ethics."

"Of course."

"Now, sir, I consider it quite possible that Miss Friedkin elected to vanish of her own free will and now prefers not to disclose her whereabouts. Under such circumstances, she might well have confided in you, knowing your absolute discretion, particularly if a medical reason was involved. If you have at this time any hard evidence that she is indeed alive and well and requires no police assistance, I will accept your assurance of that fact and withdraw my request for more data."

"I have no such information," the doctor said.

"Then, sir, I suggest that we get down to cases."

"Very well; how can I help you?"

"In your opinion, was Miss Friedkin generally in good health, as far as you know, at the time of her disappearance?"

"Yes."

"Did she have any possible incipient condition that may have developed further later on?"

"Not to my knowledge."

"Then would you describe her as a fully normal young woman, physically speaking?"

"Yes. She was slightly underweight and I recommended some changes in her diet, but there was no medical causation for that insofar as I am aware."

"You told all of this to Sergeant Perkins?"

"I did."

"Now, Doctor, I will have to enter a different area. In the short time that I have been on this case I have encountered some conflicting statements that I hope you can resolve for me. I would not ask this if it was not important to my investigation."

"I so assume, Mr. Tibbs."

"Do you know if Miss Friedkin ever consulted a gynecologist?"

"I believe that Dr. Abrams saw her on one occasion."

"Did you refer her to him?"

"Yes."

"Was her family aware of it at the time?"

"I can't say. Since Doris was of age, I didn't inform them and I very much doubt that Abrams would."

"It is my understanding from Mr. Friedkin that Doris had had some sexual experience prior to her disappearance."

Dr. Simon leaned back and raised an eyebrow. "How do you define sexual experience?" he asked.

Virgil caught the subtle change in the doctor's manner and altered his response accordingly. "In the usual way."

"You are asking me to confirm that?"

"Yes, if you please."

Dr. Simon paused for a few moments of considered deliberation. "Are your investigation, and your subsequent reports, a matter of public record?" he asked.

"No, sir, they are highly confidential. The Friedkin case, in particular, is kept in a special section reserved for unusually sensitive material."

"On your assurance that my response will remain completely confidential, that is correct. I am quite surprised that Mr. Friedkin was aware of it."

"He told me that his daughter had been a rape victim, but only after I had somewhat forced his hand."

"I see."

That told Tibbs a great deal and shaped his next question. "As a matter of judgment, Doctor, would you be inclined to credit the story that she had been raped?"

"I would say that Doris was not given to lying," the doctor answered carefully.

"Excuse me, sir, but that's not entirely responsive. Let me put it this way: did you, or any other physician to your knowledge, treat her for physical or mental injury as a result of such an attack?"

"Not so far as I am aware."

Tibbs had been laying his groundwork carefully; now it was time to probe for the real piece of information that he needed. "Dr. Simon, I rather gather that Miss Friedkin was having a more or less regular sex life prior to the time that she vanished."

Simon realized that this was a key question, and he gave it

a careful response. "That might be putting it a little strongly, Mr. Tibbs. I would certainly describe Doris Friedkin as a young woman of good character — particularly by today's standards. However, at her request I did prescribe 'the pill.' I certainly do not believe that she was promiscuous."

"One man and one only?"

"Not necessarily, but certainly she was, at the least, highly selective."

"Did a pregnancy occur?"

The doctor was carefully precise. "At one time I suspected that that might be the case and I sent her to Abrams. She disappeared not too long after that."

"Did Dr. Abrams give you his opinion?"

"He ran a test, but it was inconclusive. Doris had had a history of occasionally missing her period. It does happen, you know."

"Dr. Simon, in the sex relations that she was having, would it be reasonable to assume that Doris was a consenting partner?"

"Yes," the doctor answered slowly, "I would say so."

"Then the rape story could have been her defense against the embarrassment of a possible pregnancy."

"It is certainly a standard explanation."

"Doctor, in your considered judgment, do you believe that she was indeed raped?"

Dr. Simon reflected and then declared himself. "On the whole, based on all of the information that I have at hand, I would be inclined to believe it somewhat unlikely."

6

TWO DAYS OF HARD WORK FAILED to reveal the identity of the young woman whose body had been discovered in Oak Grove Park. Bulletins circulated through the country failed to turn up any valid lead. A number of young women were missing, but in every instance some available piece of data disqualified the Jane Doe that still awaited disposition in the Los Angeles County morgue.

Bob Nakamura had taken on a good part of the detail work, but even with his help, things moved no faster. When the end of the line was apparently reached, Virgil leaned back in his office chair and offered an opinion. "The most likely thing now," he said, "is that that girl, whoever she was, isn't yet known to be missing. Every year thousands of girls go somewhere to take a job and then don't write home, or phone, for weeks. After a while someone thinks to inquire. We'll probably get her that way."

The phone rang. Virgil picked it up and learned that Dr. Philip Peck was on the line. Because the name wasn't familiar, the operator supplied a quick fill-in. "He's the forensic dentist you wanted to talk to."

"Right!"

Within a few seconds he was speaking with the specialist directly. "What can you tell me, Doctor?" he asked. "In particular, I'd like any possible data on what part of the country she may have come from."

"First of all," Dr. Peck answered, "I'll tell you right now that I can't answer that. There isn't that much difference in dental practice between, say, the East Coast and the West Coast."

"I understood that there were some differences in gold work."

"That isn't so. I've seen excellent work from both sides of the country, and some garbage. In this case there is a little gold work, but almost everything about the subject's dental work is entirely conventional and routine. There are no dentures, no root canal procedures, nothing but three very ordinary fillings and one gold inlay. If it will help you any, I would say that it was caused by some kind of accident rather than decay, but even that's not conclusive."

Tibbs was disappointed, but he kept trying. "You've charted the whole mouth, I take it."

"Oh, certainly. I also took impressions so that a stone model can be made if necessary. But the charts contain all of the significant data."

"How about printing the charts in the dental magazines and asking for an I.D. if possible?"

"Certainly you can do that, but I have to tell you that if she had been my own patient, I don't think I would recognize the charts. There is simply too little work and it is, as I said, entirely conventional. Also, as many as four different men may have worked on her, not necessarily all in the same part of the country."

"So I have a blank."

"Not entirely. The staff here will check all incoming charts very carefully; that's your best bet. We may have something for you at any time."

Virgil settled for that and hung up. "No make," he said.

"We'll get it," Bob reassured him. "Remember the anonymous body in the nudist park swimming pool?"

"Yes, but there were some indicators there."

"How about clothing labels?"

"J. C. Penney. I checked; they tell me that it's all but impossible to trace the particular dress, and there isn't much of it left. Underwear, no clue. Shoes, no clearly visible markings. No jewelry at all, not even a watch."

"Pathology?"

"Quite difficult; she was pretty well gone. No fractures or other skeletal abnormalities. No bodily scars."

"Contact lenses?"

"I checked. No."

"Bathing suit marks?"

"None — and not likely this time of year."

"Just a girl."

"Just a girl."

"Somebody's daughter, possibly somebody's wife."

"No," Virgil said.

Bob looked up. "Don't tell me," he said.

"That's right," Tibbs responded. "Even in this day and age. A virgin. So I've got that to work on, at least."

The restaurant manager was almost effusively cooperative. "I've been expecting you," he told Tibbs as he settled himself in a booth with his guest. "Ever since I read in the *Star-News* that you had been assigned to the Doris Friedkin case."

He signaled to a waitress who came at once to the table. "Have you eaten?" he asked.

"Yes, thank you."

"Coffee?"

"Fine."

"Two coffees, and some Danish."

The girl nodded and left. "I presume," the manager went on, "you've gone over the statements I've already made to the police."

"In detail."

"Then ask me anything you want to, but I don't think I've got anything to offer that hasn't been covered several times already. Agent Hagerty got it all, believe me."

"Chris is an excellent investigator."

"That was my impression, and he had a year's head start on you. But forgetting all that, what can I tell you?"

"First, let me confirm some points: you were here personally when Doris did her disappearing act?"

"Yes, I was. Naturally I'd be here when the rose princesses were being entertained. They come here every year, and of course that's very good for our business."

"I'm sorry," Tibbs said. "I didn't get your name."

"Martinson, Edgar Martinson. I've been the manager here for four years."

"This is a very good restaurant; it has a nice atmosphere."

"Thank you — we go to a great deal of trouble to keep it that way. We don't encourage patronage that . . . doesn't fit our image."

That touched a nerve and Virgil could not help reacting. "Would you like to continue this interview in your office?" he asked.

Martinson reacted almost violently. "No, of course not!

You misunderstood me completely. I was referring to the longhairs, the hippy crowd — the barefoot gang. No, no — we welcome all respectable guests here, and we're strictly an equal opportunity employer. We have two Chicano busboys."

Virgil resisted the impulse to smile at the manager's last remark. The waitress interrupted them. She put down two cups of coffee and a plate of miniature Danish buns. Martinson was eager to have Tibbs try them. "They're made in our own bakery — and we think they're the best. We use real butter, of course, and plenty of it. You can't get real quality unless you use real ingredients." He held out the plate until Tibbs took one of the offerings. "Our coffee is special too, it's not the usual restaurant stuff. It's specially blended and aged for us in Venezuela."

"You pay very close attention to details."

"The secret of our success, Mr. Tibbs."

Virgil tried his coffee and found it exceptionally good. "Mr. Martinson, by any chance are you one of the owners of this establishment?"

A quick shake of the manager's head disavowed that. "No, I wish that I was. I do get a quarterly bonus, though, if the business meets its quota."

"Now, once more, tell me in detail about the rose princesses and the day that Doris Friedkin disappeared."

"All right, although I expect that you know most of it already. Each year about eight girls are chosen to be the rose princesses; most of them come from Pasadena City College. They try to pick lookers, naturally. Once the girls are chosen, they go through a lot more than the public sees. For instance, they're told how to fix their hair, and the clothes they wear during the period of the Tournament are de-

60

signed for them. They're kept very busy; sometimes they appear at three different luncheons on the same day. It's a pretty hectic schedule."

"How do most of the girls take it — on the basis of your experience?"

Martinson took the baited bit of flattery without hesitation. "Most of them love it. They're in the public eye, and they're being admired. Not too many girls can resist that."

Virgil nodded. "That sounds very reasonable. Now on the day that Doris Friedkin disappeared, you were entertaining the princesses here for luncheon, I believe."

"Yes, that's right. And it wasn't just an appearance — it was their real lunch. I still remember what we served them — chicken à la king. It's unusually good here."

"Did you notice Miss Friedkin at all?"

"Yes," the manager leaned forward and became confidential. "I did for several reasons. First was the obvious one: her family is famous — she is, or was, Herbert Friedkin's daughter. That adds up to a hundred million bucks, more or less."

Tibbs baited another hook. "Do you think that had a lot to do with her being chosen a rose princess?"

The manager screwed up his face momentarily and appeared to consider the matter. "I don't think so," he said finally. "She was a doll, money or no money. A little skinny, maybe, and not much in the way of a bosom, but in a quiet way she was pretty close to a knockout."

"What was her mood — do you remember that? Was she gay and happy? Or did you perhaps get the impression that she had something on her mind?"

"Hagerty asked me that too, and I remember the answer I gave him. She was quiet; I remember that she left most of her food. When she got up, before the dessert was served, to go to the ladies' room, I guessed that it was the wrong time of the month for her. When you're in the restaurant business, Mr. Tibbs, you learn a lot about people and their habits. When she was gone an abnormally long time, I was sure of it."

"Did she give any evidence of being ill — other than what you suggested?"

Martinson quickly shook his head. "Not that I could notice. Of course she hadn't had anything to drink. She didn't have a lot to say to the other girls, but she wasn't mad or anything like that. I would have noticed it."

"Did she seem to be distracted? Put another way, did she seem to have something on her mind?"

Martinson shook his head. "No, she was quiet, as I said, but she didn't seem worried. Some of the other girls did, but that was obvious. You see, the choice of the rose queen hadn't been announced and it was going to be one of them. So naturally . . ."

"And Miss Friedkin was a candidate, of course."

"That's right, but — well, maybe this is reaching too far, but I formed the impression that she didn't really care. A girl in her position has everything anyway, trips around the world all the time, things like that, and she wasn't at all the pushy sort."

"If you had been choosing, would you have selected her?"

For the first time Martinson was uncertain. "I looked them all over," he admitted. "What man wouldn't? To be honest about it one of the others looked like the winner to me. She was something, the best-looking blond I ever saw."

"Did she make it?"

"No. As a matter of fact, the girl who did was just about my own last choice."

Virgil took another of the Danish rolls despite himself. As he did so, the waitress appeared and refilled his coffee cup. "Now," he said. "Forget what you told Chris Hagerty and all the others. Clear your mind of all other impressions and tell me exactly what happened when Doris vanished. Don't skip anything, even the slightest detail."

Martinson had been waiting for that question and he relished it. "All right, here it is from the top. I remember it vividly, so you can believe what I tell you. You said every detail. I saw that Miss Friedkin had dropped her napkin. I had another sent to her immediately — we use cloth ones, of course. Ordinarily that would be meaningless, but it occurred to me, in view of what happened, that it could have been a signal to someone."

"A very astute thought, Mr. Martinson. Please go on."

"About a minute or two after that, she got up to go to the ladies' room. She took her purse with her. It was a fairly large one, which suggested to me that she might be carrying sanitary napkins. She knew where it was, or she may have noticed the sign — it's visible from where she had been sitting. Anyhow, she went to the ladies' room. The plates were removed and the dessert was served. It was light, but very tasty; most of the girls finished it all. By the time they had, Miss Friedkin still hadn't returned. At that time she had been gone, to the best of my recollection, between ten and twelve minutes. I thought that she might be having some kind of trouble, so I asked my hostess to check the ladies' room and find out if anything was wrong. She came back in less than a minute and told me that the room was empty."

"And there is an outside door near to the entrance to the ladies' room?"

"Yes, there is. It opens onto the back alley. We keep it unlocked during business hours as a safety measure even though, once in a blue moon, somebody sneaks out on us without paying."

"I'd like to see that door," Tibbs said.

"I'll show it to you now."

The two rest rooms opened off a short corridor which began at a corner of the dining area. It was conveniently located, but Virgil noted that it was effectively out of the sight of anyone seated in the dining area. When he opened the door at the end, he discovered that anyone going out that way would only have to walk a short hundred feet to the nearest cross street.

"As I said," Martinson repeated, "now and then someone sneaks out on us, but it doesn't happen often enough to be a problem. If anyone does that, they can never dine here again."

"Is there any other possible way that Miss Friedkin could have left the restaurant?" Tibbs asked.

The manager shook his head. "This has to be it. If she had come out the front way, I would have seen her, and others on my staff. She was wearing the official rose princess costume for the day, as all the girls were."

"How distinctive was the dress?"

Martinson pursed his lips in a pretense that he was giving the matter deep thought. But when his answer came, it had been ready and waiting. "It was a very lovely dress, but if you saw it and didn't know what it was, you might not have paid too much attention. There are new costumes each year, of course, all of them custom designed."

"Then if Miss Friedkin did go out of this door, as you suggest, she might have walked down the street without attracting undue attention?"

"Yes — I would say so."

Satisfied, Virgil went back to the table where his notebook awaited him, and sat down once more. "Just for the record," he asked, "is there any other exit from the ladies' room? Even a window that could be used in an emergency?"

"No, there's no window at all in the ladies' room and the walls are all solid construction."

Virgil nodded and made another note. "Now think carefully, sir: during the time that Miss Friedkin was absent and you were expecting her to reappear, did you by any chance hear anything to suggest that a car might have picked her up in the alley?"

Martinson shook his head emphatically. "Mr. Hagerty went over that with every member of the staff that had been on duty at the time: positively no one heard anything. And the parking attendants stated that there had been no traffic of any kind in the alley for a period of at least twenty minutes. Then a garbage collection truck went through. Hagerty interviewed the driver and his helper; they saw and heard nothing."

"I know; I read the report." Virgil deliberately closed his notebook and slipped it into his pocket. "Now, Mr. Martinson, I want to ask you one more thing. This is completely off the record; you understand what I mean by that."

"I do; it is strictly confidential."

"Yes, and also you will not be held responsible in any way for what you may tell me. Officially, I don't know of it."

"I understand."

"Then here is my question: is there anything that you

have not told us because you did not remember at the time, or because you were being careful for the sake of the restaurant, or for any other reason?"

"I don't quite understand."

Tibbs spoke slowly and carefully. "Sometimes, Mr. Martinson, during an investigation people do not volunteer information for any one of a number of reasons. Often they don't want to become involved. Sometimes they fear someone. They want to protect a reputation; of an individual or of a company. They may have a mental oversight that it would be embarrassing to admit to later on. Or perhaps a reservation made only after careful thought — a judgment, perhaps, based on long experience."

"I see."

Martinson sat very still, at least appearing to think very hard. After a pause of many seconds he looked up and then quite deliberately finished his coffee. "I'm sorry," he said. "I can't think of a thing. I answered hundreds of questions a year ago and there isn't a thing I can add now. Nothing at all."

"Thank you," Virgil acknowledged. "You've been most helpful." He shook hands and left.

Back in his office a few minutes later, he sat in deep and silent thought. Bob Nakamura was there, but he knew better than to make an unnecessary sound. He was careful to turn the pages of the file he was reading in almost total silence. When Tibbs sat like that he had something, and Bob Nakamura knew it.

7

B Y THE AFTERNOON OF THE SECOND DAY the public response to the announcement that the Doris Friedkin case was being reinvestigated was already considerable. Every phone call, every communication of any kind whatsoever, was taken down in as much detail as possible. Nothing was discarded as too ridiculous for serious consideration. The phones rang almost constantly, as Jerry Ferguson had known that they would, but somewhere in the bushels of chaff a grain or two of valuable information might lie concealed.

By far the largest number of callers suggested that the body recovered in Oak Grove Park might be Doris Friedkin and some went so far as to claim that they could prove it to be true. Since the dental evidence had totally ruled that out, the callers were cordially thanked and promised that the possibility would be thoroughly checked out.

A spiritualist called to advise that Doris was dead and that communication had been established with her from the next world. A séance with the press present was proposed. The name and address of the caller were taken and she was marked down for an interview. Two desert rock hunters called to say, cautiously, that they knew where a body was located; they had hesitated to come forward previously. That report was given full credence and flagged for immediate attention.

A number of people phoned in to suggest that Doris had eloped with a boyfriend or lover whom her family, being sincerely religious, had refused to approve. A young man called in person to say that he had met Doris, he was sure, in a kibbutz in Israel; for a consideration he would reveal where she was. The investigation file grew rapidly and still every communication of any kind was given the most careful attention.

A flurry came when a young woman called with the startling news that she was Doris Friedkin. Two investigators left immediately to interview her; they returned with the information that the young woman who had come forward was five feet ten in her bare feet — six inches too tall to be the missing girl. Her name was Doris Friedman and she had been in the area for only a few weeks. She had been thanked for her help, despite the fact that the newspapers had contained a thorough review of the case of the missing rose princess.

A crudely done ransom note was received at the Friedkin home. It differed from the usual format; for an unstated amount it promised that Doris would be delivered safe and sound at a place to be revealed. Herbert Friedkin, who had long ago posted a ten thousand dollar reward for any information at all leading to the finding of his daughter, turned the letter over to the FBI. Almost every member of the Pasadena Police Department received part of the barrage. Meanwhile the mills of patient, careful investigation ground on.

In the midst of it all Tibbs's phone rang with an internal

call. Jerry Ferguson was on the line. "I think you'd better take this one," he said. "It could be something."

A patch connection was made and a man's voice came through. "Mr. Tibbs?"

"Yes. How can I help you?"

"It is possible that I may have some information for you concerning the missing young woman — the Friedkin girl. Could I talk with you, confidentially?"

"Certainly," Virgil responded. "Immediately if you would like. Where are you?"

"In Los Angeles. Let me be frank, sir — what I have to tell you may possibly compromise my own position. You can understand my hesitation."

The voice was cultured, obviously that of a man somewhere in middle age who had been well educated. It had probably taken him a good deal of soul-searching to come forward and a single wrong word could lose it all. Virgil was therefore extremely careful in his language. "I will be glad to meet with you, sir, and if you can help us, in return I will do everything possible to protect your position. One question if I may: have you been concerned because you may have personally committed an infraction?"

"That's part of it," the man admitted.

"Then let me say this: if you are willing to help our investigation, we are certainly not going to take advantage of your generosity. Do I make myself clear?"

"I believe so. As I understand it, you might be willing to overlook . . . an indiscretion."

"Unless it is something very serious, sir, you can depend on that."

The man hesitated for only a moment. "Then why don't

we meet, in say an hour, at the top of the Occidental Center. I believe that I will know you."

That remark did not escape Tibbs. "That will be fine, sir. We can have coffee together."

The touch of informality accomplished its purpose; the caller was audibly less tense as he confirmed the appointment and then hung up.

After he had completed a few minutes of additional work, Virgil picked up an unmarked official car and hit the Pasadena Freeway southbound toward Los Angeles. He drove through the Stack, where four freeways converged on four different levels, and on down the Harbor Freeway until he reached the turnoff for the towering Occidental Center that dominated the skyline at the southern end of the downtown area.

He parked in the garage and took a series of elevators up to the restaurant that commanded a panoramic view of the vast city that surrounded it in every direction. He paused in the lobby long enough to be seen, then he stepped into the men's room. When he emerged, a man approached him.

Tibbs took him in quickly: about fifty, very well dressed, carefully groomed, no rings or other jewelry, normal size and build, every external indication of better than average success.

"Mr. Tibbs?"

"Yes, how do you do."

The man shook hands cordially enough, but he did not mention his name. Virgil let it pass as they entered the spectacular dining room and were promptly shown to a choice window table. As they were being seated, Tibbs looked again at the seemingly endless city that was literally spread out at his feet and then at Catalina Island, on the horizon at least twenty miles away. The day was crystal clear.

His host spoke a quiet order and then they were alone; there was no one close enough to overhear their conversation.

"Mr. Tibbs," the man began, "please excuse my rudeness in not introducing myself before. I made a blunder. My name is Walter Rosenblatt and I am an executive, on a fairly high level, of a major insurance company. Will that suffice?"

Virgil nodded. "Certainly, Mr. Rosenblatt. Since you have voluntarily come forward to help us, naturally I'm going to protect you, and your position, as much as I can."

"I've got to admit, that's a considerable relief." Rosenblatt took a sip from his iced-water glass. "I've been living with something on my conscience for a long time. I have been very reluctant to expose myself, but now it's evident that I can't hide any longer."

He looked toward the waiter and saw that the man would be returning to their table shortly. He switched the conversation to the spectacular view and mentioned that he liked to dine in that restaurant quite frequently.

"I noticed that the headwaiter knew you," Virgil commented, "and how you were treated."

Rosenblatt tightened a little after that, and Tibbs realized what an effort the man had made to phone in and declare himself.

When the coffee had been served and a plate of light finger food had been put on the table, Rosenblatt began his story. "I will put this as simply as I can, Mr. Tibbs, and ask your indulgence. I am married and have been for some

71

time, but my relations with my wife are not good. We are very much at odds with each other. She is ambitious almost to an insane degree and she is unrelenting in her demands that I try to politic my way upward whatever the cost — to myself or to others. I simply can't subscribe to that. As a consequence, I have for some time sought my sexual satisfaction elsewhere."

"Unfortunately," Virgil commented, "that's all too common a situation."

Rosenblatt drank coffee, as if he was trying to draw strength from the beverage. "A little more than a year ago, I was in Pasadena to attend a meeting. I was fairly frequently in your city because my secretary lived there. I had a key to her apartment. Two days before she had left for a vacation in Europe, so I was very much alone."

He paused and looked at Tibbs, apparently trying to measure the reaction to his words up to that point. Virgil nodded his understanding, and his implied sympathy, as well as his continuing interest.

"After leaving the meeting, while I was going to get my car, I encountered a young woman, alone and unescorted. She seemed bewildered and uncertain. Under the circumstances I approached her and asked if I could be of any service. She was clearly young, slender, and in a quiet way most attractive. Her general appearance and deportment certainly did not suggest that she was soliciting."

"In what part of town was this, Mr. Rosenblatt?"

"Toward the eastern end of Colorado Boulevard."

"Thank you, please continue."

"Without burdening you with unnecessary details, she told me that she had had a serious falling out with her family and was afraid to go home. She had only limited funds with her, but she made it clear she wasn't asking for money. Rather, I think, she wanted someone to advise and help her."

Rosenblatt resorted to his coffee. "I am not proud of this next part, but I will tell it to you exactly as it happened. I thought of dropping her off at the police station, but not very seriously — I admit that. Instead I told her that I had the keys to a vacant apartment and that she would be welcome to use it for the night. She was obviously a girl from a good home, but when I made that suggestion, she looked up at me and said, 'Why not?' I therefore drove her to my secretary's place and there we had a drink together. She told me her name was Mary, which was neither here nor there; I did not identify myself to her."

"I think you were most considerate," Tibbs said.

Rosenblatt shook his head. "I can't claim that I was being entirely objective. I will say that if she had asked me to leave I would have done so, but she did not. She seemed to assume that I had invited her to spend the night with me. I was satisfied that she was of age; she told me that she was twenty-two. So I did stay. We slept together and naturally we were intimate. It was not her first experience; thank God for that."

He signaled the waiter who poured more coffee at once.

When he was ready, Rosenblatt continued. "In the morning she made my breakfast for me; despite the difference in our ages, I had more companionship with her during that hour than I have had with my wife for the past fifteen years. She was a delightful girl and the night seemed to have restored her. She told me that she knew what she was going to do and that she was certain that she had made the right decision. She was considerably more than a pick-up to me, I ask you to believe that."

"I do," Virgil said.

"I'm glad for that. Before I left, I did two things. I had not been able to . . . protect her . . . the night before. I gave her a number to call in the event that she found herself pregnant as a result of our relationship, and a code word to use."

"Your attorney, I assume."

"Exactly; we went to school together and his situation was closely similar to mine. I also gave her a hundred dollars. I was careful about that: I called it a loan and promised her that if she ever needed a friend I would be available. I was entirely sincere in that, not the loan part, of course — I simply didn't want her to regard it as a fee for her services. And it wasn't intended that way. She had not asked for a thing. We left the apartment together — she insisted on that to reassure me that she was not taking anything with her. At her request I dropped her off on a residential street where she said that she had friends."

"Mr. Rosenblatt, do you recall the date on which you met this young woman?"

The insurance executive nodded, gravely this time. "It was the same day, as you have probably guessed, on which Miss Friedkin disappeared."

"Another guess, Mr. Rosenblatt, if I may. If you had met Mr. Friedkin at any time, well enough so that you knew each other, then if you subsequently learned that his daughter had disappeared, you would be in an extraordinarily difficult position. And innocently, of course."

Rosenblatt looked at him with fresh interest mixed with

concern. "Apart from the innocent part, you're completely correct. I do know Herbert Friedkin."

"Mr. Rosenblatt," Tibbs said, "you did spent the night with a young woman, but by all indications it was with her complete consent. If she was Herbert Friedkin's daughter, you had no way of knowing that unless she introduced herself that way. So you were entirely innocent of deliberately abusing his friendship. Had you ever met Doris as his daughter?"

"No."

"By your account, I can't see how that would have been possible, but I asked just to make doubly sure." Virgil reached into his pocket and extracted a small folder. He opened it and showed the photograph it contained to the man across the table.

Rosenblatt studied it for almost half a minute before he committed himself. "It looks a great deal like her," he said finally. "I'm sorry, I can't give you an absolute answer, one way or the other."

"Assuming for the moment that it was Doris Friedkin that you met, did she tell you anything about her plans, or perhaps indicate what she might be most likely to do?"

That was a key question and Tibbs had a hard time keeping his outward expression calm. The answer could mean a genuine breakthrough in what had been a solid wall of dead ends for more than a year.

"The most specific thing, Mr. Tibbs, was the place where I dropped her." He passed over a slip of paper. "That isn't an exact address, she didn't want to be driven to the door, but she did say that she had a friend very near to there who would help her. Find that friend, and you may have something to go on."

Virgil had thought of that, of course, and as a result he had dared to hope. With the beginning of a solid clue in his fingers, he spoke in a tone that indicated his complete sincerity. "Mr. Rosenblatt, you have my assurance that I will hold this conversation in the closest possible confidence. I would like to able to contact you again; I may have some additional questions."

The insurance executive passed over his card. Tibbs looked at it and was mildly surprised when he saw the title that it carried.

"Thank you. I'm very much indebted to you, as you know. One thing more: during the time that you were with the young woman, did you note any physical peculiarities at all — anything that might help to identify her?"

Rosenblatt thought carefully. "I'll be as candid as I can," he said. "She was quite pretty, I already told you that. A brunette, her hair was almost black. I don't believe that it was dyed. She was five feet three or four — possibly five, but no more than that. Her eyes were dark also, but I can't give you the specific color. She was slender, but well shaped. Her breasts were small, but almost perfectly molded. Her skin color was slightly pale."

"That's excellent," Virgil told him, "all of this is very solid information. Obviously you are a very observant man, and thank heaven for that. Can you think of anything else?"

Rosenblatt was human enough to react to the praise, one of the professional investigator's most useful tools. "One small item: she did mention Canada one or two times. I rather gathered that she had had a friend at one time who had fled to Canada to evade military service. My impression was that she both liked him and was ashamed of him at the same time. The problem was her age: she was a little too young, I believe, to have known a draft dodger, unless she had become attached to him when she was sixteen or seventeen."

It was all that Virgil could do to conceal his mounting interest. "Did she indicate any particular part of Canada? East Coast or West Coast?"

"Come to think of it, she did mention Vancouver once — I'm almost sure of that."

Excitement ran down Virgil's spine and even his fingertips felt the stimulation. He made a careful effort to control his voice and at the same time let his appreciation show through. "Mr. Rosenblatt, what you have told me may prove invaluable. Please understand how much I appreciate your calling me. Officially and personally, I consider that you conducted yourself as a gentleman."

The insurance executive leaned back as a massive weight seemed almost visibly to come off his shoulders. "I am profoundly grateful to hear that," he said.

"Before I go, one last question. Did the young lady have any other physical characteristics that you can recall? Did you note the shape of her ears? Were there any slight scars? Anything at all?"

Rosenblatt shook his head. "As I recall, her hair covered her ears; I am almost sure of that. I saw no evidence of dental work; in fact she had pretty teeth, I do remember that."

He looked up. "I'm being stupid; I did note something else. I hope that you won't think that I subjected the young lady to any intense scrutiny, even though it was quite evident that she didn't mind. She had an almost invisible two-inch incision where she had had her appendix out. I didn't see it at all until the bright light of morning."

77

Virgil felt like a man who had been standing on the gallows, hearing his reprieve read, and then had had the trap spring under him. He knew very well that Doris Friedkin had never had surgery of any kind before she had disappeared.

8

As soon as the last man was in his office, Captain Bill Wilson got up personally and closed the door. By the time he had seated himself once more, those who had been summoned to the meeting knew that he definitely meant business.

"I'll begin," the captain said, "by telling you that Chief McGowan has made some changes in the command structure of the department. As of now, I have taken over the responsibility for the Investigative Division from Captain Cockel. He's going to head another division — that will be announced in due course.

"As of now, gentlemen, I have two major things on the docket. I don't want to be quoted on this outside this office, but the more important, as of now, is the case of the Jane Doe who was recovered strangled at the north end of Oak Grove Park. We need to get some answers. So far all we have to go on are these facts: she was approximately eighteen to twenty-five years of age, she was reasonably attractive, she was in all probability in moderate circumstances since she was wearing a popular line of chain store clothes. She was certainly unmarried unless she chose to split immediately after the ceremony and I can't readily credit that. She had been dead approximately ten days when she was found. Her fingerprints could not be taken due to the condition of the body and the forensic dentist could not give us any real information beyond a detailed set of charts. She had had only a limited amount of work done."

"How much did the autopsy give us?" Dallas Perkins asked. He already knew what he expected to hear, but something might have come in that hadn't reached him.

Captain Wilson tapped a folder on his desk. "I have it all here; it was a complete and thorough job. Despite the condition of the body, it was determined that she was in normal good health, not pregnant, of course, since she was a virgin. All organ samples were normal. She was not diseased in any way. The stomach contents indicated that her last meal was a good quality hamburger, fries, a glass of milk, and probably no dessert. There were traces of ice cream, but that was all."

"I'll give you what I've been able to make out of that," Virgil Tibbs offered. "I believe that she was killed at night, or in the early evening. The stomach contents suggest dinner; certainly it wasn't breakfast. She did not eat alone, and probably had more than one companion."

"Explain that," Wilson invited.

"The trace of ice cream. If she had ordered a sundae, or a dish of ice cream, she would have eaten more than that, unless she disliked it — and that is highly unlikely."

"So you believe that someone offered her a taste of theirs?"

"Exactly. When I got that far I called the coroner's office and asked if they could give me anything on the flavor of the ice cream. They couldn't be too specific, but they did find bits of chopped almonds. Unless it was topping, and that isn't usual, it was probably one of the more exotic flavors. That would support the idea that she had been invited to have a taste."

Wilson saw the rest of it. "And the idea of sampling someone else's dessert is a little more likely in a crowd than it would be with just one companion."

"Yes, sir — plus one more thing. She was attractive and from the physical evidence, a girl probably not too easy to date. Therefore, if a single escort had taken her out, he probably would have stood her a better quality dinner. That's a little thin, I admit, but I've got one more thing: the hamburger was good quality with an adequate amount of meat. That suggests a place such as Bob's on Colorado which is popular with the kids of her age. Of course a lot of other places put out a good burger, but the point is, their menus are almost all standardized and they don't carry the oddball flavors of ice cream."

"Therefore," Perkins suggested, "she could have been with a crowd of four or five who piled into a car and went to one of the ice cream shops."

"Exactly. However, those places are so well patronized I don't think that showing them the artist's sketch of the girl as she was would help us. Even if we do get a statement that she was in, something I strongly doubt would be reliable, where does that get us? Nowhere."

Bob Nakamura broke his silence. "Captain, I honestly believe that we've taken this about as far as we can at this end. I've been checking known sex offenders, but the MO doesn't fit. If one of those birds had gotten hold of her, and had strangled her until she was unconscious or otherwise powerless, then she wouldn't have died a virgin. Also note that she was strangled from in front. I assume from that that she knew her attacker. She would hardly have let a stranger get that close to her."

"Was she killed where she was found?" Wilson asked.

"No," Tibbs answered him. "Plain logic. Presumably it was night. Jane Doe, being the kind of girl she was, would never willingly have walked up into the northern area of Oak Grove Park, no matter what kind of a story she might have been told. She would have had too much time to think about it."

"Perhaps she did just that and was killed when she realized what she was up against," Lieutenant Perkins suggested.

"I don't think so, Dallas. Getting her just to go down into the general area would have been difficult."

"Perhaps, just perhaps," Nakamura contributed, "she had decided that she had been a virgin long enough. There is a first time for everyone, you know, unless they pass up sex altogether."

"I considered that," Virgil responded. "It's not too far-fetched. She was certainly about due, unless she had very strong religious convictions. But assuming that she had decided to have her first sexual experience, can you see her willingly lying down on the ground in that area, with the sand, the still moist raw dirt, and the good possibility of annoying insects in the bargain? No way!"

"I'm inclined to agree with that," the captain said.

"I would suggest one or two additional points," Virgil added. "First, I believe that one person carried her up to the place where she was discovered by the scoutmaster. She was not very heavy and in a fireman's type of carry, it would be a reasonably easy job with very little risk of being seen in that area at night. The only thing that bothers me is the car. The murderer had to have one and since we patrol down there, it would be much too dangerous to leave it long enough to carry the body that far, assuming that the homicide had already been committed. Secondly, the evidence strongly indicates a man. A powerful woman could have done it, but it is much less likely."

"Unless," Dallas said, "it was a woman whom Jane Doe trusted and therefore went with her."

"It could be," Virgil conceded, "but that still doesn't answer the first unresolved question. Who the hell was Jane Doe?"

Back in his office Virgil sat still at his desk and stared at the wall. There was a small pile of work waiting for him, but he ignored it. Ideas were churning through his mind, tantalizing ideas that all gave promise, but stubbornly refused to come out of the kaleidoscopic morass into something approaching a clear and sharp focus. Bob Nakamura understood perfectly and picked his moment to speak.

"Look," he said. "Even though this is a nation of more than two hundred million people, sooner or later someone is going to call in somewhere to report a daughter missing, or possibly a sister."

Tibbs was only half listening. "I think she came from the East Coast," he said.

"Why?"

Virgil looked at him. "The probabilities. If she was from anywhere around here, in more than two weeks she would have been missed. But, on the other hand, if she came out here from the East, then there is a better chance that she might be thought to be on the road, traveling, and negligent about writing or phoning home. It's not firm, but it's indicative."

"How did you make out on your interview?"

"A total dead end. I met a man worth knowing; he admitted to fornication in order to give me some information that could have helped. That's an embarrassment to some people."

"What's next on the Friedkin thing?"

Virgil pressed his palms against the top of his desk and took a fresh grip on himself. "I'm going to have to do it the hard way," he answered. "And that will be rough on some people. I might as well get started."

He flipped open a telephone index and checked the business number for Herbert Friedkin.

In New Brunswick, New Jersey, Arthur Kallman was beginning to feel a mild concern. Nancy still hadn't written or called, and that wasn't like her. Despite some of the people who were her more or less constant companions, she was still, in his opinion, a "good" girl. After considering the matter in his mind for some minutes, because he didn't want to alarm his wife, he spoke to her in as casual a tone as he could command under the circumstances. "Mary, I would feel a little happier if we had heard from Nancy. Just to let us know that she's all right."

By one of those empathies which can exist between people who live together and who share more than the titular bed and board, Mary Kallman had been thinking the very same thoughts. Now she looked up from her reading and tried to match her husband's casual tone. She did not quite succeed and he detected it. "She will," Mary said. "You know how young girls are. And we have been out quite a bit; she could have tried to phone several times."

"We're home now," her husband noted.

She smiled. "But we can hardly expect her to know that, can we?"

Arthur Kallman looked at the telephone, that miraculous instrument that could put him into almost immediate communication with the police any time that he chose. "I didn't say this before," he told his wife, "but I made up my mind yesterday that if we didn't hear anything in today's mail, or get a phone call, I was going to make inquiry."

Mary countered him. "It's too soon for that. The police are very busy people; you know how much violence there has been in the papers lately. And we don't have anything definite to tell them."

"Yes, we do," Arthur disagreed. "Our daughter has been gone for almost three weeks without a word from her of any kind. And I don't like it."

"Then call if you want to." Mary said. She did not even admit to herself that she hoped that he would. It was her job to be cautious; if she didn't behave that way in the supermarket, they would never have been able to keep within their food budget, even when Nancy was away at school.

Arthur hesitated one more long moment, then he looked up a number in the directory and picked up the phone.

It was almost an hour later when a police car stopped in front of their home. It was unmarked and the man who pushed the doorbell was in plain clothes. It was not until he had identified himself and displayed his credentials that Arthur Kallman knew definitely that he was a policeman.

To make things as painless as possible, he performed a formal introduction. "My dear, this is Sergeant Morrison from the Police Department. My wife, Mary."

"Good evening, Mrs. Kallman," the sergeant acknowledged. "May I sit down?"

"Of course. Would you care for some coffee?"

"Not now, thank you. I would like to ask some questions, if you don't mind."

At that moment Mary Kallman wished that her husband hadn't gotten them involved; she wasn't sure she would know what to say.

The sergeant produced a notebook and a Cross pen. His suit, they noticed, was of good quality and pressed.

"I take it that your daughter's name is Nancy Kallman and that she lives with you here at this address."

"Yes, that's right," Arthur agreed.

"May I have her age, please."

"Twenty."

"Her occupation?"

"Student, but she wasn't going to school this semester."

"And the reason for that, sir?"

Kallman hesitated for a bare moment, wondering how much to tell. "We had medical advice to keep her out for a term," he said.

"I see. Mr. Kallman, when did you last see her?"

When her husband hesitated, Mary Kallman supplied the information. "Three weeks and one day ago. She left with some friends to drive to the West Coast. She had some relatives there she wanted to visit. We haven't heard from her since she left here."

"Close relatives?"

"No, quite distant as a matter of fact." She laughed a little tightly. "This may sound absurd to you, Sergeant, but I don't know exactly who they are myself. Nancy claimed that she had located a branch of our family and when the doctor suggested a change of scene for her for a little while, we approved her going to look them up."

"I know that this is a personal question," the sergeant prefaced, "but can you tell me why the doctor made that recommendation?"

Arthur knew that it was his duty to handle that one. "Nancy had been engaged. She was quite emotionally involved, but I'm sure it was no more than that. We are strong church members, so we are very strict about . . . matters of morals. Nancy fully supports our beliefs in that regard. When the engagement broke up, quite suddenly, Nancy was very depressed. It was especially hard for her because her intended quite suddenly married another girl. You can understand Nancy's feelings after that — and ours."

"I certainly can, sir, I have a family also. Now some specifics, if you please. How tall is your daughter?"

"Five feet four."

"Five feet three and a half," Mary corrected him.

The sergeant made a careful note. "Her weight?" he asked.

"One hundred and five." Again, it was Mary who answered.

"I take it then that she is of slender build."

"Yes, but she has a very nice figure. Not the overblown type, just what is right for a modest girl who takes care of herself."

"That's fine," Morrison encouraged. "The color of her hair and eyes?"

"She is a very dark brunette," Arthur responded. "Her eyes are dark too. She is really quite pretty."

"Do you have a picture of her?"

"Yes." Arthur Kallman glanced at his wife. "Remember those engagement shots we had taken?"

Instead of answering Mary Kallman got to her feet and left the room. She was back within a minute with two studio portraits that had been conventionally retouched. The sergeant looked at them with minute care, so much so in fact that Mary noticed it. The policeman caught that and used his head. "I don't see any evidence of birthmarks or anything like that."

"Oh, no — she has a lovely complexion," Mary volunteered.

"I'm certain of that," Morrison said very carefully. "Just one more question, if you don't mind, and I won't trouble you any more. Could I have the name of your family dentist?"

Arthur Kallman reacted to that. "Why?" he asked.

Morrison was an experienced man and he knew better than to alarm anyone prematurely. "It's strictly routine," he said with conviction. "When anyone is missing, we like to have their dental charts on hand. It's simply one of the tools we use. We always ask for the name of the family dentist."

He convinced them, as he had hoped that he would. He wrote the doctor's name down and then rose to go. "As soon as I have anything definite to report, you'll hear from me," he promised. "You've both been extremely helpful."

"We really didn't want to bother you," Mary said.

"I understand, ma'am, but since you haven't heard from your daughter for this length of time, I want to assure you that you did the right thing."

With that he left them. He wasn't sure of anything, but the information they had given fitted the report he had restudied just before he had left for the Kallman house. Only one thing troubled him: the obvious cover-up concerning Nancy's destination. It simply wasn't reasonable that such a carefully raised girl would have left to cross the entire country in search of relatives that neither of her parents could identify.

Obviously, something was being held back.

9

ERBERT FRIEDKIN PICKED UP A PHONE on his desk and spoke to his secretary. "I am not to be disturbed until further notice for any reason," he directed. "With the usual exception."

"Yes, sir."

That done, the industrialist turned back to Tibbs. "Now you have my undivided attention," he said. "That phone will not ring unless there is news of Doris — and I fear that that isn't very likely."

Virgil did not comment on that; instead he produced a sizable pad of ruled paper and prepared to make notes. "I am about to make a considerable nuisance of myself," he warned. "I am building my own case file and there are a number of gaps that I want filled. I need your help."

"You have it, without reserve."

"By any chance, Mr. Friedkin, do you have any recordings of Doris's voice — tapes, perhaps, that she might have made?"

"Not to my knowledge, no."

"Did she ever mention to you recording her voice for any reason whatever?"

Friedkin thought for a moment. "She might have done

so — many of her friends had cassette equipment, and so did she, as a matter of fact. I will have that matter looked into, if you would like."

"It would be very helpful; I want a voice print of her if possible. Next: I would like to know as much as you can tell me about her financial resources. Cash, securities, any other property she might have been able to convert quickly and easily into cash."

"She had a bank account of her own to which she had access. Then there is a trust fund of considerable size, but I still have control over that. There is some real estate in her name, but none of it has been sold — I thought of that one myself."

"How much cash do you estimate she may have had with her at the time of her disappearance?"

Friedkin leaned forward. "I was asked that before, and I can't give you a very good answer. A few days before she vanished she drew out a thousand dollars, but that wasn't unusual. She bought all of her own clothes, for example, and paid for them out of her own funds."

"Is there any record of her having spent any of that ready cash?"

"No, but I should make one point clear: some day in all probability she will come into a very substantial inheritance. From the beginning I have tried to teach her the wise and prudent use of money. When she was ready, I gave her a generous allowance with the understanding that she was to use her own good judgment and that I wouldn't ask for an accounting."

"And that allowance was . . . ?"

"A thousand a month. That wasn't expected to include medical expenses, cars, or other major items that might arise. To the best of my knowledge, she used her funds prudently for a young lady in her position."

"It could have been possible, then, that she could have made gradual withdrawals and held some of the funds aside, accumulating them for some particular purpose."

"Yes, that's true, but I very seriously doubt it."

Tibbs did not press the point. "What exactly, are her language skills? More accurately, what were they when she disappeared?"

Friedkin gave him a penetrating look. "That's a new one," he admitted. "She was fairly good in French, she had three years of it in school. A smattering of Spanish. She had no interest in Hebrew, but somehow she had picked up a little Italian — nothing more than a few phrases."

"Could she carry on a conversation in French?"

"A simple one, perhaps."

"Would you say that she had an aptitude for languages?"

"Only if she was really interested. In that case she could do exceptionally well at almost anything. French never really interested her, therefore she did well enough to pass satisfactorily, but no more."

"Did she tint her hair?"

"No, she was naturally very dark-haired."

"To your knowledge, did she ever buy a wig?"

"Yes, she tried one once. Her mother and I didn't care for it, and I don't believe that she did either. She wore it once and then threw it away."

"Do you have definite knowledge, Mr. Friedkin, that it actually did leave your house?"

"I can't absolutely swear to it. It was a reddish affair in what I believe is called page boy style. To be honest, she did look quite nice with it on, but it wasn't her — not to us."

Virgil was busy making notes. "Was she in any way double-jointed?"

"No."

"Now, sir, I'd like to take up the subject of her tastes. Did she show any particular interest in music?"

"Unfortunately, she seemed to prefer much of the common variety that goes with her generation. She liked ballad singers and other people who have voices of some kind and who normally sing on key."

"Did she ever favor any particular type of message singer? Joan Baez, Bob Dylan, any of those?"

"I don't recall that she cared for either of those. She mentioned a John Denver once."

"Her favorite instrumentalist?"

"The Indian sitar player, I can't remember his name."

"Ravi Shankar?"

"Yes, that's it. She played a recording of his for me at one time. He is obviously a virtuoso of tremendous powers, although his music is foreign to my own particular tastes."

"Your favorite artists, sir?"

"Heifetz, Zuckerman, Segovia, Mehta — if you allow conductors."

"Does Doris have any notable dramatic talent?"

"I'm pleased that you've returned her to the present tense. She had no ambitions to become an actress. She did appear in two or three school productions, never in a leading role — she preferred to avoid the limelight. One thing: she is a very clever mimic. She can take off almost anyone, man or woman, and hit the nail right on the head. She did Richard Nixon so well it was uncanny."

"I'd definitely call that talent," Tibbs said.

"Very possibly so."

"Her hobby interests?"

"None, really. She can ride a horse quite well, but she declined a mount of her own when I offered it to her."

"Can you mention any motion pictures that she particularly liked?"

Friedkin actually grinned. "Yes, *In the Heat of the Night*."

Virgil seemed uncomfortable. "Thank you, but we can let that one pass. How about some others?"

"All right. Including pictures shown on TV, she liked *Casablanca, Love is a Many Splendored Thing, Sayonara,* most of the James Bond films. She never showed any taste for westerns or situation comedies."

"You are being most helpful, sir — you are a keen observer."

"Not really. She talked quite a bit about the things she really liked. She saw *Casablanca* at least a dozen times."

"Who were her favorite authors?"

"That's harder. She liked mysteries, but who doesn't — I read them myself. She doesn't care for what are commonly called gothic novels. She likes Steinbeck and read almost all of John Masters."

Virgil was busy with his notebook. When he finally looked up, Friedkin had a question of his own. "Is this getting you anywhere?" he asked.

"Yes, sir, it is," Tibbs answered him. "In what we have talked about so far, you have provided one very significant clue — one that wasn't in our case file. Now, sir, some more questions."

It was more than an hour later when Tibbs finally left the big executive office. His mind was churning once more, because with reasonable luck, he had his teeth into something.

Virgil was closeted with Chris Hagerty, who had worked very closely on the Doris Friedkin disappearance the first time around. He was glad to go over the reports he had filed a year before. "Virg, we shook that restaurant, and the personnel, down all the way to rock bottom," he said. "The stories they told all jibed, with the usual minor disagreements that always crop up when people are really trying to tell the truth. We checked out every one of them, whether or not they had had any contact with the table where the rose princesses were being entertained or the area from which Doris disappeared. Nothing. We found a few minor things: one of the men in the kitchen had a couple of outstanding traffic warrants and we cleared those up. The manager had a rather nice mistress: I interviewed her myself."

"Did you find anything, anything at all, that didn't completely fit?"

"Strangely, no. Normally, where so many people are involved, little things crop up, but this time we drew blank. Virg, she simply got up, went to the ladies' room, and that was that. She had never had contact with anyone connected with the restaurant that we could uncover, apart from the fact that she had eaten there occasionally in the past and presumably knew where the ladies' room was."

"And, possibly also, that there was a door close by that led to the outside."

"That could be, Virg, but she wasn't the sort of person likely to open it to see. The picture I got of her shows her to be quiet, somewhat reserved, and accustomed to a great deal of money."

"Then, as you see it, there would be no point in my shaking everyone down again?"

"You're welcome to go ahead — I certainly won't mind. But in that restaurant there is a considerable turnover of personnel as a usual thing. Busboys, waitresses, and minor kitchen help tend not to stay on the job too long unless they have a particularly lush job. The place is good in almost all respects and the salaries are above average, but they aren't outstanding. So you'll have some problems."

Tibbs shook his head. "I'm sure, Chris, that if you did it, there won't be much left for me to rake over; I was just double checking to make sure. One thing: in your opinion, did she go out that back door?"

"She had to, nothing else was possible. To leave normally by the front door, she would have had to go almost directly past the table where the other rose princesses were seated; she could not have escaped being seen. The rest of the doors are out of the question. There is one off the kitchen that is used to bring in supplies and two others that are for emergency use only and are equipped with operating alarms that would trip if they were used. I checked them out and both of them were working."

"Why no alarm on the door she apparently did use?"

"To accommodate the cleaning service that looks after the washrooms; they come in every day. The management knew that it was a possible exit for deadbeats, but in three years they had lost only two checks that they know of that way. That made it cheaper to leave things as they were rather than go to the expense of installing an alarm and having to turn it off every time the cleaning personnel came by."

"Second question, Chris: after she went out that door, how did Doris leave the area?"

Hagerty leaned back. He was a very tall man and his leanness emphasized it even more. "I was afraid you'd ask that," he declared. "She didn't take a taxi, that's definite. She might have boarded a bus, because there is a stop close by that's out of sight of the restaurant, but four of us ran that one through the wringer to the bitter end and the chances are very much against it."

Tibbs was absorbing everything carefully and quietly. "So she either simply walked away or else managed a ride we know nothing about."

"True. We combed the whole surrounding area, talked to all of the shopkeepers and everyone we could find, and no one saw her. The rose princess dress she had on was quite elegant, but not a conspicuous standout — or so I'm told. However, I'm inclined to believe that she would have been noticed. We tried everything to get someone to come forward, but nobody did. Correction: some did, but they didn't check out. She plain vanished."

Virgil locked his fingers together and pressed them very tightly. "Then someone gave her a ride," he said, "or else she had it planned and had a car parked nearby on a side street."

Hagerty clasped his hands and rested them on top of his head. "I agree. Naturally we thought of that and went after the car angle particularly hard. No one saw anything that we could use, but that isn't conclusive, of course."

"I like the idea of a conspiring friend," Tibbs said.

"Or a coincidence, but it would have to be a remarkable one: remember that she came out in an alley. Just to walk

97

out and immediately sight a friend who would give her a ride and then keep his or her mouth tight shut thereafter is asking too much. I won't buy it."

"Any candidates for the friend?"

"We checked out several. Most of them satisfied us. You might have a go at a boy named Barry Samuels; his address is in the file. He had an alibi and a good one, but I had a very slight feeling that he could have said more if he had wanted to."

Virgil was suddenly quite grim. "That's good enough for me," he declared.

The make from the New Brunswick police came through shortly before three in the afternoon. Since Virgil was out, Bob Nakamura took it down in detail and promised a call back. He suggested that notification be held up until a brief conference could be arranged at the Pasadena end. There would undoubtedly be a number of questions to be resolved before the parents were told and any possibility of a mistake had to be eliminated first.

As soon as he was finished with that call, he made one to the Los Angeles County Coroner and passed on the information; after that he allowed himself a brief moment of repose. By the grace of God one major problem had been cleared away; the Jane Doe found in the park now had a name. The moment that Virgil walked back into the office, Bob gave him the news.

The Negro detective was grim. He dropped into his chair and stared at the wall before him. "I've been hanging onto a vain hope," he admitted. "I wanted her to have been someone alone in the world without any parents to notify. There wasn't any chance of that, of course."

"Very little," Bob agreed.

"God damn it!" Tibbs exploded. He was not loud, but his words shook with intensity. Rage was burning inside him and for a very few moments Bob feared that he was going to lose control of himself.

"Call me an idiotic sentimentalist if you want to," Virgil declared bitterly, "But I can't simply wipe her out of my mind. She was a pretty thing who'd been saving herself for the right man. That isn't too common any more. I can't escape the feeling that she was a nice person, now she's a half-rotted corpse that's been cut to pieces in a PM: so much human garbage — I hope she had a soul." He lapsed back into a dangerous silence.

When he sensed that it was the right moment, Bob spoke quietly. "We've had a good many S-5's in traffic accidents, and I'm afraid there'll be more."

Tibbs was still boiling. "Yes, but they weren't deliberate. And when we nail the bastard that did it, what will he get? Seven years, probably, and then he'll be out again."

"What do you want?" Bob asked.

Virgil looked at him. "Make a guess," he invited.

After another minute Bob tried something else. "What did you get?" he asked.

"I went and had another look at that alleyway. I timed various possible movements that Doris Friedkin could have made after she came out the back door of the restaurant and checked the angles of vision from the nearby houses and other occupied places."

"Did you learn anything?"

"Indirectly. It's quite possible she could have gotten out of that door and down the short alley without being seen. After that it depends on an unknown factor: how conspicuous that rose princess dress was. I've arranged to see one."

"Properly modeled, of course. Mary Goldie can put it on for us."

"Charming," Tibbs responded. "But there is also the idea of asking one of the rose princesses, who still has the dress, to do the honors."

"Scratch one lady cop."

"Unscratch Miss Peggy Collins who has consented to oblige." Virgil was beginning to come back to the world of reality; his anger had subsided somewhat and he was more in possession of himself.

"You do get around. When may we expect Miss Collins?"

Tibbs glanced at his watch. "It might be worthwhile to hang around for a few minutes."

"We ought to have a photographer."

He was rewarded by a slightly weary look from across the office. "He's on his way," Virgil said.

The photographer arrived first; Miss Collins was announced from the front desk ten minutes later. When she appeared at the office door, it was apparent at once why she had been chosen as a rose princess the year before. She was exceedingly pretty and radiated an ebullient personality that surrounded her like an aura. She paused for a moment and then came in with a welcoming smile as though she were the hostess rather than a guest. "Hello," she offered. "You're Virgil Tibbs?"

"Yes, Miss Collins."

"Good. Now please introduce this other nice-looking man to me."

Virgil was already on his feet. "This inscrutable Oriental with the somewhat revolting features is one Robert Nakamura, my partner."

"Hello, Bob."

Nakamura grinned. "Hello, Peggy. Come, sit over here and let me tell you exotic tales of the Mysterious East."

"First, don't you want to look at my dress?"

"Virgil will look at the dress, I will admire the contents."

Peggy went through the gestures of a fashion model, turning from one position to another with practiced ease. As the photographer recorded her performance on film, both men studied her and the attractive garment that she wore. When the impromptu fashion show had been completed, Tibbs became businesslike.

"What do you think?" he asked.

"If I met her on the street," Bob answered, "I wouldn't notice the dress too much. I'd see the girl."

"So would I, but remember: it wasn't this girl."

"I know, but Friedkin was also very attractive; everyone agreed on that."

"She certainly is," Peggy contributed. "What you want to know is: if she were walking down Colorado Boulevard in this dress, would a lot of people notice her because of it — is that right?"

"Exactly," Tibbs answered.

"Then maybe I can help you. Men wouldn't pay too much attention; they'd see Doris. Women, on the other hand, would be more inclined to see the dress and they might possibly know what it was."

"Peggy," Virgil asked, "how much of a departure is this dress from what you might ordinarily wear on the boulevard at noon, assuming that you were dressed up to go somewhere?"

"It isn't that different — that's an honest answer. It's supposed to be an original design and very special, but actually it has to be right for several different girls, and they hadn't even been chosen when the dresses were made. So it couldn't be too far out — is that clear?"

"Very." He nodded a dismissal to the photographer. "While you're here, may I ask some questions?"

"Sure — go ahead."

"First, we don't have a wide selection, but how about some coffee or a Seven-Up, something like that?"

"Here?"

"Right here — I'll have the houseboy bring the refreshments."

"You have to watch those blacks," Bob retorted. "Give them an inch and they'll take a mile."

Peggy was delighted. "Is there any root beer?" she asked.

Bob rose. "There is and I'll get some." He left.

"You answered a lot of questions at the time that Doris vanished, didn't you?" Virgil opened.

Peggy nodded. "Yes, we all did. Two or three times."

Tibbs visibly relaxed and studied the young woman before him. "Peggy, this is a new ball game: all I'm trying to do now is to find Doris — nothing more. I have considered the idea that she may not want to be found."

Again Peggy nodded. "That's what most of us thought."

"Then let me tell you this: if I do find her, and she doesn't want her whereabouts known, I'll report to her family that she's alive and well, but prefers not to come home."

"And you won't tell them where she is?"

Virgil shook his head. "Quite often we find somebody who is perfectly all right, but prefers to be left alone. When that happens, we let the relatives know that the person is well and happy, but we don't reveal anything more. Doris is an adult and she is entitled to her privacy."

Peggy became more grave. "I see." She was clearly think-ing, which was exactly what Tibbs wanted her to do.

"How long had you known Doris?" he asked, very gently.

"About four years."

"Were you good friends?"

"Good enough. Not too thick, but we got along."

"Then maybe you can tell me this: how serious was she about her religion?"

The unexpected question had its effect. Peggy hesitated and then looked at him. "Just between us?" she asked.

Virgil nodded. "Strictly between us, nobody else."

"Then here's the truth — she didn't like being Jewish. I don't mean that she was ashamed of it, just that she didn't *feel* Jewish, can you understand me? She talked about it with me once. She wanted to be just an American girl, with-out any hang-ups."

"Do you think she believed in God?"

"I know she did, but her family is sensitive about what they call 'the faith,' so they made it hard for her to date non-Jewish boys. They didn't forbid her, or anything like that, but they made it pretty clear that her husband should come from a Jewish home. That turned her off. She really likes her folks, or she did, but the religious part didn't appeal to her at all."

"Did she ever consider joining some other religious group?"

"She didn't talk about it, but it could happen. You see: Doris is quiet, but she's pretty brainy too. And when she wants to, she can throw off that shell in a hurry."

Bob came in with two drinks; he put them down and then quietly left the room. Peggy picked up hers and drank an inch off the top.

"Can you give me an example?" Tibbs asked, making it casual.

"Off the record?"

"Absolutely."

"Well, one time she came to a small party at my house. Just girls — my folks were out. We got talking about the strip shows that were all over town at that time — remember?"

"Yes, I saw a couple."

"Good, then you'll understand. Just for fun, we picked Doris as the girl least likely to succeed in that job. She didn't say anything, she just got up, put on a cassette, and gave a demonstration."

"Was she good?"

"She was terrific! None of us had any idea she could do it, but she was sensational."

Virgil drank half of his root beer. "And I had to miss it!" He deliberately warmed a little. "Well, maybe someday . . ."

"Don't rule it out," Peggy said. "And I'll tell you something else: the fact that you're black wouldn't make any difference to Doris — any more than it would to me."

Tibbs steered away from that one. "Peggy, still strictly between us, why do you think Doris chose to disappear? Don't tell me you don't have any idea, that's the official answer. I'm asking you absolutely off the record."

"According to the paper, you're working for Mr. Friedkin."

Virgil shook his head. "I'm working for the people of this city — and that includes you. And I can't be bought."

"First I want to ask you something," Peggy said. "Are you married?"

"No."

"Have you ever been?"

"No."

"Have you ever been to bed with a girl?"

"Yes."

"More than one?"

"Yes."

Peggy eased back in her chair. "Do you know why I asked you those things?"

"Of course. Were you satisfied with the answers?"

Peggy pushed her lips together and then nodded. "All right: I'll trust you, if you'll promise me that this doesn't go into writing — anywhere. And that you won't tell anyone."

"You have my word," Tibbs said.

"Right after we were picked as rose princesses Doris was upset. Not emotionally, she's not the kind to blow her cool. Physically upset. She was a little sick at times; that's why she left in the middle of the lunch to go the ladies' room."

Virgil nodded. "I guessed the same reason," he said. "As soon as I heard that she got up right in the middle of the meal."

Peggy put it into words. "I think she was pregnant," she said.

10

BARRY SAMUELS WAS DRESSED in casual clothing, but it was of very high quality and had cost a considerable amount of money — something that he was aware of every moment. He had dark, narrow features punctuated by a pair of close-set eyes and a prominent nose that accentuated the sharpness of his glance whenever he looked at his visitor. Young Mr. Samuels was still in school, but he had about him an aura of maturity that suggested nature had spotted him twenty years of experience sometime during his puberty. In his scheme of things every minute had to count, therefore he resented having to talk to the police once more after he had made a full statement more than a year ago.

The fact that he was not going to be cooperative was as obvious to Tibbs as the make of wristwatch that he wore — a very thin gold model of almost stark design. It would have been suitable for a man well past forty who had heavy responsibilities to discharge and a very expensive mistress. Flattery wouldn't work with this sharp young man, but something else might. This subject would measure everything by his own self-interest, and that was the way to get to him.

"I'm going to lay a few things out on the line for you," Virgil began with a strong no-nonsense tone in his voice. "You gave an incomplete account of your involvement with Doris Friedkin's disappearance the last time that we discussed the subject with you."

"I answered all the questions you asked." It was intended to be a positive statement, but it contained the suggestion of the defensive.

"I know that you did, but that isn't what I'm talking about." Tibbs picked up a thin sheet of closely typed paper and displayed it. "I read Agent Hagerty's report in detail; during your interview with him he said to you, 'Now I want you to give me a complete account in your own words.' You will notice the word 'complete.' That meant you were to report everything that you knew with no omissions whatever. You didn't do that. "

"What makes you think so?" Barry demanded.

That was music to Virgil's ears; it was an admission of guilt whether the speaker knew it or not.

"I'm going to make it easy for you," he pressed. "At the time you had no way of knowing that she was going to disappear semi-permanently; at least I'm willing to give you the benefit of the doubt on that."

"How could I know?"

"She could have told you," Tibbs almost snapped. He was playing his man carefully, keeping him just enough on edge without letting him become hostile. "For the time being, assume that she didn't. That means that you were unaware of the future course of events, which gives you a partial excuse."

"For what?"

Virgil ignored him. "According to your story at the time, you had gone to Los Angeles with a friend."

"That's right," Barry interjected.

Virgil picked up the report and scanned it once more. It was unnecessary — he knew every word that it contained — but it emphasized the fact that it was part of the official record. "Actually, you said Beverly Hills." He fixed his subject with a grim, penetrating stare.

"All right, Beverly Hills," Barry defended. "That was a year ago, dammit! How the hell am I supposed to remember?"

"You remember," Tibbs told him. "You had some dates with Doris; you knew her well. Her disappearance was dramatic and filled the news for days. You were involved; you'll remember in detail when you're sixty. So out with it. I know your friend backed up your story — he had to."

"And after a year you want to bust him. You're chasing shadows, you know that."

That was the point Virgil had been working toward; it was time to use the landing net. "I don't make deals," he said in a more normal tone of voice, "but in this particular instance I'm not out to bust anyone. That includes you and your friend. Let me put it this way: at the time that Doris vanished, did you have any idea that she would be gone for so long?"

"Of course not!"

"How long did you think it would be?"

Barry avoided the obvious trap. "Hey, wait now . . ."

Tibbs pretended to retreat. "I'll accept your statement that you had no idea she would be gone more than very briefly. Sooner or later, everyone wants to do that — to get away for a while; to leave personal problems behind, to feel a little freedom."

"And is there anything wrong in that?"

Virgil shook his head. "No, there isn't; that's why we have vacations, but they aren't always enough of an answer." He leaned forward a little. "I can put myself in your position: Doris wanted help from someone with enough sense to keep his mouth shut, someone she could trust. So you kept your mouth shut even when the matter became serious and we were called in. After that, you had no acceptable opportunity to change your story and you kept your word to her. Now it's another matter. I think you have sense enough to know that. Do you?"

"Yes," Barry said. It was the only answer he could give.

"I'm trying to find her because she may need help. But I can keep my mouth shut too. If she's all right, then whatever you tell me now stops here. If she does need help, or if something has happened to her, it's time to stop playing games. But I'll still protect you if I can."

It was quiet while Barry thought. It was time to unburden himself and he knew it. He had heard of the relentless Virgil Tibbs and he wanted out — precisely the attitude Tibbs had been carefully building in him.

"I want a guarantee of immunity," Barry said.

"In other words you want to put everything on the public record?"

"No, dammit, I want to keep out of trouble."

"You've got your chance right now. If I'm satisfied, we'll conveniently forget what you told us the first time around. Otherwise, you'll have to take your chances."

Barry knew that that was a deal; he could have challenged Tibbs's statement that he didn't make any, but he had too much sense to make that blunder. He had a good out and it might not come back again. Also he didn't know how much the resourceful Negro detective had already uncovered in the case that was supposed to be all but dead. In stock-market terms, which he understood, it was time to sell.

"Doris and I weren't too thick," he began, "but I did see her from time to time. Her family preferred me to the guy she was more or less going with. He was still a kid and they knew it, and there were other reasons."

"I know."

"O.K., you get it. Now Doris was quiet most of the time, but she knew what she was doing and she knew her way around."

Virgil nodded. "That checks. I know a lot more about Doris, in some respects, than her parents do."

"You're not the only one. Something happened to her that got her up pretty tight. Part of it was her old man's money: because of it she was expected to act a certain way all the time, and she didn't like it."

"She didn't want to be high society," Tibbs suggested.

Barry looked at him with something approaching mutual understanding. "No way, and her old man is pretty starchy. So she wanted to split. She had her own money and besides that she could write checks on her father's account. But she'd starve before she'd do that. Anyhow, we understood each other. She told me what the problem was and I told her I'd help her. It was pretty much all set when the rose princess thing happened. She didn't want any part of it, but her old man pushed her into the ring and she got picked."

"Under the circumstances," Virgil said, "that probably just made things worse."

"A lot worse. She was knocked up, you know that."

"Yes. Off the record, how was she in bed?"

Barry x-rayed him with a hard look. "Off the record, sensational. It was one of the few things she had on her own, something she allowed herself. We weren't together that much, but we both knew it wasn't anything serious. Our families kept shoving us together so what the hell."

"Were you going to take care of her?" Tibbs asked.

"Of course, but she didn't need it — I told you she knew her own way around. She planned to go to a little hospital in Santa Monica that specialized in that sort of thing. She was an adult and it would have been legally O.K."

"But when she was chosen as a rose princess, all of her time was tied up and she had to miss her appointment."

Barry lifted his shoulders. "So you've got it. Now you see the rest of it. She'd gone to a doc who told her he didn't think she was pregnant. He wasn't sure at that stage. Later she found that she was, and fairly well along. She had only a little time to get in under the wire."

"At which point she asked you for help, figuring that you could deliver."

"What would you have done?" Barry challenged.

Virgil was cool and at ease. "In your position, I'd have helped her. You owed it to her. Also, I would have been inclined to keep my own mouth shut, knowing that she was all right and only wanted a little time to herself."

Barry uncoiled a little. "Man, you could be human after all! I don't know why in hell you're a cop."

"Because I like it. Someday, if you get ripped off, you may be glad that we're around."

"All right, maybe. Anyhow, Doris told me that if she didn't get rid of her problem quickly, it would be too late. So I arranged to meet her outside the back of the restaurant,

111

on the side street. She came out right on schedule, I picked her up; so bust me for it."

"Where did you take her?" Tibbs asked.

Barry shook his head. "Look, I've leveled with you, now you know how she got out of that restaurant. I took her to a friend of hers. That's all I'm going to say. I'm not going to put somebody else's neck on the block."

"You don't have to," Virgil told him. "Just one thing: you wanted immunity. A good way to earn it would be to keep absolutely quiet about our little discussion. To everyone. Got it?"

"No tip-offs, in other words."

"That's right. It wouldn't work anyway."

"No, I guess not. Can I go now?"

Things were beginning to shape up and Virgil was satisfied. "Why not?" he said.

When Arthur Kallman answered his doorbell and found Sergeant Morrison on his front porch, he instinctively knew what to expect. "Come in, Sergeant," he said, and stepped aside to let his guest enter. The way that Morrison walked confirmed his suspicions. The news was bad — very bad.

Kallman called in his wife and in so doing tried to prepare her, at least in part. "Mary, Sergeant Morrison is here to see us." He knew that she would understand. Nothing would make it easy, but at least she would not come into the room all smiles and then have to be told a terrible thing.

When Mary Kallman did come in, it was instantly clear to her husband that his message had been understood. He turned to look at the police officer and realized that Morrison understood as well. "Suppose we all sit down," Arthur said. He sat with his wife and held her hand while Morrison, with careful tact, took a single chair opposite.

"You have some news of Nancy," Arthur said, to make it easier both for Morrison and for themselves.

The policeman nodded quietly. "Yes, sir, I have. And I am afraid that it isn't very good."

Arthur closed his eyes for a moment and gripped his wife's hand very tightly. "Is it definite?" he asked.

"Yes, sir, it is."

Mary spoke in a strangely calm voice. "She's dead."

Morrison let a long interval of silence answer for him, it was the kindest and the gentlest way. When the truth had seeped through the room, he put it into words because it was his duty to do so. "I'm very sorry. Please accept my very deepest sympathy."

After a few moments Kallman found his voice once more. "You have been very considerate, Sergeant. Thank you for that. Was it an accident?"

"No, sir."

Mary suddenly leaned forward, her eyes widened with horror. "She didn't . . ."

The policeman shook his head. "No, Mrs. Kallman, not that."

Arthur looked at the quiet sergeant. "It wasn't an accident, she didn't do anything desperate herself, then . . ."

Morrison pressed his lips hard together. "This isn't easy to tell you, sir, but she was found in a very wild part of a large park in Pasadena, California. There is no evidence to suggest that she went there by herself."

Mary resorted to an old expression she had unconsciously learned as a girl. "Then she met with foul play."

The sergeant answered her calmly, but without delay. "Yes, Mrs. Kallman, that is what we believe happened. It may be some comfort to you to know that she was not sexually assaulted, or anything like that."

"Then why . . . ?" Arthur asked.

"We don't know yet, Mr. Kallman. The Pasadena police are investigating and they will keep me informed."

Morrison waited to measure the way in which the Kallmans were reacting to the news. There were many questions that he wanted to ask as soon as possible, but he was a humane man who genuinely respected the privacy of others. His problem was resolved for him when Arthur Kallman sat up a little straighter and addressed him.

"Sergeant Morrison," Arthur said. "Is there anything we can do — to help?"

The policeman produced his notebook. "Yes, sir, very definitely there is, if you and Mrs. Kallman feel up to it. We need some information desperately."

"We'll do all we can," Kallman promised.

Something in his tone, earnest as it was, tipped Morrison off. "I want you to understand, sir," he declared carefully, "that whatever you may be able to tell us, is very strictly confidential. We prefer to keep things that way."

The impact of that statement was almost visible on both of the Kallmans. Definitely there was something that they didn't want to have generally known. Arthur, however, was an intelligent man and he had his priorities sorted out in the proper order. "I very much appreciate that, Sergeant," he said. "There are certain matters we would rather not have published."

"They will not be," Morrison promised.

"Then in that case, sir, perhaps now would be the best

time to get this over with. First of all, if it makes any difference, I am not Nancy's father. Or I was not ..."

"I suspect that you were a very good father to her none the less," the sergeant said.

"I tried my very best to be," Kallman declared. "Nancy knew, but we loved each other just as though I had been her natural father."

Mary Kallman continued, because she wanted to lift the burden from her husband. "If ... you need to know ... I can tell you the facts concerning Nancy's birth."

Morrison was entirely sympathetic. "It could be very helpful, if you don't mind too much."

Mary massaged her face with her palms and then straightened herself beside her husband. "Nancy is my daughter," she began calmly enough. Then she realized what she had said and momentarily lost control of herself. The sergeant sat very still, giving her all the time she needed to recover her composure.

When at last she did, she began once more on a different tack. "I came originally from California. I had a very good job there as a private secretary. I was quite happy, and then I met a wonderful man."

She stopped once again and looked at her husband. Arthur tightened his fingers reassuringly around her hand and nodded his head just enough to encourage her to continue. Morrison watched, and hated the necessity of putting them through this.

Mary Kallman intentionally made her voice flat and factual as she went on. "He was married, something I'm sure you've heard many times before." She found a fresh well of strength and looked at Morrison face to face. "I'm not defending myself when I say that his wife, almost from the day that he married her, was not a well woman. It had been an obligation type of marriage, entered into because it was expected of both parties by their families. He did everything he should have as a husband, but he received almost nothing in return."

She stopped and measured the effect of what she had said. The comforting silence that filled the room gave her a measure of encouragement and reassurance.

"I was aware of the situation, but I did not intrude myself — I would never do that. Then, when things had gotten about as bad as they could, he told me that he was going to file for divorce. At that time he asked me if I would be willing to wait for a decent interval and then — marry him. I said that I would. At that time it was a wonderful dream come true, and my conscience was clear because I had done nothing whatever to bring this about."

"I can very well understand your position," Morrison told her. "To make things easier, I take it that he was Nancy's father."

Mary lowered her head for a moment. "Yes. He moved to an apartment and we saw something of each other. Then he was told that after many years of marriage, his wife had become pregnant: something they had both thought would be impossible. When he came and told me, I knew what it meant: he had no choice then but to remain his wife's husband, at least in name. We were both completely . . ." The word eluded her and she did not try to supply it.

She was close to tears. "We had looked forward so much to being married — to each other — we seized one moment of realization. It was my fault, not his. That was when Nancy was conceived."

With that confession behind her, Mary found the rest

easier. "When I discovered my own condition, Nancy's father did everything he possibly could for me. It was my own decision to have my child — I wanted that part of him even though I was not entitled to it."

When she could not continue, Arthur Kallman took over for her. "If you had known Nancy, you would know how wise that decision was. Mary's employer was a man of affairs with many contacts. When she confided in him that she would have to resign, he was more than considerate. He arranged a job for her here and had the personnel papers sent through as 'Mrs. Mary Stepanik.' Someday I want to meet him just so I can tell him how much that kindness meant."

Mary finished the account. "When Nancy was born, I confided in my doctor. He issued a birth certificate showing Nancy as legitimate and her father deceased." She looked quickly at Morrison who at once shook his head.

"Don't worry at all about that," he reassured her.

"Thank you." Mary's eyes were wet as she smiled at her husband. "Two years after that I met Arthur, the finest man possible. After we had been going together for some time, I told him the whole story. When I finished, he kissed me and then asked me to be his wife. After we were married, he formally adopted Nancy so that she could have a true father and take his name. Ever since then we've been completely, wonderfully happy until . . ."

Morrison helped her once more. "When Nancy went to California, it was to meet her natural father," he suggested gently.

"Yes," Arthur answered. "She wanted to do that very much and we both approved of it. You can understand why."

"Of course. Was he expecting her?"

Arthur Kallman shook his head. "No, sir. Nancy wanted to arrange to see him on a suitable pretext before she told him who she was. After that, it was to be her decision whether she did so or not. We have always been completely open and honest with her, and we found it to be the right way."

"I wish that everyone could be as prudent and considerate," Morrison commented. "It would make our work a lot easier, and prevent many tragedies."

That was a bad slip and he knew it, but it was too late to recall his words. He covered very quickly by asking a question. "May I have the gentleman's name?"

Surprisingly, Arthur answered that. "If it is necessary, then we will give it to you. But if it can be avoided . . ."

Morrison stood up. "Mr. Kallman," he said, "It's a rare privilege to meet a gentleman like you. You have my admiration, sir."

He turned toward his hostess. "Mrs. Kallman, would you object to giving me the name of your employer in California? It might help a little at that end. We will be very careful with the information you've given us."

"I don't mind that at all," Mary answered. "It might possibly help." She looked at her husband. "Because Nancy was planning to meet him too if she could. His name is Mr. Herbert Friedkin."

11

Virgil Tibbs sat quietly, savoring the presence of his companion. Intervals of relaxation were too few in his life and he did not enjoy many to equal the peace that surrounded him at that moment. Across the table Marsha Briggs looked back at him, a cigarette held in her tapered fingers, returning his silence with silence, his cool detachment with her own sophistication.

From the thirteenth-floor dining room of the Pasadena Hilton the city was again spread out inviting inspection, its flaws and secret vices hidden from almost a hundred and fifty feet above.

Because he could not help it — the habit was too deeply ingrained — memories came back to Virgil of a deprived boyhood in the Deep South, of the race riots, of the angry and hopelessly frustrated attempts of some God-beseeching Negro people to be allowed to eat at the bus station, of the violent deaths that had taken place. In Virgil Tibbs's mind there came back yet once again the sight of his first victim of murder; a seventeen-year-old black youth who had been mistaken for someone else and who had died with an unde-livered report card still in his pocket. He had spent most of his short life in classrooms, preparing himself for whatever kind of life he would be permitted to live. He had "shown promise."

As he had bent over the body of that once living human being, in Virgil Tibbs's adolescent mind there had been born the dedication that he would someday do something to punish cold-blooded, wanton murder. It had grown as a gradual thing, not forged in a furnace of blind hate, but it had endured. Now he sat at one of the choicest tables that the elegant room had to offer, dining with a young woman who was catching far more than her share of masculine eyes. And he was the homicide specialist of an important, modern police organization that protected a major American city.

Willie Jones had not lived to see all this, but his representative was there, dressed in a hand-tailored suit that would have exceeded young Willie's wildest dreams of eventual glory, if he had ever allowed himself to have any.

"I want to ask your help," Virgil said. "Do you mind?"

"What kind of help?"

"Just conversation. I'd like to lay out something for you and see what you think."

"Why not ask a policewoman?"

"Because they think like policewomen; that's part of their job."

Marsha put her cigarette briefly to her lips and blew a thin veil of smoke into the air. "Don't tell me that you don't have a regular girl friend," she chided him.

"The girl I see most often was born and raised in Japan."

Marsha yielded. "All right, I'll try."

"Consider yourself to be a young woman of position who has found things piling up too fast for her, to the point where she is seriously considering taking some sort of drastic action."

"In other words, consider myself Doris Friedkin." When Tibbs gave her a penetrating look, she spoke again without emphasis. "I read the papers."

"Very well, you are Doris Friedkin. You have just been chosen a rose princess with a very hectic schedule to face, with all of your individuality snatched away until the Tournament will be over. You will be told what to do, what to wear, how to fix your hair, when to go to bed and when to get up. Even what to eat and where. So you decide to split."

Marsha took a last taste of her cigarette and snuffed it out. "So I get up in the middle of a meal with the other princesses and go to the ladies' room."

"Yes."

"Alone."

"Yes."

"I'm pregnant."

Virgil's face betrayed nothing. "What else do you think?"

Marsha thought only briefly. "I might just go out, hoping that I could catch a cab or something like that, but then whatever I did could be traced. I'd do one of two things: I'd simply walk away, hoping that I wouldn't be recognized, or else I'd have someone meet and help me."

"Who?" Tibbs asked.

"The man who would have to respond, the one who had knocked me up. Do you agree?"

"The thought had crossed my mind. Where would he take you?"

"Where I told him to, to a friend I could trust, who

wasn't under any obligation to me, someone dependable."

Virgil looked at her. "Man or woman?" he asked.

Marsha was slightly scornful. "Another woman, of course. No other way."

The music began to flow in from the cocktail bar. "Thank you," Tibbs said. "I think you're right. One more point, where would you go after that?"

Marsha touched her napkin to her lips. "As far away as I could get," she answered. "Where neither you nor anyone else could ever find me."

Herbert Friedkin was becoming accustomed to unexpected visits from Virgil Tibbs, but he found that they brought him a strange comfort. The more that he saw of the Negro detective, the more convinced he became of his abilities. He sensed that a notably efficient job of investigating was being done and despite the fact that the trail was long cold, some definite results were entirely possible.

He was therefore somewhat surprised when he learned that the subject of the interview was not to be his missing daughter. "Mr. Friedkin," Virgil began, "let me preface by saying that this is a private and confidential police discussion in which I'm enlisting your cooperation."

"You have it," Friedkin said.

"Thank you, sir. I'm now concerned with the young woman who was found murdered in Oak Grove Park; that case is also my responsibility."

Friedkin was puzzled. "I don't see how I can help you there."

"Do you recall employing a young woman named Mary Stepanik some time ago? Say a little more than twenty years."

The financier stared at him for a moment. "Mary, of course I do! She was my private secretary for some time and, quite frankly, the best one I ever had."

"I understand that you helped her materially with a personal problem at the time she resigned." Tibbs was quietly factual.

The shutters dropped. It was a subtle thing, but instantly detectable. "Could you explain a little more fully?" Friedkin asked.

"I am aware, sir, that Miss Stepanik had a romantic affair that resulted in her pregnancy. At that time the abortion laws were still very strict and she was in a considerable difficulty. You came to her rescue."

Herbert Friedkin slowly nodded his head. "Since you are clearly in possession of the main facts, I'll discuss it. Otherwise, I still consider myself bound to respect her confidence."

Virgil admired that. "She spoke of you recently in glowing terms, Mr. Friedkin. Obviously her trust in you is well justified."

"How is she?"

"Physically very well, I understand. Now what can you tell me about the events of that time?"

Friedkin still hesitated. "For what reason, Mr. Tibbs?"

"To help me catch a murderer."

The industrialist relaxed. "When you put it that way, obviously it becomes my obligation to help you in every way that I can. Mary, when I knew her, was exceptionally well qualified as a private secretary — I've already indicated that. She was also very presentable if not actually a beauty. It was always my feeling that the man who would eventually marry her would be making a very fine choice."

"You were yourself married at that time, I take it."

"Very much so, and most happily. You have met my wife."

"Well put, sir. Briefly, what happened?"

Friedkin pressed his lips together for a second or two before he responded to that — his reluctance was still visible. "During the time that she was working for me Mary met a man who became very much interested in her. I knew him slightly. He was married, but it was my understanding that he was having some serious domestic problems and that divorce was imminent. To the best of my knowledge, he conducted himself as well as either of us could expect."

Herbert Friedkin paused and considered something intently for several seconds; then he made a decision. "I'd like to withhold his name for the time being if I may. As I said, I happen to know him."

Tibbs yielded a point. "For the time being, of course."

"Thank you." The feeling of restraint deepened and Virgil felt it clearly. Then Friedkin continued. "I don't see how I can avoid mentioning this, so I will tell you that a major reason for his unsatisfactory marital situation was his wife's almost complete refusal to participate in any sexual activity with him. And as you know, that is a valid basis for divorce everywhere, and it was at that time."

"Certainly."

"Mary and he were attracted to each other very strongly. Mary told me, very much in confidence at the time, that he had asked her if she would be willing to wait for a while after his divorce and then marry him." The industrialist sat up to inject a fresh thought. "Let me make it clear, Mr. Tibbs, that in my opinion Mary herself did nothing whatever to widen that schism, at least nothing deliberately. That would have been entirely out of character for her."

124

"I understand, sir, and I accept that."

"Just before the divorce proceedings were to begin, something happened — the wife became pregnant. It became a highly emotional matter. She didn't want the child; she was terrified of motherhood. Her husband, on the other hand, felt completely trapped; he couldn't divorce a pregnant wife and abortion was out of the question at the time. And, of course, Mary's hopes were washed away. Under the extreme tension of that situation Mary seized a brief interval of happiness while she could. Personally, I cannot blame her."

"Nor can I," Tibbs said.

"Fortunately, she came to me and told me the whole story. I offered her two alternatives: a trip abroad where she could obtain a legal and safe abortion, or a transfer to an eastern subsidiary where they could make good use of her abilities. She chose the latter, so at my direction a close personal friend of hers who could be trusted retyped her personnel records to show her as a recent widow."

"It was certainly generous of you to go to all that trouble."

"It was actually very little trouble, Mr. Tibbs. Compared to what she had to go through, it was nothing at all. Now, please, why are you so interested in all of this past history?"

For carefully considered reasons, Virgil began to tread with added caution. "Perhaps you can guess, sir. Miss Stepanik had her child — a girl. Since she was understood to have lost her husband, no questions were ever raised. Then she subsequently met and married a man who knew the whole story and who adopted the little girl as his own."

"Mr. Tibbs, don't tell me . . ."

"I'm intensely sorry, Mr. Friedkin, but the young lady whose body we found was, in fact, your former secretary's daughter. She had come out here in the hope of meeting her natural father, with the full approval of her parents back in New Jersey."

Friedkin sat very still for several seconds, his eyes shut. When he spoke, his thoughts were hardly in the room. "Poor Mary," he said.

Virgil sat quietly and let him take his time absorbing the news. He had been in many similar situations before and he understood them.

"I must confess," Friedkin said at last, "that I had, and still have, a very high regard for Mary herself. She was with me for more than five years. How is she taking it?"

Tibbs did not want to say, "As well as could be expected," but he was in no position to improve very much on that. Also, he was acutely aware that the man before him had lost his own daughter and had no idea of her fate. He resorted to telling the strict truth. "I haven't met her," he said simply.

Friedkin brought himself back to the present. "How may I help you?" he asked.

"In two ways. First, I will have to talk to the young lady's natural father, you understand why. Since you know him, perhaps you will be kind enough to ask him to get in touch with me."

Friedkin leaned forward and let his forearms rest on the top of his desk. "Do you want me to break the news to him?" he asked.

"What is your feeling on that, sir?"

"Perhaps it would be better if I prepared him for any questions that you may want to ask. Assuming that I can get hold of him, you will probably hear from him shortly. What was the other thing you wanted to ask of me?"

"Just one question: did you hear from the young lady at any time before her death?"

"No, I did not, but why would she wish to contact me? I'm certain that we never met."

"It's quite simple, Mr. Friedkin: Nancy knew the whole story of her birth and what happened at that time. She was fully aware of what you had done for her mother, and she had heard your name many times. She wanted to meet you and thank you herself."

"That was her name — Nancy?"

"Yes. Nancy Kallman."

Friedkin covered his face with his hands for a moment or two and then brushed his eyes. "Forgive me," he said, "I'm a human being, dammit, and I can't help being affected." Presently he went on. "She did not try to reach me; I can be certain because ever since Doris disappeared, I've made myself accessible just in case someone might have a message for me. Is there anything else I can do?"

"No, sir, and thank you for your time."

Virgil Tibbs returned to the Pasadena Police Station with a long list of things to be done. The first item on his agenda was to run a complete recheck on all of the known sex offenders in the area — more than ninety of them. The fact that Nancy Kallman had not been sexually assaulted was not in itself conclusive, particularly in view of the fact that she had been strangled. It was quite possible that she had been accidentally killed while her attacker had only been trying to subdue her. After discovering what he had done, his raging passions could have turned abruptly into cold fear in the face of death.

A full investigation turned up nothing. Since the time of death could not be accurately determined, alibis were relatively useless.

Bob Nakamura took on the tedious task of contacting all of the parole and probation officers in Southern California to find out if any of them had noted any unusual emotional problems in the people under their jurisdiction. Nothing productive came of that. Next he checked out the Travelers' Aid and all of the other information agencies to which Nancy might have turned. He drew another complete blank.

The final report from the coroner's office contained nothing new. Tibbs released the body for shipment to New Jersey and burial there. The casket was sent sealed with orders that it was not to be reopened under any circumstances whatever.

The obvious lead, the friends with whom Nancy had come to the West Coast, proved exasperatingly hard to pin down. None of them could be located. The car should have been relatively easy to spot with New Jersey plates, but the California Highway Patrol and the Sheriff's Department both failed to turn it up, as did all of the other law enforcement agencies in the greater Los Angeles basin.

Herbert Friedkin phoned personally to report that he had spoken with Nancy's father who had been in Hawaii for some time. The man was willing to meet with the police when he returned; in the meantime he advised that he had heard nothing from Nancy and had had no idea that she had planned to see him. He confirmed that they had never met.

Playing the percentages, Captain Wilson ordered an intensified coverage of the Oak Grove Park area, particularly at night. Anyone concerned enough to watch and keep track would have noticed a marked increase in the number of white Matadors that cruised through the park driveways; less conspicuous were the unmarked official cars and the borrowed vehicles from used car lots that also helped to maintain the surveillance.

From New Jersey Sergeant Morrison reported that none of Nancy's traveling companions had either written or phoned home. All of the concerned families had been alerted, but nothing had broken the unnatural silence.

One small thing did jell; Virgil checked with the Pasadena City College and learned that the speech department had a recording of Doris Friedkin's voice. That filled in a badly wanted item; he lost no time in getting it and having a cassette copy made. The quality was good, something he appreciated as he listened to it over and over again, memorizing the voice pattern and the inflections. Then he took it out to have a voice print made.

When he got back, Bob Nakamura was on hand with some ideas to discuss. Virgil closed the door so that they would not be interrupted and listened to what his partner had to say.

"I want to talk about your interview with young Samuels," Bob began. I've been thinking over your account of it. In the first place, you told him that you didn't make deals, then a little later you offered him one, is that right?"

"Yes, it is."

"I'm assuming that you did that in order to let the subject feel superior — smarter than you were — so that he would become incautious and tell more to the poor dumb cop."

"Exactly. Barry Samuels has a flaming ego. I just blew on it a little."

"And it worked."

"Yes."

"Now he supplied information up to the point where he admitted picking up Doris Friedkin and taking her to a friend's house. Then you stopped."

"Yes, I did."

"Virgil, it wouldn't have taken you two minutes to get the name out of him. Why did you let him off the hook?"

Tibbs actually smiled, something he had not had much opportunity to do of late. "Simple, and notice my restraint — I didn't say 'elementary.' Of course I could have gotten the name out of him, but if I had done so, he would have called the girl and warned her that I was on the way."

"I think he called her anyway."

"Of course he did; I insured that by asking him to keep our conversation strictly confidential. But if I'm guessing right, he told her that he hadn't given her away, that I didn't know who she was, and that if I came back at him to get her name, he would warn her."

"Do you think that he doesn't want Doris found?"

"I think that he wants to protect himself and that that's the only consideration that means a damn to him. If Friedkin was pregnant when she disappeared, he may well be responsible. I also like Randy Joplin for that role, but he swears to high heaven that he never had her. He may be telling the truth, because he readily admits to an active sex life with a variety of other girls. He attributes his success to his good looks and his family's money."

"A nice young man."

"Yes, just the kind we ought to recruit for the force. Now that the Nancy Kallman killing is in the slow agony stage, I plan to interview Doris Friedkin's friend — the one who helped her. I think that I may make some hay there if I go in as a friend rather than as a police officer."

"Have you anyone in mind?"

"I have Miss Peggy Collins in mind."

"But she was one of the rose princesses; that scrubs her!"

Virgil shook his head. "That's exactly what I assumed at first, but put the facts together. The first time around every one of Doris's known friends was interviewed in depth, more than once. Every girl's movements were checked and verified up to seventy-two hours after Doris vanished. But the rose princesses were not — it was assumed that they were all tied up."

"And you've found out that they weren't."

"After that memorable luncheon, the girls were excused until five-thirty when they were to report back in their evening costumes. So Collins, or any of the other princesses, had plenty of time to get into the act."

"So far, I'll buy it. Now why the ravishing Collins — apart from the fact that you would obviously like to have the pleasure of seeing her again?"

Tibbs tilted back in his chair and put his legs on the corner of his gray metal desk. "Several little things. Consider her personality: she isn't the retiring type — she's very open and the kind of a girl willing to take a chance on something if she likes the idea."

"True — but thin."

"Granted. But now recall our conversation as I reported it to you. After you had stepped out of the room, I explained to Peggy that if we found Doris and she didn't want her whereabouts revealed, we wouldn't tell anyone where she was. As soon as she understood that we keep such matters confidential, she said to me, '*And you won't tell them where she is?*' Those were her exact words."

Bob mused. "I did miss that the first time around."

"Next," Tibbs continued, "when I asked her how well she had known Doris, she acknowledged that they had known each other for four years. She specifically claimed that they hadn't been too thick, but a moment later she was able to tell me that Doris didn't espouse the Jewish faith, but that she did believe in God — I asked her specifically about that. Peggy knew intimate details about Doris's relations with her family on religious matters; that puts her in the class of a confidante."

"A confidante who knows that Doris is alive and well and who let it slip."

"Another thing: she frequently spoke of Doris in the present tense. She said, 'Doris is quiet, but she's pretty brainy too.' Since the girl has been gone for more than a year, almost anyone would use the past tense automatically. Even the Friedkins did that; her own mother said to me, 'Doris never had to wear glasses at any time.' And that was during our first meeting."

"You've got me thinking," Bob admitted.

Tibbs meshed his fingers and studied them for a moment. "You may remember something else: Peggy's description of the party where Doris did a striptease for her girl friends. I said to Peggy, 'And I had to miss it!' Then, quite intentionally, I added, 'Well, maybe someday . . . ' "

Bob quickly leaned forward. "I do remember. Peggy answered, 'Don't rule it out.' You're right, she does know where Doris is!"

"She certainly knows more about her vanishing act than she has told us so far. She also made a considerable point about the fact that she didn't object to my ethnic origins whatsoever, so I shall test that statement. I'm going to invite the lady out."

12

WITHIN A MATTER OF A FEW HOURS, things began to break.

In Venice an alert patrol officer who had been on the force less than four months spotted a fairly ancient Chevrolet with New Jersey plates turning right on a red light without stopping first. He flicked on his red lights and made the traffic stop within two blocks. As soon as he could read the back plate he phoned in the I.D. as a matter of routine. He also knew that a Chevrolet with Jersey plates was involved in a murder investigation.

The driver stopped promptly enough without visible protest. Just before the officer got out of the car, the computer read-out was radioed to him. As a result he undid the top of his holster and had his hand on his weapon as he bent over to ask the driver for his license.

The young man behind the wheel offered no resistance. When he was asked to follow the patrol car to the police station, he did not understand the reason — or he pretended not to. "I busted the light, I know," he admitted. "But that's only a ticket, isn't it?"

"The watch commander will be glad to answer your questions, sir, if you'd be kind enough to follow me." He worded that carefully, so that it would at least sound like a request. Then feeling inwardly that perhaps he had already made his first big bust, he returned to his car and drove back to headquarters. The young man in the New Jersey Chevrolet followed as he had been instructed to do.

At almost the same time Officers James Riley and Charles Watkins, on patrol in their Matador, were checking on the report of a lost child in northeastern Pasadena. They were not unduly alarmed; it appeared to be a simple case of an eight-year-old who had wandered away from home in the very early evening, but they were alert nevertheless. As they had so many times before during the past few days, they drove slowly through Oak Grove Park, which was only a short distance from the child's home. The windows of the car were down and as they looked, they also listened.

Some faint sounds that reached them could have been meaningless, but nevertheless they pulled over and with a portable radio and flashlights began a search.

It had lasted for only two or three minutes when, quite close by, they heard someone running. At the same moment a child cried out. The officers required no further evidence; Watkins took off in pursuit of the runner while Riley headed for the sound of the crying child. When he found her, and rapidly noted her condition, he spoke urgently into his radio.

The response was extremely fast; three additional cars came on the scene within the next two minutes. By the time that two more units arrived, one of the police helicopters was already overhead, shining its powerful floodlight down into the suspect area. From headquarters Dallas Perkins drove with lights and siren to the site to take command. The two officers who were stationed at the missing child's home were notified that she had probably been found, but to withhold the information from the parents pending confirmation and more data. They both knew what that meant; because they had children of their own, they shared in inward shock despite their training and experience.

Lieutenant Perkins arrived on the scene just as Jim Riley came out of the brush carrying the little girl in his arms. Her clothing matched the description of the child for whom they had been searching.

"How bad?" Perkins asked.

"Pretty bad, Sergeant. She's bleeding from the vagina."

"Ambulance?"

"Let me take her; it'll be faster. Someone should hold her."

"Right."

Less than thirty seconds later Riley pulled his car away and hit the red lights. Beside him another officer held the child carefully as they sped, the siren splitting the air, toward Huntington Memorial Hospital.

Meanwhile six other officers had joined the search for the suspect. Agent Chris Hagerty heard crashing sounds; he broke into a small clearing to find Watkins in a desperate struggle with a burly man dressed in dark work clothes. Hagerty flung himself into the action and with his much more than six feet of height, he had powerful leverage. Even then it was not easy; the suspect fought like a wildcat. When Watkins was caught off guard for a moment, he received a vicious kick in the abdomen that dropped him to the ground in agony.

The suspect picked that moment to try and break away, but two more officers blocked his way. They did not use their weapons; the quarters were much too close and in the darkness any shooting would have been extremely hazardous. Instead they resorted to purely physical action and then it was a matter of seconds. By the time that Watkins had recovered enough to get to his feet, they had the suspect flat on his face and Hagerty was cuffing his hands behind his back.

He was transported to headquarters and booked on suspicion of child molestation, statutory rape, and resisting arrest. By the time that the process had been completed, Sergeant Bill Orr had been briefed and was ready to conduct an immediate interrogation. After the suspect had been given his rights and otherwise prepared, Orr was ready to begin.

Identification was swift and relatively easy. The suspect gave an alias, but Orr broke that down within five minutes; half an hour later a full rap sheet had been received in communications. It told a deadly story, including the fact that the suspect was on parole in Indiana after having been convicted of raping a housewife in the presence of her six-year-old daughter.

With that information at hand Orr really bored in. Within an hour the suspect admitted having raped the child after he had enticed her into the park. He had declined legal advice, but he asked for "help." He showed no remorse, claiming that he was too mentally sick to be responsible for his actions.

The interrogation then turned to the death of Nancy Kallman. The suspect admitted having been in the area at the time, working in a car wash. When he was shown a picture of the girl he suddenly dried up, became morose, and refused any further communication. It was Orr's decision to end the session at that point; toughened as he was by some of the things he had had to witness during his career, he was so repelled by the man he had been talking to he needed a respite. The suspect was taken up to the fourth floor jail and put into a maximum security cell to await legal action in the morning.

In an unmarked official car, Virgil Tibbs drove westward on the Santa Monica Freeway, fuming, like so many others, at the reduced speed limit that so few observed and that made driving strictly according to the law all but an impossibility. He was deep in thought. Certain ideas were germinating in his mind and they were far from conventional. But the more he considered them, the more they invited further exploration. It was as though some unseen phantom was whispering silently into his ear, "You're getting warmer!"

The house where a young man was awaiting him was long run down and devoid of paint. Part of it could be blamed on the salt sea air, part of it on neglect, and part of it on the economics of inflation and the prevailing carnivorous interest rates. It was the kind of place where young people with limited resources could find accommodations if they weren't too particular. Billy Owens fell into that category.

The story he told Tibbs was on the surface consistent and blameless. He owned the Chevrolet and to prove it he displayed the registration certificate which was made out in his name. He had wanted to visit the West Coast during the cold months — he had no taste for the ice and freezing slush of the East Coast — and California held some hope of being a land of opportunity.

He had signed up two friends to split expenses with him, one male and one female. Then someone had told him that

Nancy Kallman also wanted to go to the Coast. With four aboard it would cost everyone a little less, probably be a lot more fun, and there would be an additional driver. It had worked out quite well all of the way. They had taken seven days to make the trip with some stopovers to visit friends who could be depended upon for a night's lodging, and to see the Grand Canyon.

Nancy had left the party in Pasadena. She had never discussed her actual destination and no one had bugged her for any explanations. Toward evening they had found themselves close to the end of their route; while driving down Colorado Boulevard in Pasadena they had spotted a coffee shop that had seemed suitable and they had all gone inside for food. It had been around eight by the time they had been seated and none of them had known where they were going to sleep that night.

The restaurant had been almost full and they had been put into an oversize booth that already held four or five others like themselves; they had been separated only by a token foot of air space between the tables. They had begun talking and within a few minutes a rapport had been established. The travelers had wanted to push on to the beach community of Venice, symbolically reaching the Pacific Ocean. They had been assured that accommodations could be found there at low rates if they were back from the water. Nancy had not concurred; she had stated that one person she wanted to see lived in Pasadena and she wanted to remain there.

"So she split," Billy concluded. "It was all just fine. She had paid her share all of the way and we were square. I gave her the name of a friend of mine in Venice where she could call me if she wanted to. One of the guys we had met there offered to drop her off at a good place to stay. He was O.K. and the girl we had met agreed that she was in good hands. So she got her case out of the car, and they left."

"What was his name?" Virgil asked. He was careful to make it appear a casual question.

"I don't know," Billy answered, "I heard it, but I don't remember."

"Barry?"

"No, I don't think so."

"Randy?"

"Maybe — but I doubt it."

"Think hard."

Billy spread his hands. "It won't do any good. I met this guy once, see, and I heard his name that one time. That's all. And that was maybe a month ago."

"The date is important," Tibbs told him, "I need to know that."

Billy was again uncertain. "I'll ask the others and call you."

"Good. Make it collect, because it's a toll call. I'll give you my direct number. If I'm not there, leave the message — I'll get it." He wrote on a calling card and handed it over.

"I will; I don't want any trouble. And . . . I'm awful sorry about Nancy."

"Thank you. If you move, let me know where you are. Don't leave the area without my permission."

Satisfied, Virgil went back to his car. He was intentionally giving Billy a great deal of rope, because it fitted the ideas that were growing in his mind.

It was time for lunch, and he was ready for his usual sandwich and milk. He drove northward into Santa Monica, stopped at a coffee shop, and then returned to his car to think. As he sometimes liked to do, he drove slowly through the quiet residential streets, looking at the houses and the gardens that were pleasant even in the middle of the coldest month. It was a warm day and despite the closeness of the ocean, the temperature was in the comfortable sixties.

He made a boulevard stop and then rolled on, taking his time as he pondered some unresolved questions. Then he remembered something: there was a lady in Santa Monica about whom he had heard. A call might be in order.

At a filling station he stopped, got out of his car, and checked the phone book. There was no listing. He deposited a dime and dialed the operator. After identifying himself as a police officer and going through a certain ritual, he was supplied with a number, and an address, that did not appear in the directory. When he came out of the booth, he discovered that by chance he was on the right street.

The small cottage where he drew up to the curb was surrounded by a neat, well-kept yard. In it there was a quite tall, but very elderly woman, who was down on her knees on a pad digging out devil grass. Even in that position he could see that she was angular, almost bony, and when she looked at him, her elongated features reminded him, unwittingly, of a horse.

As he got out and approached her, she rose to her feet. "Perhaps we can save some time," she said. "I am not interested in cemetery plots, dancing lessons, real estate investments, or senior citizen housing projects. I'm living on a very small pension and it's growing smaller every day, thanks to the Federal Reserve System. You're not selling magazine subscriptions; you wouldn't be driving if you were."

Virgil smiled with appreciation. "Absolutely correct, ma'am," he said. "Your analysis was most complete."

A certain scornful look put him in his place. "The word 'complete' cannot be modified," she declared. "A thing is either complete or it is not. You watch too much television. Now what do you want?"

Tibbs confessed his sin. "I'm fully aware that 'complete' cannot be modified, I was just hoping that you would tell me so. Am I forgiven?"

"Who are you?"

Virgil produced his card and offered it to her.

"I don't have my glasses, but I think it says 'Tibbs.' "

"Yes, ma'am, it does."

"So you're another policeman. Well, we need all we can get around here. I take it that you wish to speak with me."

"If you can spare a few minutes."

"Come in, I'll make some tea. You do like tea, don't you?"

"My lady friend is half Japanese; she was raised over there."

"That means you drink it, whether you like it or not."

The tall, gaunt woman led the way into her small home. She waved her guest to a chair and then, without comment, left to boil water. Grateful for the change in atmosphere, and for the gentility that surrounded him, Tibbs took in the modest furnishings of another generation. On the small mantelpiece was a framed portrait of a man who offered no urbanity and who obviously had disliked having his picture taken.

He was still studying it when his hostess returned, standing like a thin ghost above him. "Do you know Oscar?" she asked.

"I'm afraid not." He got quickly to his feet, but was motioned back down again.

"That's just as well. My retirement is complete and I intend to keep it that way." Presently she handed over a cup and saucer, offered sugar, and then set down a small plate of cookies. "Now why did you come to see me?" she asked.

Virgil was careful. "I understand the terms of your retirement, but I need a woman's point of view on something — a woman of long and vast experience."

"I trust that the subject is within the usual standards of propriety."

"Definitely, ma'am, or I wouldn't have stopped by. This concerns the case of a missing heiress, a Miss Doris Friedkin."

The features of the thin old woman showed added signs of life. "Go on," she invited.

"Briefly, she disappeared."

"I am aware, Mr. Tibbs; I retain my eyesight and my paper is delivered each day."

"Then I shall take you into my confidence. I have discovered how she escaped from the restaurant where she was lunching with the other rose princesses, who helped her, and I know where she went from there."

"Then why do you need me?"

"For the next step. She went to see a girl friend she could trust."

"Naturally!"

"She has been missing for more than a year, but I have some reason to believe that she is alive and well."

"Then she is either out of the country or else married to someone who is keeping her well hidden."

"I favor the former. Furthermore, I'm inclined to believe that she is in Asia — or at least went there."

The old woman raised her teacup. "Tell me why," she directed.

"Because of her tastes in music and literature. When I asked who her favorite authors were, I was told that she liked Steinbeck and had read almost all of John Masters."

"Steinbeck is very popular, of course, although I do not approve of the type of language he sometimes felt called upon to use. Masters, of course, is well known for his many books about India."

"Exactly. When I asked which motion pictures she had enjoyed, I was given *Casablanca, Love Is a Many Splendored Thing*, and *Sayonara*, plus the James Bond films."

"And what is your analysis?"

"*Casablanca* is a classic that everyone likes; it's shown a great deal on TV. The James Bond pictures are youth cult items. I was much more interested in *Love Is a Many Splendored Thing*, which is laid in Hong Kong, and *Sayonara*, Michener's great love story based in Japan."

"Have you anything else?"

"When I asked who her favorite musician was, I was told it was Ravi Shankar, the celebrated Indian virtuoso of the sitar. Both the artist and his music fit the pattern. It was mentioned to me that she has had trips around the world. But she showed no particular interest in Europe; her father told me that while she is reasonably proficient in French, she showed no interest in developing that language skill any further."

Tibbs' hostess thought for a moment. "Since she disavowed Europe after having been there, and since she liked both books and films about the Far East, and its music, I would agree that Asia is indicated."

Virgil leaned forward and clasped his hands. "Now my question: assuming that this young woman wished to leave the country of her own accord, how might she, in your opinion, have arranged it?"

For several seconds there was no sound but the ticking of an old-fashioned clock. Then, almost as if she thought herself to be still alone, the elderly gaunt woman began to speak. "She would need immunizations, her passport, and, of course, some funds. If she had been planning her own disappearance for any length of time, she could have hoarded some cash or purchased traveler's checks. I don't believe that any identification is needed to buy them."

"Please go on." Virgil drank his tea as he listened.

"Since she had already been abroad, she would have her necessary little yellow health booklet. She would probably need a cholera booster, but that would be very easy to obtain. Did you locate her passport, by the way?"

"Yes, her father found it among her effects — at my request."

"Was her inoculation record with it?"

"He didn't mention it."

There was another few seconds of silence. "It is very dangerous to use someone else's passport, Mr. Tibbs, and I don't believe that she obtained a duplicate of her own — that would involve too many explanations, particularly on short notice. A photograph can be replaced, but it takes an expert forger to do it and she would probably not know where to find one."

"Then what do you suggest?"

The very elderly woman was still thinking. "All you really need for a passport is a birth certificate, an application, and some photographs. She could have her picture taken anywhere and the form is no problem — it narrows down to the birth certificate."

"Are you suggesting that she got a second passport?"

"No — there must be some sort of a check on that. But there is another possibility: today passports can be applied for at many post offices. It is possible, I think, that if her friend did not have a passport, but did have her own birth certificate, she could have loaned it to the Friedkin girl."

"Then she would have trouble herself later on getting a passport for her own use, if she needed one."

"True, but young people don't always think that far ahead. It might be worth investigating."

Virgil got to his feet. "Thank you," he said, "for your time and counsel."

"You're more than welcome, young man. Forgive me if I don't see you to the door."

"Of course. Thank you again."

Virgil carefully let himself out, looked once more at the neat yard as he returned to his car, and then drove away.

He had hardly entered the doorway of his office when Bob Nakamura caught his attention. "We've got a break in the Kallman case," he reported. "You know the child rapist suspect we have in custody; Bill Orr and some others took him back to Oak Grove Park. He led them up the trail and showed them where he left the body of the girl. It was the right spot — just where she was found."

Tibbs sat down and let himself unwind. "God be praised," he said. "At least that one's off our backs."

Bob shook his head. "Not so fast. The suspect claims that he didn't kill her."

"*What?*"

"That's right. He's already copped out to raping an eight-year-old child, so he isn't trying to protect himself. His story is that he was in the park — he admits why — and that near the driveway he saw a girl lying on the grass. She appeared to be unconscious, so with rape in his mind he picked her up and carried her a short way up the trail. It was close to a full moon, so he could see quite well."

"And then?"

"He says that he tried to revive her; he thought she had passed out from drinking too much and, according to him, the marks on her throat weren't visible in the moonlight."

"That could be," Virgil said. "The discoloration might not have been noticeable at that time."

"To continue: when he discovered that she was dead, he was terrified. All thoughts of sex went out of his head, he was only aware that he was alone on a park trail with a dead female; with his record he would have been nailed, he thought, if he were to be caught with her. So he picked her up again and carried her well up the trail to where he was sure she wouldn't be found for at least a day or two. He stayed out of the park until long after he had heard that she had been found."

"Dammit!" Tibbs exploded, "It's just crazy enough to be true. And if his hands don't fit the markings on her throat . . ."

"They don't: the coroner's office made exact measurements and sent us a diagram. The suspect in custody has hands like hams — too big."

"All right," Virgil said, "at least it clears up one thing that had me stopped cold — how the girl ever got that far up the trail without one of our patrols spotting a parked car at the lower end. The driver could have dumped her in a few seconds and then cleared out. Enter second murderer. He carries the body up the trail and then conceals it where it was eventually found. And don't tell me he isn't a murderer — he's an accessory after the fact."

Bob didn't take offense. "How did you make out with your car owner?" he asked.

"He's the right one and he was scared enough to be co-operative. He's going to talk to his traveling companions and phone me with the exact date that they arrived in Pasadena."

"Five will get you fifty that he doesn't."

"No bet — because I'm going back to see him tomorrow afternoon. Meanwhile, I'm asking Santa Monica to co-operate and put a tail on him." He picked up his phone.

Santa Monica was willing; supplied with the address and the car license, an around the clock watch was promised. In return, Virgil promised to return to their jurisdiction any time that he might be needed.

Something more than an hour later he got a return call from the beach city. "You're not going to like this," he was forewarned.

"Let's have it; I'm ready."

"We haven't been able to locate your subject. However, we do have some information."

Tibbs grabbed for a note pad and a pen. "Yes?"

"About two this afternoon he took his car to a used car dealer and sold it for cash. Since he had the registration, there was no problem. As part of the deal, the buyer drove him home. There he apparently packed in great haste and split. He's definitely gone, we have no idea where he is, and we don't have a line either on any of his companions."

13

THE PASSPORT OFFICE WAS GLAD to cooperate. "The subject," Virgil told them, "is a Miss Peggy Collins. Presumably her first name is Margaret, but I don't want to tip her off by making an inquiry."

"Have you tried the voter registration lists?"

"I have — she registered under the name of Peggy. I'd appreciate it if you would check all applications under the name of Collins for both the week before, and the week after, Miss Friedkin disappeared." He supplied the date.

"You think it possible then, that she got a passport *before* she vanished?"

"It's quite likely. A lot of people were looking for her afterward; she could have had a hard time hiding and getting a passport at the same time."

"Perhaps her friend did it for her."

"Possibly, but there would be the picture problem, and I know that you check."

"Indeed we do. I'll call you back."

"Fine, thank you."

That done, Virgil began a check of the consulates in the greater Los Angeles area to learn if a Miss Peggy Collins, or a Miss Anything Collins, had applied for a visa. Since visas were not required by the countries of Western Europe, he confined his inquiries to the Pacific nations. He got no immediate answers, but promises of cooperation.

Next he devoted some attention to Mr. Barry Samuels and ran a rather thorough background check on that young man. He turned up his footprints in a number of places; among other things he learned that Barry seldom missed any of the X-rated pictures that played in the adult theaters of the city. His possible involvement in a paternity matter had been very quietly and efficiently squelched through an expensive legal firm. He was definitely an operator.

Randy Joplin was discovered by a patrol unit to be parked long after hours down in the Arroyo Seco area. He had a girl in the car with him, but there was not sufficient evidence of any misconduct to charge him. He was advised to move his car and he did. Virgil heard about it because one of the officers involved happened to know of his interest in young Joplin.

The suspect being held in the rape case changed his mind and retained an attorney. Acting on legal advice, he refused to talk on any subject without his lawyer present. That forestalled any further interrogation which could have been productive. Because there was enough hard evidence on hand to make a very strong case against him, no one wanted to blow it by even remotely infringing on the suspect's rights. When California got through with him, there was still the matter of his parole violation back East.

At last the passport office called back. Virgil crossed his fingers and asked the big question — did they have anything definite?

They did. On the day following the disappearance of Doris Friedkin, a Miss Alicia Collins had applied for a passport in Inglewood. She had paid the extra fee for immediate service and had been given a passport on the same day.

The excitement of a fresh scent filled Virgil as he took down the data. Then he jumped into an official car and headed immediately down the freeway toward Inglewood.

There were several passport photographers immediately around the government office, but it took less than forty minutes to find the right one. The proprietor did not like to be disturbed by anything apart from the ringing of his own cash register, but he grudgingly checked his files, which he kept for a period of two years, and turned up a negative. "Sometimes they order more prints," he offered, "so I keep records. It costs money, but it pays off enough to make it worth while."

"I want an eight by ten," Tibbs told him. "Yesterday. I'll wait."

"It'll cost you six bucks."

"O.K."

With the inward thought that he should have asked for more, the owner disappeared into the darkroom and emerged in a surprisingly short time. "I put it in quick fix," he advised. "It's washing now."

"How long will that take?" Virgil asked.

"About five minutes."

"I also want the negative."

The proprietor stiffened. "I don't sell my negatives," he countered.

Virgil preferred to use his card, but this time he showed his badge. "I'm investigating a murder case," he announced, quite truthfully.

"She's dead?" the photographer asked.

Tibbs shook his head. "That's confidential."

"I getcha." He returned to the darkroom and came back with a negative in his hands. "It's no loss, since she won't be ordering any more prints," he said as he handed it over. Five minutes after that he delivered a hastily dried print.

Virgil laid six dollars on the counter, got a receipt, and then headed back to Pasadena. At first glance the girl in the photograph didn't appear to be Doris Friedkin, but makeup and wigs could make remarkable changes.

The police artist compared the newly obtained print with the blow-ups of Doris Friedkin and nodded his head. "It looks like a make," he said. He put a sheet of thin paper over the print and quickly sketched in the features just as they appeared. Then he put the print aside and added to his picture the hair style that Doris had been wearing when her last known portrait had been taken. He was halfway through before the evidence emerged, but with each stroke of his pencil the resemblance grew stronger. When he added a bit more shading to the eyes, the face of Doris Friedkin looked up from the paper.

"Great!" Tibbs said.

Bob Nakamura came into the room and looked over his shoulder. "What've you got?" he asked.

Briefly Virgil filled him in. He looked at the sketch once more carefully, savoring his victory. Then he pressed his lips together in a grim smile. "I am now going to have a little heart-to-heart talk with Miss Alicia Collins," he announced with satisfaction.

"Where are you planning to hold the séance?" Bob asked.

In the suddenly heavy atmosphere Virgil looked at him.

"I made the check you asked for at the Bureau of Vital Statistics," Bob announced. "Miss Alicia Collins, address etcetera verified, departed this life of leukemia some four years ago. The City of Hope is a good bet for further details."

It took Virgil a few seconds to recover. When he had done so, his brain began to function once more. "So that's it," he said, largely to himself. "Collins had a sister, possibly a twin."

"No," Bob supplied. "Not a twin."

"Then they were both within a year or two of each other."

"A cigar for the gentleman; Alicia was nineteen months the older. Peggy's real name is Margaret — you were right about that. There was very little publicity due to the tragic circumstances — a lovely young girl stricken by a fatal affliction in her teens."

"And somehow our Miss Peggy had her sister's birth certificate."

"Undoubtedly. And furthermore, Alicia would never be applying for a passport of her own."

Virgil nodded. "So it all fits. Now I shall speak with Peggy and after some soul-searching, and possibly a few tears of remorse, she will spill."

Peggy opened the door to her home personally to welcome her visitor. "Come on in," she invited. "You can relax, we've got the place to ourselves. What may I offer you? We've got lots of different things — even root beer."

"For the moment, nothing, thank you. I'd rather just talk."

Peggy waved him to the davenport; when he had seated himself she plopped down not too far away. "All right, go ahead," she invited. "I'll help you all that I can."

The tone of her remark seemed quite open and sincere,

but Tibbs detected a very slight tinge of fear. Obviously Peggy didn't want to lie, but she sensed that she might be facing a crucial test. He decided that it would be best to give it to her in one lump immediately. "I'm quite interested," he said almost casually, "in the passport that was issued to your late sister Alicia something over a year ago."

It was so quiet that the faint traffic sounds of the city could be heard filtering through the closed windows. Peggy sat perfectly still. Even the expression on her face did not change. Virgil let her take her time; the davenport was very comfortable and he was in no hurry. There should have been a clock ticking somewhere, but internally the room was entirely still.

At last Peggy spoke. In a very soft voice she formed her words and used them almost reluctantly. "Now I understand what a detective is."

Since that didn't call for any comment, Virgil remained quiet.

"Am I busted?" Peggy asked.

"No — not as far as I'm concerned." He relented and gave her a half smile. "Technically you conspired in the obtaining of a passport under false pretenses, but that isn't my area."

"Are you going to tell on me?"

"Probably not," Tibbs answered. "You weren't trying to steal from anyone or defraud the government. I have that in mind."

For the first time, Peggy was visibly uncomfortable. "I thought that it was all over," she confessed. "That it would never come up again. Then that poor girl was murdered in the park and the lid blew off everything. Tell me, was she raped?"

Virgil sensed that she was not motivated by curiosity — it was a genuinely humanitarian question. For that reason he decided to answer it. "No, she wasn't. As a matter of fact, she was a virgin."

Peggy recoiled a little and Tibbs knew why — she was visualizing the examination that had had to be made of the body of what had been an unusually chaste girl. Then she shook her head a little as if to clear the unwelcome thoughts away and changed the topic. "Sometimes the police make deals, don't they? Like Agnew and Nixon and all that."

Politics wasn't Tibbs's field either and he refused to get involved in that area. "Deals are made," he replied. "Immunity is sometimes granted in return for testimony. And plea bargaining is a way of saving a great deal of time and the taxpayer's money. It always depends on the circumstances, who is the accused, and the gravity of the offense. The DA has a great deal to say about it."

"Could we make a deal?" Peggy asked. "You see, if you snitch on me, I'm ruined."

"I'll do my best not to. As I see it, you weren't guilty of any vicious act — you simply tried to help out a friend in trouble. You weren't well advised, but we all make mistakes sometimes."

Peggy looked at him. "I'm going to say something. In the first place, I don't believe that people should be sorted out by colors. So I see you just as a man; a little old for me, perhaps, but a very attractive man I really admire. And not that old either — I'm sorry I said so. May I call you Virgil?"

"Why not?"

"All right, Virgil, you're a cop and all that, but you're a human being and I admire you for it. Now don't misunderstand me — I'm not trying to bribe you or to make a deal that way, but do you have any aversion to white girls?"

"No — certainly not."

"You know that Mother and Dad are divorced; she's living with a rich swinger down on Miami Beach and having a great time. Dad is gone most of the time — business trips. Right now he's in New York."

Tibbs forced it out into the open. "Just what do you have in mind?" he asked.

"Only this: that if you'd like to call me up sometime, when you're not working, I wouldn't mind."

For a frozen moment images came flooding back and he was once more, despite himself, a small Negro boy in the Deep South listening to his father's solemn, almost fearful advice, warning him about the terrible danger of white women. He had learned then, for the first time, that others had paid with their lives for even appearing to be interested in some white woman, no matter how slatternly. That day was now passed, but it had been forcefully instilled into him that he would have to protect himself by every means since he would soon be old enough to come under suspicion. It had been that way and his father had done the right thing in warning his son.

Now a white beauty was offering to go out with him and if he refused, he would have a woman scorned on his hands.

He reached out, took Peggy's hand, and let her soft fingers rest against his palm. As a young woman she was intoxicating, but he tried to put that out of his mind. "When this case is over, I may do that," he said. "Now let me keep a little of my pride as a man; I don't want to buy your help on that basis — do you understand?"

Peggy closed her fingers around his own. "Of course I do, I'm not that stupid."

"Raincheck?"

"Definitely — and don't wait too long."

"Let's speed the day," he said. "When did Doris make up her mind to split?"

"The night before she actually did. She had a row with her parents — they probably didn't tell you that."

"No, they didn't."

"Not a flaming one, but enough. She wanted to tell them about her condition and get their help — it would have been easy that way — but her father is a terrific stickler for all the old-fashioned morality. Strict chastity until marriage and all that. He's really a nice guy, but on that point he's impossible."

"So she knew that she couldn't look to him for any help. And her doctor?"

"Great, but also old-fashioned. He would have advised her to have her baby, she knew that. He wouldn't help."

"Did she ask you to help her before that?"

"No, right afterwards. She called me up; she has her own phone in her room and, of course, it's a private line. That's when she told me that she'd made up her mind. She asked if she could come over to see me the next afternoon. I knew what she meant, of course, so I told her that I'd like that, because Dad was away again."

"How did you set up Barry Samuels to cooperate?"

Peggy let a little scorn creep into her voice. "We paid him," she answered, "for the taxi service and to keep his mouth shut. That's the way he is."

"Let me put it all together," Virgil said. "Doris told you

that she wanted to get away. She was pregnant and that was her principal reason."

"Yes."

"Who knocked her up?"

"I honestly don't know — she never told me. That's the truth."

"How about Barry?"

"She despised him!"

"Is Randy Joplin a candidate?"

Peggy laughed. "Mr. Desperation; he wants every girl in sight and it makes him furious if he can't have them. He thinks he's so good-looking that no woman can resist him. He's a clown!"

"But he does make out, doesn't he?"

Peggy disposed of him by lifting her shoulders and letting them fall again. "Everybody does sometime, I guess," she said. "But his ego is so big, he's made a laughingstock of himself. That's why he doesn't get anyplace."

Tibbs went back to the main topic. "It was arranged, then, that Doris would leave the luncheon at a certain time and that Barry would pick her up."

Peggy nodded.

"He brought her here and since you were alone in the house, it was a good haven for her. Then you gave her Alicia's birth certificate so that she could get a new passport."

"She really wanted to use her own," Peggy explained, "but she was afraid that her father would check up and find out that she was overseas. She didn't plan to be gone very long."

"She went the next day and got a passport in Inglewood under your sister's name. She wore a wig."

"Yes, she had one — and she changed her makeup; I helped her with that."

"She had put some money aside, so that was all taken care of."

"Yes. You see, with the Friedkins, money never mattered very much. They had so much of it, they never had to think about it."

"When did she leave the country?"

"That same night. She did it quickly, before any search would be started. They would think, she believed, that she had just gone away for a day or two. The Friedkins don't like to let the police and people like that into their private affairs."

Virgil looked at her and deliberately softened his manner. "Peggy, you've been a big help. I'll cover for you to the best of my ability. You know that I'm not going to embarrass Doris either; I told you that intentionally when you were in my office."

"How did you know that I knew?"

"I just had an idea. Now one last thing: where did she go?"

Peggy shook her head. "I'm leveling with you now, you know that. She left on China Air Lines that same night — they had a late departure, but I wasn't there and I don't know any more about it. We agreed that she wouldn't write. I thought she would be back in, maybe, a month, and I was expecting her. I never dreamed that she'd be gone this long. I only hope that somewhere she's all right, that's all."

14

Virgil Tibbs sat at his desk laying out little slips of paper. Bob Nakamura had seen him do that many times before; it was a kind of jigsaw puzzle, but instead of assorted, variously-shaped pieces, it was made up of facts and likely conclusions. Each three-by-five piece of notepaper had one salient fact written on it. The way in which they were placed, and the patterns that they formed, helped Virgil to marshal his thoughts and to see which way he was going.

Even from where he sat, Bob could see that there was one long progression, but it was broken in the middle by a conspicuous gap. "Damn it!" Virgil said.

"Can I help?" Bob asked.

"No. Something just didn't check out, that's all, and I was almost certain that it would."

"What's it about?"

"Telephones, for one thing."

"There are a lot of those," Bob commented.

Tibbs, apparently, did not hear that. He still sat staring intently at the complex pattern he had formed, his eyes moving from one point to another.

"Have you been down to the telephone company?"

"Yes."

"Did you take a warrant?"

"No. I'll do that, and submit a letter from the chief, if I have to present the results as evidence in court. Right now I'm trying to put something together, but, confound it, it won't fit."

"What's out of phase?"

"A boy named Billy Owens."

"My uncle might help, he's very good at that sort of thing."

Virgil displayed interest. "Who's your uncle?" he asked.

"Mr. Moto."

"Shut up!"

It remained quiet for another ten minutes. Tibbs continued to study the pattern before him, but he did not add a single slip, or move one. Finally he laid a desk blotter over the whole thing and got to his feet. "I'm going downtown to see a man," he announced. "Hold the citadel, will you, and take any confessions that come in."

"What man?"

"Possibly a distant relative of yours, but I doubt it because he's quite good-looking. I need an expert and he's one."

"Good luck," Bob said.

Virgil left without replying.

Tyler Tanaka sat at his desk with his hands clasped before him. Immediately outside of his office a dozen members of his staff were busily engaged in their various fields of specialty. The sign outside the door of the large suite read JAPAN-ORIENT TOURS, but the company was not listed as a travel agency. It was, in fact, well hidden in one of the principal office buildings in the center of Los Angeles's Little Tokyo.

"You understand, Mr. Tibbs," Tanaka explained, "that this is strictly a wholesale operation. Technically we are tour operators; we sell our services through local travel agents throughout the country. We don't retail to the public at all."

Virgil nodded. "I'm aware of this, it was carefully explained to me. I was also told that you know more about travel in the Far East than probably anyone else available."

"A gross exaggeration," Tanaka said.

"But most of your operations center on the Orient and Far East."

"Yes, that's correct."

Virgil ended the sparring. "Mr. Tanaka, this is a highly confidential matter; I prefer that you not discuss it with anyone."

Tanaka nodded his acceptance of the terms.

"A little more than a year ago a young woman left Los Angeles via China Air Lines for an unknown destination. No one has heard from her since that time. I have already learned from the local consulates, and the visa services, that she apparently had no visas whatever in her passport."

"Was she an experienced traveler?"

"Yes, she had been around the world at least twice with her family."

"Within the past four years prior to her last departure?"

"Yes."

"Then she would have had certain visas already. Both Japan and the Republic of China issue multiple-entry visas good for forty-eight months."

Tibbs shook his head. "She had a new passport, just issued."

Tanaka gave him a sharp glance. "I take it that she's officially missing and you're out to find her."

"That's right."

"Therefore the question is: where could she have deplaned without a previously arranged visa."

"Exactly."

Tanaka turned slightly toward the window while he marshaled his thoughts. "Here's what you want, I think," he began. "She could have stayed in Japan briefly as a transient passenger without a visa; the same pertains to Korea and the Republic of China. The Philippines require an advance visa, so Hong Kong is the first place she could have gotten off for any period; a visa is no longer necessary there. By the time she arrived there, she would probably be quite tired and her time would be inverted. Normally that takes a day or two to straighten out, westbound. Coming this way, it's considerably harder."

Virgil was listening carefully. "So Hong Kong is a possibility."

"Yes, but there are some objections to it if she disappeared as you say. The colony is quite small and while it does an enormous tourist business, the Hong Kong authorities have a computer that keeps a careful check on each individual visitor. If anyone doesn't leave on time, it isn't too hard to find him — or her."

"Could she have crossed into Red China?"

Tanaka shook his head. "The border is very carefully controlled in both directions; visitors are kept away from the crossing points unless they have the proper travel documents. Add to that the great suspicion of the communist Chinese toward anyone not specifically known to them and you have, for all practical purposes, an impossibility."

"So Hong Kong isn't a good bet."

"For a permanent hideout, definitely not, but she could have stopped there for a few days of rest, shopping, or sightseeing."

Tibbs made a careful entry in his notebook. "What else might she have done?" he asked.

"Bangkok," Tanaka suggested promptly. "Thailand is a good-sized country and a visa is issued on arrival. All you have to do is fill out a landing card."

"Is it reasonable to believe that she might have stayed in Thailand for a year or more?"

"Not too likely, because there are much better bets for that sort of thing close by, notably India and Nepal. But, since she's been around the world at least twice, and therefore knows her way in the Orient, she could well have gotten off at Bangkok and lost herself in the city for a while. Also, in Bangkok she could have applied for visas to such places as Malaysia, Burma, Indonesia, or almost anywhere else."

"Is there any way you could trace that out for me?" Virgil asked.

Tanaka shook his head. "Either you'll have to do it in person or else get someone there to handle it for you. By mail it would take forever, and I think you'd need the diplomacy of personal contact."

"How about India?" Virgil asked. He was careful to keep his tone unchanged, but his inner emotions were harder to hold under control.

"That's a very good chance. In the first place, India no

longer requires visas in advance — they finally woke up to the problems they were creating and the money it was costing them to maintain a restrictive position. You can get a three-week visa on arrival. However, there's another thing: India is a vast, greatly overpopulated country that right now is overloaded with young people who have overstayed their visas and who are almost impossible to locate and deport. They are all over the country, living in ashrams and studying music, meditation, yoga, or what have you. There are a lot of them in Kashmir and quite a spillover into Nepal."

"Could she have remained in India for a year?"

"Yes, that's quite possible. India has enormous problems and the influx of young people that remain illegally is just one of them. It's a little like the serious problem we have with illegal Mexican immigrants here."

"So you would vote for India."

"It would be my first choice, then Nepal. How was she fixed for funds?"

"Plenty, I believe."

"Then check with the Indian authorities in Delhi, and expect that that will take some time. Also it would be worth while to investigate Nepal. Do you know if she used any drugs?"

"I believe she didn't."

"Nepal is a haven for those who do, because supplies are cheap and readily available: the hashish shops put out signs. Food is inexpensive in the Tibetan restaurants and the government isn't too strict, except in enforcing the Hindu religion. Located as it is, Nepal is extremely hard to police and the country has only limited resources. It's right next to communist-occupied Tibet in a very sensitive part of the world."

"One last question, Mr. Tanaka: to locate this young woman, would I have to go over there myself?"

His host was definite. "As you've explained it to me, there isn't any other practical way."

Virgil stood up. "I'm much indebted to you," he said. "Thank you for your time."

"Anytime, Mr. Tibbs, don't ever hesitate."

To Tibbs it seemed almost like a flashback — the scene in the Friedkins' living room. They were even sitting in the same positions, just as they had been on the first evening when he had called. He was dressed a little differently, and the coffee service was of another pattern, but otherwise almost nothing had been changed. Except the circumstances. Now he would have to handle things very carefully, but he was fully prepared and quite ready to begin.

He stirred his coffee and then spoke. "Mrs. Friedkin, and Mr. Friedkin, at the instruction of Captain Wilson I have been looking once more into the matter of your daughter's disappearance — as you well know. With the invaluable help of some of my colleagues, I have been able to make just a little progress."

He put it that way to be sure that they didn't jump ahead of him to the conclusion that he had found Doris; he wanted to avoid that at all costs.

Herbert Friedkin, too, was very much in possession of himself. He kept his composure intact as he asked, "What can you tell us?"

Deliberately Virgil looked at them both. "First, I have now established, to my own satisfaction, that Doris was not kidnapped and I have reason to believe that she did not meet with any form of foul play."

166

"Thank God!" Grace Friedkin burst out. "How did you ever learn that?"

It was a somewhat critical point, but Tibbs was prepared for it. "I can tell you that I have been able to determine, quite specifically, why and how Doris vanished from the restaurant where she had been having luncheon with the other princesses. In this instance, time was my ally; the year that has passed actually made it easier for me to learn certain things. Incidentally, I'd like to confirm a point: can you recall if you had any kind of a family misunderstanding with Doris on the night before she disappeared?"

Friedkin thought for only a bare moment. "You must have talked with her," he declared. "There's no other way."

Virgil quietly shook his head and then took his time drinking his coffee. "No, sir, I did not. If I had found her, I would not be sitting here without telling you."

Friedkin drummed his fingers on the arm of his chair while he collected himself once more. Then he answered the question. "Since I presume that you are not yet the father of a late teenager or a very young adult, Mr. Tibbs, I can only tell you that occasional spats and flareups are normal, healthy, and expected. It is true that we had a few words with Doris the night before we last saw her. Naturally it has stuck in our minds, but I can assure you that it was nothing unusual. Certainly not grounds for her to leave her home under the impression that our love for her was in any way diminished."

"What was the subject, sir?"

Friedkin didn't want to answer that, but he realized that he had to. "We cautioned her concerning a young man that she was seeing. We considered him most unsuitable for her, and we said so."

"Had she been seeing him to the point where it could be construed as possibly serious?"

"I very much doubt that," Friedkin said. He looked at his wife, who nodded her agreement. "For one thing, he never even took Doris to meet his parents."

"Have you met the young man's parents, sir?"

"Casually, yes — but no more than that. They are fine people; he is the president of an important insurance company here locally, but the boy hardly does them proud."

Virgil had a sudden flash and took a gamble. "By any chance are you referring to Mr. Walter Rosenblatt?"

"Mr. Tibbs, how do you do these things?"

It was a moment of trial for the talented Negro detective: he could admit to a successful shot in the dark, or he could take credit for something he didn't really deserve. Since he had for most of his lifetime practiced the virtue of keeping his mouth shut during times of doubt, he convinced himself that he was justified in doing so once more. He covered himself by asking another question. "In your opinion, is this young man likely to reappear, after Doris returns?" He hated to build possible false hope that way, but he couldn't think of any different way to put it.

"I can be definite on that point," Friedkin answered him, still a little shaken. "He was married, only last week — to another girl, of course. I'm surprised that you don't already know that."

"I had missed it," Tibbs confessed. "Now, I have a little more information for you. I have sound reason to believe that very shortly after she dropped out of the Tournament of Roses in such an abrupt manner, Doris left for overseas. This also, I believe, was of her own free will."

"That's not possible," Grace Friedkin said. "Her passport is still here. I saw it just the other day."

"I know, Mrs. Friedkin, but she went just the same."

"Did she stow away?"

"No, she obtained possession of some travel documents that were adequate for her purpose at the time. I have no definite evidence concerning her welfare after she left the country, but up to now I have no reason to believe that she has met with any kind of a disaster."

"You're quite confident that she did go overseas?" Friedkin asked.

"Yes, sir, I am."

"Mr. Tibbs, you amaze me. In a comparatively short time you have outdistanced both your own department and three separate private detective agencies, all of which have excellent reputations. How in the world did you accomplish it?"

"Through regular police channels, Mr. Friedkin."

"You have me convinced, sir, but I think you're being too modest."

Virgil did not comment on that; instead he shifted the topic as he had planned. "I have now reached the point where I feel, quite strongly, that further inquiries concerning Doris should be made on the scene in the Far East. I'm sure that you can find someone to handle them for you, someone who is familiar with the Orient and who has the necessary language capability. When you have your man, I'll be glad to give him a full report with everything that I have and how it came to me."

Friedkin shook his head. "Is there any special reason why you cannot continue on the case? Surely your department must have handled many other matters that have involved other jurisdictions."

"For one thing, sir," Tibbs said. "I've never been in the Far East."

His host brushed that away with a gesture. "Mr. Tibbs, the day when it was a vast adventure to go abroad is past. Today you can go to Calcutta in about the same time it used to take the train to reach Chicago. And expense is certainly no factor."

"Mr. Friedkin, I respectfully remind you that I'm a policeman in the city of Pasadena and I have my job to do here. As a matter of fact, I have an unsolved homicide on my hands right now and it's my responsibility to clear it up."

Herbert Friedkin considered the matter with some care. He was fully accustomed to having his expressed wishes accepted without question, but he could not deny the logic of his guest's position. "Thank you," he said when he was ready. "I'll get some advice in the morning. In the meantime, let me again express my complete gratitude for what you've already done."

The point of that remark did not escape Tibbs, but once again he deemed it most prudent not to comment either way. He took his departure and was once more shown to the door personally by his host. He glanced again at the striking Buddha with the remarkable eyes that was in the entryway, and then went out to breathe the cool night air.

Fifteen minutes later he was in his apartment and ready to relax. He took off his shoes, mixed himself a drink, and ran his finger down the sizable collection of records that comfortably filled a large case against one wall. He pulled out Ravel's *Daphnis and Chloe*; that would provide him with nearly an hour of fascinating, intricate, and exotic music perfectly suited to his mood. He put the record on his sound system, set the volume at a decent level, and dropped his coat and tie across a chair: he could hang them up properly later.

He had been seated, unwinding, not more than two minutes when his phone rang.

Automatically that meant trouble: like most policemen his number was unlisted and a call at that hour meant that something had come up and he was needed. Reluctantly he picked up the phone and spoke his name.

This time he had been wrong. The voice was soft and feminine, but not unduly artificial. "I called to say good evening. Do I need to tell the world's greatest detective who this is?"

"The world's greatest detective is keeping bees on the Sussex Downs," Tibbs replied. "How are you, Marsha?"

"Fine, but a little lonesome. There were a couple of guys up here tonight that tried to paw me over. The manager handled it, but I didn't like it."

"Naturally not."

"Isn't that Ravel you have on in the background?"

"My favorite — do you like him?"

"Of course. Have you had dinner yet?"

"So to speak."

"Then prepare to receive a lady, bearing food. That is: unless you'd rather not."

"You are welcome, your food will be welcome, and the bar is open. Also there is Ravel and Falla too, if you like him."

"I adore the *Three Cornered Hat*."

"Tonight's the night."

"That's one way of putting it," Marsha said and hung up.

Beginning shortly after nine in the morning a series of phone calls were made between various high officials of the City of Pasadena. None of them was protracted. Captain Wilson conferred with Chief McGowan, the chief then phoned the city manager, who in turn called the mayor. The still unsolved killing in Oak Grove Park came up, as did Herbert Friedkin's many very substantial gifts to the city and its citizens. It was noted favorably that the financier had not taken advantage of his position as a major benefactor of the community. He had only asked a question that was more a request for information than anything else.

"As far as I'm concerned," the city manager said to Chief McGowan, "officially all of our citizens are totally alike in the eyes of the law and this administration, and they are all entitled to the best protection and assistance that your department can give them."

"I absolutely agree," McGowan responded. "You may recall the exhaustive effort we made when Tommy Bowman disappeared, and he did not come from a wealthy or influential home."

"I know that, Bob, and I also know that this city owes Herbert Friedkin a helluva lot. You are running the police department and what you say goes. If you want to spring Tibbs long enough to chase down the lead that he has dug up, I certainly won't disapprove of your action. You have another good homicide man, don't you?"

"Yes — Heatherton."

"Then I presume he could carry on while Tibbs is away. But you call it and either way I'll support your decision."

The mayor said substantially the same thing, adding the thought that since he more than anyone else was in possession of all of the available facts, Virgil Tibbs was certainly the proper man to see the thing through to its conclusion. "Not for quotation," the mayor added, "I'd rather like to see your department pull it off — find the Friedkin girl if that can be done. I can cite a dozen reasons for that."

Bob McGowan had the word; he notified Captain Wilson who sent his instructions down the chain of command. At three that afternoon Tibbs bared his left arm and accepted the cholera shot he had to have. He then allowed himself to be revaccinated and took his little yellow booklet to be stamped by the Public Health Service. By evening a steady pain had settled down in his arm; he took two aspirins and diverted himself by rereading *The Valley of Fear*. He went to bed early, lay on his back, and stared up toward the ceiling. The discomfort in his arm made itself felt, but his mind was otherwise occupied. Step by step, detail by detail, he fitted evidence together in his mind: hard evidence that he could prove, other evidence that was a result of meticulous observation, mental note-taking, and careful deduction.

He had two major problems for which he was responsible, but the more he considered them separately, the more they seemed to be somehow invisibly linked together. But he could not pin down the connection: it stayed tantalizingly just out of his grasp and each time that he tried to reach out and seize it, logic intruded itself and told him that any such link was impossible.

It was as elusive as ectoplasm, and possibly as unreal, but he could not purge the idea from his mind. He worried over it for a long time before the demands of his body asserted themselves and he at last fell asleep.

15

DAVID YIP, the manager of the Hotel Fortuna, sat back in his chair and presented his best smile to the visitor in his office. As Virgil Tibbs looked back at him, he wondered what incomprehending person it had been who had first declared that all Chinese looked alike. Obviously Mr. Yip was Chinese, but that fact was incidental and entirely submerged by his personality.

His English was close to flawless, and so was his attire; the suit he was wearing had been hand-done by an expert tailor from one of the finest of materials. In addition to these externals, Virgil recognized in Yip a man of startlingly quick wit, a high level of urbanity, and the possessor of distinguishing good looks. There was another element that was less easily defined, but it suggested that David Yip would have been as completely at home on the boulevards of Paris as in the crown colony of Hong Kong. He was an international: a man not fenced in by any borders, either political or cultural. And, Virgil also decided, he had about him the aura of a man who by the grace of a generous fate, was automatically a smash success wherever women were concerned.

It was also obvious that for all of his evident charm, Yip would miss nothing of what was going on.

"Suppose we begin," Yip suggested, "with you telling me how you happened to choose the Fortuna, and what I can do to help you." As he spoke his manner was openly pleasant and his face was innocent of guile.

"I learned before I came here that the government has a computer that keeps track of all visitors to Hong Kong."

Yip nodded quickly. "That's absolutely correct," he confirmed.

"I was able to persuade the authorities to check back for me. Something over a year ago a Miss Alicia Collins visited the colony and, according to that interesting machine, she stayed here — at the Fortuna."

"She was traveling alone?"

"She was."

"And you'd like me to confirm that from our own records."

"Not necessarily, Mr. Yip." Virgil relaxed and allowed his own face to become innocently pleasant. Two could play at that game. "It was my hope, sir, that someone here might recall Miss Collins. I realize that you have a great many guests, but I also observed, in the lobby and in the elevator, that a high percentage of them are Chinese. It seemed possible, therefore, that Miss Collins might have left an impression that would last until now."

"Mr. Tibbs, since you are so observant, you realize that here in the heart of Kowloon, right on Nathan Road, we have a very substantial flow of traffic; after an entire year it would be most difficult for anyone in the hotel to recall any single young woman among the hundreds of guests we han-

175

dle every week." There was cooperation in his tone despite the fact that his words were not encouraging.

Tibbs looked at him quietly and then asked a quite unexpected question. "Mr. Yip, may we agree that this conversation is completely confidential?"

If that caught Yip off base at all, he did not reveal it in any way. "Certainly — of course, Mr. Tibbs. We're quite accustomed to respecting confidences here. We'd be out of business if it were otherwise."

As he spoke he concluded his own appraisal. The man who was questioning him was a Negro, but that was an accident of birth and no racial issues were about to arise. His judgment in this regard was supported by some information he was not about to reveal. Also his guest was a gentleman, highly intelligent, and on the winning side of the fence. As he reached these conclusions, the hotel manager did not alter his expression; his face still had the very pleasant "how may I help you" look that it wore so well.

"Then speaking under the rose, Mr. Yip, I would like to suggest, without offense, that Miss Collins is remembered here, and by yourself personally."

That was a harder one for David Yip to handle. He managed to look slightly puzzled, interested, but entirely innocent all at the same time — a remarkable achievement made possible by years of finely honed experience. "I don't quite follow you," he said.

Virgil Tibbs was entirely relaxed, because he had already read clearly his interviewee's attitude toward himself and that told him how to proceed. "Mr. Yip, I am quite inexperienced in international travel, but during the three days since I left my home, I have observed that a high percentage of traveling Americans, to this part of the world at least, are middle-aged to elderly. I can think of quite a few reasons for this."

"That's quite true," Yip told him.

"I also determined that a significant percentage of these travelers are schoolteachers, librarians, and others who quite often are unmarried ladies. However, I did notice that when you mentioned Miss Collins a few moments ago, you specifically referred to her as a young woman."

Yip laughed lightly. "I believe that everyone thinks of a young person when the word 'miss' is used. And also a good many international travelers are single young women — often with romantic hopes when they book their tours."

"I certainly concur." Tibbs smiled back. "There was, however, one more thing. You carefully avoided saying directly that no one would remember Miss Collins or did. I must respect that highly, sir. Not everyone would be so meticulous in speaking the exact truth. A flat denial would have been easier."

David Yip was interested despite himself; Tibbs, in his opinion, was worthy to have been born Chinese. "May I ask the reason for your interest in Miss Collins?" he asked.

"Now we're getting somewhere," Virgil answered and for the first time he passed his card across the manager's desk.

Yip read it carefully, glanced at the back to see if it was also printed in Chinese, and then altered his demeanor. "So you are a police officer! I had assumed something like that when you told me that the authorities here gave you some information from the tourist files. Normally that wouldn't be done. Tell me, is this an official call?"

"I prefer to call it informal," Tibbs answered. "I have no authority here, although I could ask for cooperation if I needed it. To answer your question: Miss Collins disappeared from her home under rather unusual circumstances something more than a year ago; she hasn't been heard from since. My job is to locate her and determine if she is all right. Technically, in the police sense, she is a missing person."

"It has, of course, occurred to you that she might wish to stay missing."

"Obviously, and if that is the case, she is an adult and that will be her privilege."

Yip thought quickly. "That makes things a little clearer," he said. "Are we by any chance discussing a young lady about five feet three or four, a dark brunette of slender build, quite decidedly attractive and possibly of Jewish origin?"

Despite himself Tibbs's heart seemed to leap into his throat. "We are," he said. "And since you are opening up for me, let me reciprocate. Her real name is not Collins."

"I somehow suspected that, despite the fact that her identity was given in her passport."

"Which means, of course," Tibbs said, "that she told you."

A silent Chinese in a white coat came in and set a tall glass of iced tea before each of the men; he then withdrew without speaking a word.

"I shall not pretend that I don't remember Miss Collins," Yip began after the pause. "I do so quite vividly. She came to consult me. I also gave her my assurance that I would not betray her confidence. You see the delicacy of my position."

Virgil tried the iced tea and found it delicious. "I certainly do," he agreed. "But let me put it to you this way: if anything I'm trying to help her — and to relieve the anxiety of her family at home. I have no intention of dragging her back if she doesn't want to go and I won't reveal where she is if she chooses to keep it a secret. Her parents have been going through a hell of uncertainty, and it's accentuated by the fact that she's an only child who also happens to be the potential heiress of a major fortune."

"And you feel that that makes her more vulnerable."

"Very much so. The scions of some very wealthy families have been nabbed, and at least one of them was mutilated."

"He had his ear cut off, as I recall," Yip said. "Your argument is persuasive, Mr. Tibbs, and I can't do anything but take you at your word. All right: Miss Collins did stay here at the Fortuna, and she consulted me about certain matters. I did what I could to help her. I also invited her out to dinner and I'm glad that I did: she was a delightful companion and she dances beautifully. Nothing romantic, you understand — it was my judgment at the time that she needed a personal contact of that sort."

"Did she tell you anything about herself?"

"Yes, she did. Obviously you know her real identity."

"Did she mention any other personal matters?"

"One or two. I suggested that I could recommend a very highly qualified physician if she had it in mind to consult one here, but she definitely declined that."

Virgil pursed his lips for a moment while he considered that; it was a new fact and an unexpected one. Also it blew one of his own theories out of orbit. "I presume that we're talking about the same thing," he said.

"The doctor I had in mind is a gynecologist. Dr. Wu Fat."

Tibbs decided to come to the point. "Mr. Yip, without putting you on the spot ethically, I'd like to ask if she told you where she was planning to go."

David Yip pressed his own lips together, tipped his chair back, and thought. "In direct answer to your question, Mr. Tibbs, she did," he said very carefully. "Whether or not I should tell you what she had in mind presents a problem."

"Let me suggest that it was India," Tibbs prompted.

That seemed to release something in Yip's mind. "Since you already have that, I will confirm that that was her intention. I hope that I succeeded in talking her out of it."

That was another surprise and Tibbs reacted to it. "I'd like to hear you on that point," he declared.

Yip took his time while he drank some of the tea. "At the time that the young lady was here," he said, "there was a considerable anti-American feeling throughout much of India. I don't know how much you were aware of it in the States, but over here it was an important matter. I'm sure you know the reasons for it, so I won't go into that. Enough to say that I advised her a single, young, attractive American girl in India could encounter some very serious problems. And they have fantastic ways of finding things out; they would have known that she came from a wealthy home almost immediately."

Virgil took his own turn at choosing his words carefully. "If I had been in your position, I'm sure that I would have done the same thing — if I had had the same knowledge, that is. But if you did succeed in discouraging her from going to India, obviously you had to suggest an alternative. It would have been the only way that you could carry your point. Even if you hadn't offered some other destination, she would have asked you."

The hotel manager gained a few seconds of extra time by drinking his tea. He had the measure of the man who sat on the other side of his desk and he knew that there was no point in equivocating. The American policeman was courteous and gentlemanly, there was no questions of that, but he was also determined. And obviously extremely capable. One way or another he would find out.

David Yip, for all practical purposes, had no choice and he knew it. Therefore he cut away the frills, saved time, and came to the point.

"Nepal," he said.

In all of his life and experience, Virgil Tibbs had never seen anything comparable to the city of Katmandu. He had heard of it, principally, as a remote way station for expeditions headed toward some of the gigantic peaks of the Himalaya. Because it lay very close to the roof of the world, it was the last urban outpost before the most formidable mountains on the globe; fearsome giants that soared upward to incredible heights that were forever shrouded in terrible dangers and unyielding perpetual snows.

He was surprised, therefore, when his first view of his destination from the air was of a richly greened valley not very much more than five miles across. The plane spiraled down into the bowl, dropped its gear, and landed on a runway barely long enough to accommodate it. As he stepped out onto the ground once more, Virgil discovered that although it was still March, the air was unexpectedly warm. He looked around him, and sensed with all of his being that he was in one of the truly far places of the world.

The people he saw were strange and different; many of them had eyes that seemed to be only narrow slits carved horizontally across their dark features. Although he knew little or nothing about the mountain people, he noted that they fell into different patterns — in features and in dress.

He could not help wondering if he looked as strange and odd to them, a man with a skin far darker even than theirs. He could not identify them as he entered the terminal, a small facility that was crowded by Sunwars, Mangars, Rais, Gurkhas, Tamangs, Gurungs, and women in odd dress with brightly colored aprons tied around their waists and long black hair worn in braids. A babble of languages surrounded him and he felt totally out of place; some of the fears of his early childhood in the Deep South surged back and he was once again filled with the feeling that because of his birth he would have to run somewhere far away and hide.

"Mr. Tibbs?"

The man who approached him was lean and narrow; his trousers that looked too small for a human adult to wear emphasized the thinness of his legs. He wore a white shirt that hung loose and free and over it a jacket that fitted him out of necessity. His complexion was sun-darkened and his narrow eyes appeared to be shaped in a perpetual squint, but for all of his unprepossessing appearance, he was pleasant and obviously anxious to please.

"Yes, I'm Tibbs," Virgil said.

"I am honored to meet you, sir. I am your guide. I shall get your baggage and put it into the car."

That was too much like being waited on and Virgil wondered precisely what he should do. The man who had greeted him was half his size and it would have been ridiculous to have allowed him to lug a substantial suitcase through the terminal while a completely able-bodied man stood by and watched.

The problem was solved when a turbaned porter appeared and silently held out a hand for the baggage claim checks. This man was there to make his living and Tibbs handed over his claim check. Then the little guide started to ferret his way through the crowd and Virgil, feeling more conspicuous than he ever had before in his life, followed. Outside, pulled up in front of the door, there was a small Japanese car that showed clear evidence of long, hard use. The guide put Tibbs in it as though it had been a Mercedes 600 and left him sitting there while he returned to the terminal to take care of some entry formalities.

Children poked their heads into the car to inspect the strange American. They jabbered about him in languages beyond hope of comprehension, pointed, and occasionally giggled. He was conspicuous, he knew it, and he could not blame the children for their natural curiosity. He held himself in control and fought down the old feelings that rose like vampires to taunt him at every possible opportunity. He smiled at the children and in a burst of enthusiasm they smiled back at him.

The vampires retreated, defeated once again.

The guide returned, handed him back his passport, and directed the driver to proceed.

It was only a short ride over an uncertain road until the car entered the small city itself. Wooden buildings that crowded to the edge of the narrow streets had fantastically carved doorways and balconies that testified to a totally different culture and method of living. A row of tiny shops appeared, one of them displayed a sign in English that read *Hashish House*, just as Mr. Tanaka had described. Clearly, Nepal had become a Mecca for dropouts from many parts of both Europe and America. One of them, possibly, could be Doris Friedkin.

The Soaltee Hotel was obviously one of the prides of the

city. It was of only moderate size, but a mighty effort had been made to bring it up to the standards of international tourist travel. As he waited to sign the register, Virgil noted the many examples of elaborate woodcarving that adorned the lobby, and saw also the posted notice that there was a casino in the basement. There was a small handful of Japanese in the lobby who were joined by others who had arrived on the same flight.

Tibbs went up to his room in an elevator that was an adventure in itself and there prepared himself for this strange and exotic city. He hung up the quiet business suit in which he had flown all the way from Hong Kong and replaced it with a pair of slacks and a knitted sports shirt. He slipped his wallet into one pocket and the thin case that contained his badge in another. He added such accessories as he expected to need and then went back down to the lobby.

Katmandu! He repeated the name silently to himself, trying to focus his mind on the reality of his location. He remembered the orchid-clad girls of Thai International Airways that had taken care of him en route, the many glimpses of vast reaches of water, and occasional patterns of land, that the plane had flown over, the stop at Bangkok where he had remained in the terminal for a brief interval before the flight had resumed with a fresh crew, and the other realities that he had experienced. But his mind, whetted as it was, still had difficulty in comprehending the speeds of modern flight. The world was a finite place after all.

The man who had brought him from the airport was patiently waiting although he had not been formally engaged. "You wish now to see some of the city?" he asked in his somewhat labored English.

"Why not?" Virgil answered. He wanted to be taken for just another American who had been able to put together the time and the funds to come to this remote place. If his quarry was here, he had no intention of scaring her away. Katmandu was small and obviously quite primitive in many respects, but he did not doubt for a moment that there was an active and highly developed grapevine running throughout the city.

He definitely wanted to go to police headquarters and inform them as a matter of courtesy that he was in their jurisdiction. There was no guarantee that anyone there would be able to speak English and he was not yet prepared to take his newly met guide into his confidence. Of course he was not carrying a weapon as he always did at home and he was certainly not going to make an arrest — he had no authority to do that — but he was obligated to make his presence known. He decided to wait for a suitable opportunity.

He got once more into the same little car and made himself as comfortable as he could. "Tell me about the city," he invited.

That was precisely what his guide was best prepared to do. He began at once a set speech which he delivered with a certain amount of conviction. "This is a completely Hindu kingdom," he recited. "The last reigning Hindu monarch is on the throne. So the laws about cows, for example, are very strict. They are all sacred, not just those of a certain color. If you were to kill a cow, even by accident, as a foreigner you would be fined two thousand American dollars and then ordered to leave the country within one day — never to return. If a Nepalese were to kill a cow, the penalty would be twenty years in prison."

"Twenty years for killing a cow?"

"Yes, indeed, sir."

"How much for murder one?"

"Murder, sir, of a human being? Also twenty years — it is the same. Buddhism is permitted here, but it is against the law to change religion and become perhaps a Christian. For this you can also go to prison. The Hindu faith is protected here with great zeal."

That topic concluded, the guide began to point out the principal sights of the city. When they reached the very center, it proved to be a small plaza hopelessly crowded by animal-drawn vehicles, street merchants, and all but stationary pedestrians. The car crept through, foot by foot, until it finally broke out on the other side.

"Are we far from police headquarters?" Virgil asked.

The guide displayed some alarm. "No, sir, it is close. Do you have a complaint to make, sir? If that is so, please first allow me . . ."

"Nothing like that, but I would like to see what the police are like in Nepal." That was the truth. "I would like to go there."

The guide looked at him as though he was losing his sanity, but he gave an instruction in a different language to the driver. As he sat beside Tibbs, he tried to understand the mind of his client who, apparently, would go sightseeing on the river Styx.

Within a matter of five minutes the car pulled up before a modern-looking building that was more impressive than Tibbs had expected. He got out, aware that he was probably tipping his hand, but he could think of no way to avoid it.

The interior suggested a police station before he was through the door. He walked up to the desk and asked, "Does anyone here speak English?"

Obviously the man he addressed did not, but he understood the nature of the request. He spoke into a telephone in a language that was a complete mystery to Virgil. Then he held up his hand to indicate a wait.

Within a minute or two a young policeman appeared and gestured that Tibbs was to follow. He led the way inside and showed his visitor into an office where a man rose from behind his desk and came forward. "Good afternoon, Mr. Tibbs," he said and indicated a chair. "My name is Lama. How are things in Pasadena?"

At that moment Virgil was almost fervently glad that he had presented himself so promptly; they were on to him much sooner than he had expected. "Your scenery," he responded, "is far greener and much more beautiful." He shook hands and then took the offered chair. "You certainly keep track of what is going on."

Lama sat down once more behind his desk. "As you are well aware, that is our job. The Hong Kong authorities were kind enough to advise us that you were about to honor us with a visit. I trust that you do not find our humble resources too primitive here."

"I've just arrived in town, Mr. Lama," Virgil said, "and all that I've learned so far is not to kill a cow under any circumstances."

"It would not be advisable, no. I presume that a letter from your chief is on its way — it will perhaps arrive here tomorrow."

"You must forgive me, sir," Tibbs apologized, "Chief

McGowan did not know in advance that I was coming here; I did not know it myself until two days ago. Would you like to contact him by telephone?"

Lama shook his head. "That will not be necessary. It is interesting that in my pursuit of your very intricate language, I read books about policemen — you understand my interest. Your name, therefore, is already known to me."

Virgil decided to clear the air. "Mr. Lama, I am not here officially; if that were the case you would definitely have been notified and your permission asked. I am on a case, but not one concerning a violation of law — yours or ours."

"Interesting," Lama said. "Do you wish to tell me any more?"

Quietly, concisely, and with complete clarity Virgil laid out the nature of his mission and outlined the information he had available. The Nepalese policeman listened without interrupting until Tibbs had finished; then he made a statement.

"On one point I must correct you — it is against the laws of Nepal to come here with a false passport. Now, do you wish us to overlook it?"

"If that is possible, it might make my job easier."

Lama waved a hand to indicate that the point was closed. Then, leaning forward, he picked up a letter that lay on the top of his desk and passed it over without comment. Clipped to it was a high-school graduation photograph of a clean-cut, handsome young man who gave signs of promise. Tibbs studied the picture, then he read the letter. It was an appeal from the young man's parents: he had disappeared some time ago and had never been heard from. Someone had told them that he might be in Nepal; was there any way that the police in Katmandu could help?

"You see our problem," Lama said. "We have a heavy influx of young people and some of them stay here as much as two years. Many, many such letters come in, and we would like to help, but . . ." He gestured toward the photograph. "None of them, not even one, looks like that now. I have in the morgue a John Doe, one with very long hair and a full beard. His clothing is derelict and tells us nothing. Cause of death, drug overdose. We made inquiries. His friends said that his name was Joe, that was all. They did not know where he was from; to have asked that would have violated his freedom — or so they said. He is now free of living, and we have no idea who he was. His passport could not be found."

"A first name isn't much to go on," Tibbs said.

"It is less than that, Mr. Tibbs; there is little chance that that was his real name. They often take new ones to please themselves."

There was no point in continuing in that direction, so Virgil came back to the point. "If you have any information in your official records about Miss Collins, I would greatly appreciate your help," he declared. "Meanwhile, if you have no objection. I'll carry on as best I can on my own."

Lama had no objection to that. "Our records will be carefully checked," he promised. "I will let you know what we find. Meanwhile, I suggest that you look in the vicinity of the monkey temple; there are many young people living out there and it is a good place to begin."

Virgil stood up and once more held out his hand. "You have been a great help," he said. "I'm glad that we've met."

"I also, Mr. Tibbs; I wish you the best of success."

When he returned to the waiting car, Virgil found his guide in an interesting state of mind. He was obviously burning with curiosity, but he did not want to damage his position by asking any unwelcome questions. He got in dutifully and tried his best to erase his inner thoughts from his face. "Shall we now continue our tour, sir?" he suggested.

"For a little while," Tibbs accepted.

The next hour was filled with strange temples, incredible carvings in wood and stone, many sorts of people in styles of clothing Virgil had never seen before, and architecture that seemed as though it had been lifted bodily out of the land of Oz. In sum total it was extraordinary, and for that hour Tibbs allowed himself to be a sightseeing tourist and nothing more. He had known that such things existed; now, for the first time, he was seeing them with his own eyes. Strange odors defied identification and occasional weird bursts of sounds something like the clashing of distant cymbals could be clearly heard. As the little car rocked its way over the uneven pavement, the totally new experience awoke a whole array of new emotions in the man from Pasadena and he realized at last that he was truly on the other side of the world.

When the driver finally pulled up back in front of his hotel, Virgil had had all of the fresh impressions that he could digest in one day. He made a date with his guide for nine in the morning, accepted the man's card, and went inside. The uncertain elevator gave him a few challenging moments as he rode up to his room; once inside he stretched out across the bed for a respite of total relaxation.

He had been resting for less than ten minutes when his phone rang. Mr. Lama was on the line. "Your scent is reasonably hot," he reported. "According to our records, Miss

Alicia Collins was admitted into Nepal about one year ago. There is no corresponding record of her leaving, so presumably she is still here. However, we do not have an address for her and she has not been reporting in every fifteen days as is required. She could be anywhere in the country, or she may have left without going through the proper formalities; this has happened many times. We will continue to look for her."

Virgil acknowledged all that, expressed his thanks, and then reluctantly roused himself: it was close to time to go down and eat. He washed, recombed his hair, and put on his coat; it still seemed awkward to him that the feel of the weapon he normally carried at all times was missing. As he rode down in the eccentric elevator the idea came to him that he might walk into the dining room of the hotel, look about him, and see Doris Friedkin sitting there. It was possible: she was used to the better things of life and he had been told that the Soaltee had the best dining room in Nepal.

When he arrived at the door a headwaiter appeared who greeted him in English and led him into the room to the unexpected sound of a four-piece orchestra that was playing dinner music. That was a gentility he had not expected in Nepal; as he unfolded his napkin he remembered the things he had seen outside and realized fully how much effort it had taken to provide such a show of elegance in the environment of Katmandu.

There were no young women in the dining room who even remotely resembled Doris Friedkin. It had been much too much to expect; Tibbs contented himself by hoping that the food would be up to the standard of the room itself.

That also, in this very remote place, would be a major achievement.

In the morning he was ready to begin phase two of his plan. He began by calling Mr. Lama and enquiring about his guide. The man was well known to the authorities, as were all of the people who regularly contacted foreign visitors and tourists. On an informal basis Lama told him that he was regarded as reliable and, since he valued his job above all else, he would probably let his throat be cut before he would willingly jeopardize Tibbs's mission.

That settled a point and made things a little easier. When the guide reported, energetic and willing, Virgil suggested that they have a cup of coffee together first. The Nepalese did not especially care for coffee, but he accepted at once, knowing that the invitation was more than casual.

Over the beverage Virgil put him into the picture as far as he deemed necessary. He revealed that he was looking for a young lady because her family was very much concerned. He was not going to arrest her, but the local authorities were interested in what he was doing. When he mentioned Mr. Lama's name, the reaction was immediate; without being asked the guide pledged his utmost cooperation and absolute discretion. Now he understood why his client had gone to the police station and his mind was vastly relieved.

He became at once a co-conspirator. "I believe that you should allow me to take you to the monkey temple this morning," he proposed. "It is a very logical place for you to go — everyone visits it. Also it is close to where many of the hippies live. You will be certain to meet some of them. Then, after lunch, it would be good for us to go to the Tibetan Self Help Center; there are also many young people around there; they come to learn the Tibetan religion and philosophy. This the government permits since it is Buddhist and does not conflict with the Hindu faith."

"That sounds fine," Tibbs agreed.

The same small car took him out into the countryside for a short distance and then up a fairly long hill. Not far from the top the driver parked at an area that marked the end of the road; here the guide explained that the rest of the trip would have to be on foot. There was a good path, he advised, and promised that it would not be exacting.

Virgil smiled to himself, wondering if the guide thought that because he was an American, he was somehow not able-bodied. Then he realized that it was part of the guide's regular patter, designed to accommodate elderly couples who were reluctant to attempt anything of a physical nature. He set off up the trail, enjoying the mild exercise and the magnificent panorama of verdant green valley that grew more visible as he climbed.

When he reached the top, and saw the temple, he gasped and stared at the sight before him. There was a large paved compound and in the exact center of it there was a massive, snow white stupa: a huge half sphere that appeared to be, and was, completely solid. Atop it there was a square tower that rose upward in a pattern of incredible architecture unmatchable anywhere else in the world.

But that was not all. Painted on two of the visible four sides of the crowning tower there were pairs of eyes that seemed to be burning holes right into his inner being. They were striking in the extreme — compelling and hypnotic. As he stared at them, and they glared back, a blast of controlled sound filled the air. Behind the stupa was the temple and in it a service was in progress; every few moments a fresh distinctive blare came from the fifteen-foot-long Tibetan trumpets that projected out of an open window. The uncanny sound reenforced the impact of the overpowering painted eyes.

The guide offered his standard explanation. "They are the eyes of Buddha," he said. "They look out in all four directions, and they see everything. They are the most famous sight in Katmandu; you will find them many times in photographs. It is to prove that everyone in this country is always in the sight of the Blessed One, and under His protection. Evil spirits and demons know this too, which is why the eyes show the great power that they do. The eyes frighten them away."

"I don't doubt it for a moment," Virgil said.

"Now, if you wish, we can enter the temple, which is behind the stupa, and visit the service. It is permitted, if you do not interrupt the monks and the lamas by taking flash pictures."

Another earth-shaking blast from the huge trumpets punctuated his words. On a stone balustrade a monkey swung up and sat, chatting to itself and looking about. It appeared to be in possession by right of ownership; as Tibbs took a step toward the little animal it bared its teeth and hissed a protest.

"Are there many monkeys here?" he asked.

"Yes, sir, there are many. They live here. The Buddhists do not disturb them. Very occasionally they bite someone, but only if they are very much annoyed."

Understanding that he was welcome, Tibbs stepped inside the temple and for a short while he remained, quietly, watching and listening to the chanting monks who were conducting a service that appeared to be without end.

When he had seen and heard his fill, he turned back down the trail with his guide following obediently behind.

He had not gone far before a heavily bearded young man held up some necklaces and offered them for sale. He was the first of many. Virgil spoke to them all, easily and quietly, and examined their merchandise. The young women who were also in evidence drew his closer attention, but he did not see anyone who might have been the long-missing Doris Friedkin. Yet she could well be here somewhere, and that thought kept him constantly alert.

He contacted fifty or more people informally, the majority of them Americans, but he did not make any purchases or learn anything that might help him. He managed to convey the idea that he had come for a week at least, which was his excuse for not buying immediately. In the eyes of a few of the people he talked to he saw the evidence of drugs, but he showed no visible reaction. He was very careful, because even a slight slip could betray his purpose and thereby almost automatically guarantee his defeat. One thing was in his favor: none of the assorted people with whom he talked seemed to pay any attention to his color or question the fact that a person of his ancestry was in such an obviously favorable position. For that he was profoundly grateful.

Back at the hotel, he ate his lunch in deep thought. Despite the fact that he had an all but unlimited expense account, he knew that he belonged back in Pasadena and he was probably needed there. He had been detailed to handle a very particular job; it was now up to him to finish it, if he could, as soon as possible. But the hippie colony was extremely fluid; many of its members went off on treks to the foothills of the commanding Himalayas, and for that they could hardly be blamed. Policing such an area was all but impossible; he knew that without being told.

When he had finished his meal, he was ready to resume his program of supposed sightseeing. Without quite allowing himself to think about it, he was aware that he was enjoying it immensely. It seemed to him that Nepal must be one of the most beautiful nations on earth; its scenic wonders were legendary and the small bit that he had already seen had been enough to captivate him. He well understood why so many others had fallen under the powerful spell of this remote kingdom and a few had chosen to remain for the rest of their lives.

His guide, who now inwardly swelled with the pride of his secret knowledge, promised him that his afternoon's excursion would be both highly interesting and quite possibly productive as far as his mission was concerned. "We shall go to the Tibetan refugee colony," he announced with careful language. "It is a most interesting place, also it is where many of the young people are found. There are new faces there every day, and many old ones. At the sales center, which you will see, there is an Australian girl who is very intelligent. Perhaps she can help us."

Virgil smiled to himself at the neat way in which his guide had included himself, and easily forgave him for it. All valid help was welcome, especially from a man who knew his way around with the skill of a professional guide.

On the way, he listened to the set speech about the place they were to visit. "The people you will see have mostly escaped from the communists who now occupy their country. To get out they had to run great risks and very many were killed trying. If they made it to the mountains, then they had to cross the Himalaya, on foot, and often without

196

proper clothing or any provisions. Up on the very high passes, some more than eighteen thousand feet, the air is very thin and the winds are terrible; many people could not live at such altitudes. Also it is very cold, but still some of them make it. They are very tough, like the Sherpa porters who are also of the same stock. Now they work here and make carpets which are like no others in the world. It is the only means they have to live."

When the tiny car reached the end of the pavement it continued onward on a dirt road that was well-packed, both by wheels and by human feet. A half a mile farther, a series of long, shedlike buildings came into view; the driver parked and prepared himself to wait indefinitely. The guide got out and Virgil followed.

Once more a well-rehearsed speech was unfurled. "Sir, the small building is the salesroom, there you can buy the carpets. The people work here from dawning until dark, carding, spinning, dying, weaving, and finishing. Each carpet is a work of art and they almost never stop operating the looms."

"They must drive themselves very hard," Tibbs observed.

"Yes, sir, they do. They hope to get their country back, and perhaps they will. But I do not think it will be very soon. Now I will show you the weaving."

The long shed into which he led the way was almost completely filled with looms, set close together in rows for the full length of the structure. In front of each one of them people sat packed closely together, as many as six before a single loom, so there did not appear to be enough room for them to move their arms. But they did, it was a sea of ceaseless motion, of hand-operated shuttles shooting back and forth, of hammers pounding the freshly woven strands down to make the resulting texture as solid as possible. But it was not so much the sight that captured Virgil as the sound; for the people were singing, all of them, in unison. Waves of undulating sound filled the long shed with patterns of tempo and melody that he had never heard before; to him they were at once strange and mystical.

"They are prayers," his guide told him, reading his mind. "They pray for better fortune, and for the return of their homeland."

Tibbs lingered for some minutes, watching and listening, and admiring the raw determination of the workers who seemed to have wellsprings of endless energy. They were human, they had to grow tired, in some places the light was very poor, but they kept up the steady pace as long as he watched. When he did at last turn away, the image of what he had seen would not leave his mind and the haunting sounds of the singing persisted in his ears.

"I think now we should go to the sales center," his guide suggested in a confidential tone. "It is not required that you buy anything, but it would be a good idea, I think, to get acquainted a little. Many of the hippies here mingle with the Tibetans, and learn from them. Some of them have even adopted their religion. I can understand this, because they are a wonderful people; they will never bow to defeat."

The sales center was a single medium-sized room with no pretenses whatever at decor or a conventional retail atmosphere. A pile of completed carpets was stacked against the center of one wall; there were also some small items — yaks made of goatskin, prayer wheels, and Tibetan hats with turned-up sides.

An attractive blond girl came forward to meet them and Virgil was introduced. "Miss Langford," the guide said carefully, "This is Mr. Tibbs who is visiting here for the first time."

The girl smiled with genuine warmth and held out her hand. "How do you do, Mr. Tibbs," she acknowledged in a rich Australian accent. "Thank you so much for coming. May I show you some of our carpets?"

That could not be refused. Two young men who had been squatting on their heels awaiting a call to duty rose at once and manned each side of the pile. As Virgil watched, fascinated by what he was seeing, they turned over the carpets one at a time. Each one was a profusion of colors mixed in brilliant, unconventional ways. Snow dogs in almost blinding hues poised alert, phoenix birds winged across cobalt skies with lotus flowers clutched in their beaks; flying dragons pursued the Pearl of Wisdom against multi-colored heavens. A few of the patterns were relatively sedate; others combined several animals in astonishing profusion with a snarling tiger in the center.

"These are all true Tibetan designs," the girl explained. "As you can see, they show great imagination. The Tibetan people adore bright colors and they can mix them in combinations no one else can match. And the quality of the carpets is superb."

"They are magnificent," Virgil agreed, "I wish that I could buy them all."

"I'll be happy to arrange that," the girl answered quickly, her eyes reflecting her good humor. "And we can also take care of the shipping."

Tibbs smiled back at her. "I will buy at least one for my home, I promise you that," he said. "This is only my first visit; may I come back?"

"Of course! The Tibetan people themselves will be glad

to know you; they are very friendly even though they tend sometimes to be a little shy."

"What part of Australia are you from, Miss Langford?" he asked.

She shook her head, acknowledging that her accent had betrayed her. "Sydney, where the famous opera house is. And please, call me Caroline."

"Gladly, I'm Virgil." He paused for a moment after glancing at her left hand, "It is 'miss,' isn't it?"

She smiled enchantingly. "That's right. For the time being, at least, I like it that way. Are you traveling with a group, Virgil?"

"No, I'm strictly on my own."

"Good. And what brings you here?"

There was danger in that innocent question, but he had anticipated it and had an answer ready. "I hope to write a piece about the young people here in Nepal, but also I'm glad of the chance just to get away for a while — to escape the rat race. Is that too American for you?"

"Certainly not, we have a lot of Americans here! Where are you from?"

"California."

She paused. "I have a suggestion; are you booked for to-night?"

"Not particularly."

"Then there's something you might want to do: the Nepal Cultural Society is putting on some dances. They're mainly for the tourists, but despite that, they're quite interesting. I've already seen them, but some of us are planning to go again. Why don't you come along? It's something you couldn't possibly see at home."

Tibbs made a swift decision. "I'd like that," he said.

The girl was pleased. "I'm sure you'll enjoy it," she told him. "We'll probably have a little party afterwards; you can come and meet some of the others."

He thanked her and then nodded to his guide, indicating that he was ready to leave. As he walked back to the waiting car he was thoroughly grateful for the invitation; he was, in fact, quite anxious to go.

Some five hours later one of the hotel cars deposited him in front of the small assembly hall where the dances were to be held. Most of the available seats were already occupied by tourists, many of whom were couples entitled to senior citizen status. There were also quite a few young people.

Caroline was there; as soon as Tibbs arrived inside she made him welcome and introduced him to fifteen or twenty others who acknowledged his presence in various ways. Some of the men shook hands, some merely nodded. A few of the girls frankly looked him over in a way that he understood perfectly. A few members of the group were in his own age bracket, so he did not feel out of place in that regard.

He found the dances interesting, but his mind was preoccupied by other things. He had noticed a dark-haired, dark-eyed girl who was not only pretty, but also the right age, and the right coloring, to be Doris. Her physical structure matched the description of the girl he had come to find, but when they had been introduced she had not spoken and he had therefore not heard her voice. She had been called Eileen, but he knew from his talk with Lama that the names he would encounter could be all but meaningless — particularly when only a first name was used.

Presently he was no longer able to resist the appeal of the

music and the gyrations of the frequently masked dancers. It was in a small potion the essence of the almost totally remote and isolated Himalayan kingdom that surrounded him. His guide had told him that prior to 1950 only twenty-four Europeans had ever set foot in the Katmandu Valley. Yet in this literally incredible land civilization had been well advanced in 562 B.C., when a prince of the kingdom had turned his back on his royal birthright to seek enlightenment and eventually to become the Lord Buddha. And, he had added, within the 6,476 square miles that comprised Nepal's total territory, nine of the world's mightiest mountains soared upward in incredible majesty almost to the base of the stratosphere.

He could not escape it, Nepal was intoxicating. Granted that the sanitation was close to disastrous, and the per capita income dangerously low, nothing could detract from the sublimity of the land itself.

When the program was over and he rose to his feet, Caroline was beside him. "You're coming to the party, aren't you?" she invited.

"You're sure it's all right?"

She laughed. "Of course; come along. Do you use grass?"

Virgil shook his head. "I don't smoke," he told her. "I have other vices."

The party proved to be a quiet affair where he was accepted without question. It was mostly young people with some not so young who lived by choice in Nepal; he was the only person that could be called a tourist who had been invited. A bearded young German and his wife produced guitars and sang together, simple quiet songs that were unfamiliar, but timeless. They sang in four languages, and well enough to have appeared professionally almost anywhere that they might wish. The aroma of hashish began to tinge the room, but Tibbs did not stir or show any sign of his awareness of the drug. He watched, listened, and tried at the same time to be an inconspicuous guest.

Then he was asked if he could sing. "Nothing you would want to hear," he answered.

His refusal was accepted; no attempt was made to coax him or force him into something when he would prefer not. He did manage to exchange a few words with the girl called Eileen; she was in the company of a man who was probably in fact, if not strictly in name, her husband.

When he felt that he had stayed long enough, Virgil got up, declined the offer of more tea, and prepared to leave. Caroline, who had been watching, came to him. "How are you going to get home?" she asked.

"The hotel car waited for me. I didn't want him to, but the driver insisted that he was used to it and that he would get some sleep. He's up the road a little way."

"All right." For a brief moment there was an unnatural silence while the impasse deepened, then the girl smiled at him. "When are you going to come back and pick out your rug?" she asked, changing both the subject and the mood.

"Perhaps tomorrow."

"You do that."

She was close enough for him to reach easily, but he did not. He was fully aware that he could have the privilege, but for reasons of his own he held back. He hoped that she would understand that it was a bit too soon, for one thing.

"Have you thought about Australia?" she asked.

The unexpected question caught him off guard and he

had to recover himself. "Yes," he answered her, "I think that everyone does, at some time or another. Especially if they have read Upfield."

"You ought to visit it."

"Perhaps I will," he said.

"And I'll see you tomorrow?"

"Definitely."

"Good night, Virgil."

"Good night," he responded. He turned and walked away while he was still in full possession of himself. The night was rich with stars, but for once he took little note of them as he walked through the darkness down to where the car and driver were still patiently waiting; the man himself grateful for the few extra rupees that he had so easily earned.

Tibbs roused him gently, then opened the door to the rear seat and climbed in. As he settled down for the short drive back to his hotel, his mind was working and he was planning carefully. He had discovered something, but to make use of it he knew that he would have to maneuver very carefully.

He almost regretted what he had noted, because the magic of this distant place had already taken a hold on him; when he tried to think about Pasadena, the too familiar pattern of its streets and structures seemed even farther distant than half way around the world; more remote even than the other side of the earth.

16

S HE ATE HIS BREAKFAST in the pleasant dining room of the Hotel Soaltee, Virgil Tibbs planned his day's activities with considerable care. His guide would be reporting in a few minutes, ready and probably quite anxious to show him some more of the fascinating sights of Nepal, but that would have to be deferred. He knew that Lama was undoubtedly completely reliable, and his guide had sworn to keep what he knew strictly to himself, but secrets had a way of being discovered in relatively small communities. If it got out that he was a policeman, everything that he was at that moment hoping for could be blown sky high in a matter of minutes. It was a risk he didn't dare to take.

When he had finished and signed the check, he returned to the lobby to find his man waiting. He exchanged proper greetings and allowed himself to be led outside where the same little car was ready with the same tireless driver behind the wheel. Before he got in he paused and asked, "When does the Tibetan handicraft store open?"

His guide did not quite understand, but the client's wishes were always law. "It should be open now, sir," he answered.

"When do most of the tourists go there?"

"Almost all of them in the afternoon, sir."

Tibbs walked behind the car where they would be out of earshot of the driver. Presumably the man did not understand English, but that was far from a certainty. "I want to talk to Miss Langford," he explained. "I think she can help me. But I don't want to do it when there are a lot of other people around. I'd like to see her alone if it could be arranged."

The guide understood and became confidential at once; obviously the game appealed to him and he responded to it with careful enthusiasm. "She is sometimes off in the afternoon; also there are two other girls who can take her place. I can make arrangements."

"I'd rather you didn't do that," Virgil cautioned. "It should be made to look very casual, just in case anyone else is paying attention."

"I understand, sir! Suppose that we go there just when she sometimes leaves for the afternoon. Or perhaps a little sooner. Possibly you will have good fortune." His tone suggested that he had no doubt whatever of the outcome.

Tibbs considered that for a moment, then he nodded. "Can you find something to do in the meantime?" he asked.

"But of course, sir, there is so much to see! Please allow me to guide you. We shall visit the woodcarvers and a place where they make the bronzes for which our country is famous."

That suggestion fitted his plans well; as Virgil got into the car he determined to try and dismiss his primary mission from his mind for at least a little while. He had considered stopping again at the police station, but it was unwise to be seen there and if Mr. Lama had anything to tell him, he would have phoned. Until the proper time came, he resolved to make the most of his opportunity to see more of this remarkable country.

The morning was fascinating. He bought two things for his apartment despite the fact that he would have to carry them some twelve thousand miles back home and the bronze was quite heavy. When he was driven back to the hotel for a somewhat early lunch, he almost regretted the afternoon that still lay before him.

After eating he took a quick shower and prepared himself for his coming interview with the Australian girl. He had detected a steadiness in her that he liked and he felt that he would be safe in seeking her cooperation in just the manner he had planned.

By one thirty he was back in the lobby where his omnipresent guide was standing by. Once more he climbed into the very compact little car that was owned by the tourist bureau. This time he did not carry anything beyond his normal personal articles; he was literally empty-handed. He still felt a little odd without his familiar weapon.

The Tibetan community was even more fascinating the second time that he saw it. As he walked toward the plain little building that housed the sales room, the song of the weavers that he heard floating in the air was as exotically hypnotic as anything his mind could imagine.

Caroline Langford was in the showroom which was unfortunately devoid of customers. As Virgil walked in she gave him a delightful welcoming smile and came forward to meet him. That made it easier for him to make his request. "I want to ask a favor of you, if I may," he said. "Could you possibly spare me an hour of your time, or are you entirely tied up here?"

She hesitated for only a moment. "I think so," she responded. "Excuse me a moment."

She was gone only a minute or two; when she returned Virgil read his answer before she spoke. "Eileen can fill in for me. You remember her, don't you?"

"Yes, of course. Are you sure she won't mind?"

The girl shook her head. "Not at all. We're both volunteers, so it doesn't make any difference at all. Now, what would you like to do?"

Tibbs returned her smile in a way that made him, quite suddenly, a remarkably handsome man. "This isn't the best possible place. I have a car waiting. The only other place that I know is the monkey temple — how does that sound to you?"

Caroline nodded her acceptance. "I like it up there — the view is so wonderful. I sometimes go and sit for hours."

The guide ushered them into the car and then displayed very good sense by not saying anything at all after Tibbs had given him their destination. It was equally quiet in the back seat; Caroline sensed that her escort wanted to talk to her privately about something significant; therefore she did not force him into unnecessary small talk. In only a few minutes the car was climbing the hill on which the great stupa and the temple stood.

This time as Virgil passed the many waiting salesmen and girls, he did not have to offer any polite refusals. Caroline knew them all and exchanged greetings as they climbed. Once more the almost unworldly Katmandu Valley lay spread out in a spectacle that conjured up again the image of Shangri-La: if that fabulous place were to exist on earth, Tibbs knew, it would not be far from where he was at that moment. It would be somewhere just to the north, in Tibet, hidden away on the roof of the world.

When they reached the summit plateau and the base of the huge white stupa, Virgil looked up once again, and for a long moment, at the compelling, dramatic eyes of Buddha that seemed to be boring into his being. Wherever he went, whatever he did from that moment forward, he knew he would never be able to forget those eyes. There could be nothing else like them on the face of the earth. They spoke of the inner power of this strange land and of its potent mysticism that seemed to rise out of the ground.

They demanded and they were obeyed, and it seemed that it had been that way since the creation itself. Once more the spell of Katmandu seized him and despite himself, he could not shake it off.

He led the way over to the balustrade which offered an invitation to sit down. As Caroline joined him there he noted again the gracefulness of her movements and her femininity laid siege to his defenses.

"Caroline," he began, "there are some things I would like to tell you, but I would like them to remain, if that is possible, just between us."

"All right," she agreed. She turned an interested, waiting face toward him.

"I come from California as I told you, specifically from the city of Pasadena. It's a very lovely place."

"All of California is supposed to be beautiful."

"I only wish that it was. Now I want to confide in you that there is a reason for my trip here, but I haven't come to do anyone any harm."

"Why should anyone think that?" she asked.

"You'll know in a minute." He paused and looked out over the magnificent valley once more, drinking in the sight. He knew that he might never see it again, and the thought pained him.

"A little more than a year ago," he continued, "a young woman left her home in my city. She did it very abruptly and without any explanations to her family, so naturally they became intensely concerned. She had good reasons, however, and knowing what they were, I can understand her frame of mind — and why she acted as she did."

He looked at his companion, but she sat quietly, waiting to hear more.

"Unfortunately her disappearance, without explanation, created one of the most exhausting cases that the Pasadena police ever had to investigate. Hundreds of hours of work went into trying to find out what had happened to her. She was an adult, and therefore had a perfect right to leave if she wanted to, but because she was a very attractive girl who suddenly vanished, there was great concern that she might have been assaulted, or even killed. No word was ever received from her, which caused her parents more suffering than you can imagine. Her father is a man of great wealth; he used every resource he could think of to try and find his daughter, but he got nowhere."

"You said that she was an adult," Caroline interjected. "Then wouldn't they reasonably assume that she had her own well-considered reasons for going away, and leave her alone?"

"No," Tibbs answered her. "They might have done that in the case of a son, but a daughter is another matter. You understand that, I'm sure. It seemed entirely possible that something drastic had happened to her."

Caroline shook her head and her hair danced in the sunlight. "I don't see why there is so much fuss about the difference of the sexes. A girl is just as able to take care of herself as a man. She's just as intelligent, just as resourceful . . ."

She stopped, her eyes fixed on Virgil's face. He had made her do it, but she could not quite read the expression that had arrested her words.

"For one thing," Tibbs said, "a son wouldn't have had to face the major problem she had. She was pregnant."

"Oh." The quiet wind made the only sounds for the next few moments.

"Let me tell you a little more," Virgil continued. "You agree that all this is to stay strictly between us, and no one else?"

"Yes, absolutely."

"Good, because I need your help: that's why I'm confiding in you. The young lady that I'm talking about comes from a very important family. They are Jewish and I have reason to believe that the young lady herself wasn't too interested in her parents' traditional faith. That happens all the time, of course — people decide for themselves how they want to worship, what they want to believe, and I believe myself that that is a good thing."

"Of course," she agreed. "It gets away from blind obedience to a code that perhaps a person doesn't really subscribe to at all."

"Exactly. I understand that well, because when I was a boy, I had to accept certain standards and disciplines that I didn't and couldn't believe in. As I grew up, things gradually changed and now I live a much different life — and one I prefer."

Caroline reached out and laid her soft white hand on his

dark brown one. "Believe me, I understand," she said. "I know how it must have been for you in America, when you were very young. And you've triumphed over it — completely. I think that's wonderful."

That came so close to breaking the pattern of his thinking, he had to take a little time to compose himself once more. Even then, there was a very slight lump in his throat as he continued. "By now I think you know why I'm here. I believe that this missing young lady, whose name is Doris Friedkin by the way, may be here in Nepal. In fact, I'm quite sure of it. I belong to the Pasadena police, but as I told you — I didn't come here to make any trouble for her. All I want to do is to have a few words with her and know that she is all right and happy. Then I will go home."

"But you could still have her arrested — here, I mean."

Tibbs shook his head firmly. "No, certainly not. She had a perfect right to do what she did; that violated no laws. It was a little inconsiderate, I think, but perhaps she didn't expect to be gone as long as she has been. Technically she did violate some passport regulations, but I doubt if that would be pressed. She has a valid passport of her own that I have with me — to give to her."

"But you'll still have to report just where she is and all that, won't you?"

"No, in fact that would be against department policy. We would tell her people that she is all right and well, but nothing beyond that if she didn't wish it."

Caroline sat very still, thinking intently. When she had reached a decision, she looked up once more.

"Since it's that way," she said, "I think I know who you might mean. Can you describe her for me?"

"Yes, she is five feet four and a half, dark-haired, slender, and notably pretty. She is a rather quiet girl, but a very talented one."

"And you said that she was pregnant."

"Yes, that was her biggest problem, I believe."

Caroline swallowed hard. "Then," she declared very carefully, "I want you to promise me that you will do just as you said: talk to her, perhaps, and then leave her alone. And not give her family her address."

"You have my word."

Caroline clasped her hands together. "All right." She looked suddenly upward. "You know that Buddha is watching you."

"I certainly do."

"She fits your description, she is American, and she does have a baby. We don't tell people that, but we all know and you could find out if you really wanted to. Now, please, be very kind and good to her; she needs it so badly!"

"You mean Eileen?"

Caroline dropped her shoulders in surrender. "Yes. But you knew anyway."

Very gently, Virgil shook his head. "No, Caroline," he said. "Not her. It's you."

She almost laughed at him. "I'm afraid not," she retorted.

Tibbs did not look at her directly. Instead he looked up, once again, at the terrifying eyes that radiated such enormous power. Then he turned and looked out over the almost magical valley as he spoke. "You changed your hair very skillfully, and even your manner, but your voice remained the same and I recognized yours almost as soon as we met. Your accent is wonderful, it is a real accomplishment. It doesn't surprise me too much, because one of the things that I learned before I left home was that Doris

Friedkin is a very clever mimic. Also she has remarkable dramatic talent. I told you that she was very quiet, but I suspect that to some degree that was forced on her. She once entertained a group of her girl friends with a performance that no introverted, very quiet girl, could ever have accomplished."

He looked at his companion, but she sat very still and only looked at him. Her face revealed nothing.

"When I learned that she particularly liked books about the Far East, I began to think about this immense part of the world. India became a focal point, because she particularly read John Masters, and he is famous for his stories of India. And she also very much liked the music of Ravi Shankar."

For the first time, Caroline interrupted him. "So does practically everyone."

Virgil nodded. "I was thrown off for a while, until I found out where she had obtained a passport — and how. Incidentally, I covered for the very nice young lady who loaned Doris her dead sister's birth certificate. It was a very neat stunt, since the unfortunate girl whose name was used will never need a passport of her own." Virgil turned his attention directly toward his companion. "Incidentally, no one betrayed anything; I learned what I did through careful, painstaking investigation."

Caroline remained quiet.

"There was one more thing," Tibbs continued, "something not very important, but quite indicative. Doris Friedkin intended to go to India, I think, but she came instead to Nepal and found her new identity here. I can't say that I blame her; this place is incredible and I'm fascinated by it. But the India idea was apparently quite strong and deep-seated. I already told you that she read John Masters extensively. He has done many famous books, but one of the best-known of all is *Night Runners of Bengal*. It deserves to be, it's a tremendous piece of storytelling. I read it some time ago, but I still remember the name of his heroine. It was Caroline Langford."

The girl beside him folded her hands in her lap. "I guess it had to come," she said. "Sometime."

He took her hand in his. "Now you don't have to worry any more," he told her. "I like the name Caroline and I'd like to call you that."

Through careful self-discipline and established habit, she still spoke in the sunswept Australian accent. "Oh, please do that! You see, I don't want to go back — for so many reasons."

Her emotion broke and tears filled her eyes. Virgil produced a clean handkerchief and handed it to her. She used it and then sat as though the weight of deadly guilt was upon her. "I know that I did a terrible thing," she confessed. "And not writing home; I lay awake nights and thought about it. But Dad has so much money he can arrange almost anything; if I told him where I was, I would have to go back and live a life that I don't want. Maybe I will have to now anyway, but I don't want to!"

"I'll talk to your father," Tibbs said. "I think I may be able to win him over. I'm guessing now, but Eileen's baby is really yours, isn't it?"

"Yes. You see, we knew who you were. I saw a movie about you before I left home, and Gunther saw it too and remembered your name. He's the German boy who sang, with his wife. So Eileen offered to help me and we all agreed on that. How did you know the sound of my voice?"

"You made a tape once, at Pasadena City College. I had it put on a cassette and memorized it. I have it with me."

A little painfully she slid to her feet and stood holding onto the balustrade, as if for protection.

Virgil gave her time and then asked, "Is it a boy or a girl?"

She was suddenly defiantly proud. "I have a son," she declared. "A wonderful son! So they can't come back at me about my old religion. I'm going to keep him, and raise him, and teach him all of the things that I've learned. And don't ask me who his father is: I won't tell you that. We had real love between us and I wanted to give myself to him." She looked up anxiously. "Unless you already know."

"No," Virgil answered. "I don't. And I don't want to find out."

She took hold of his arm, almost pleading for his support and help. "Thank you for that," she said. "I'll never marry him; I can't and I don't want to — not now. Someday, when I do find my husband, he will want us both — my son and me. And that's how it's going to be."

"Let me know when the line starts forming," he said. It was calculated, and he knew that she would understand.

She chose to take him literally. "I'll tell you something. I've learned a great, great deal this year — more than you can imagine. I've learned to appreciate a man like you." She reached out and took hold of him as though he were her personal tower of strength. "Please, can we be friends?"

Only partly because she wanted him to, he took hold of her and pillowed her head on his shoulder. "From this moment forward," he promised.

"Till death do us part," she added.

She was warm, intensely feminine, and vastly appealing.

Virgil held her for a few seconds longer, then he gently let her go.

"When do you have to go back?" she asked.

"When I am finished. Not before."

Her chin rose. "Then you aren't finished! It will take you several more days to do that. Will you come with me and let me show you things? Will you come with me to Tiger Tops, and on to see the Himalayas — the greatest spectacle on earth? Please, *will you?*"

There *were* some things yet to be done, some questions still to be answered, some discussions to be held. He looked at the eager, hopeful girl beside him and then up at the demanding eyes that stared out across the valley. From where he stood he could see two pairs of them, and neither was looking at him.

"Yes," he answered.

17

VIRGIL TIBBS SET DOWN HIS SUITCASE, unloaded the pack-
ages he had crowded in his arms, and fitted the key that
would unlock the door of his apartment. When his way
was clear he picked up his suitcase once more, which
suddenly seemed to be twice its former weight, and carried
it inside. He felt as though he had just enough energy left to
go back and reclaim the things he had left in the corridor
outside.

He had been flying almost continuously for so many
hours — time had almost lost its meaning for him. Furthermore, it was upside down; his body protested that day was
night and night was day and would continue to do so for
days to come.

He went back the few steps necessary and picked up the
heavy package that contained his bronze statue. With his
other hand he once more gathered in his rolled-up Tibetan
rug and found enough fingers free to get hold also of the
wood carving. As he went back inside, aware of the musty
air that had been static during his absence, he wondered

how he had managed to carry everything at one time. He felt a great mental letdown; he was glad to be home, but in his mind he still had the fresh images of the greatest mountains in the world and of a distant kingdom that had given him some of the richest days of his life.

He shut the door and opened the windows to air the place out. Spring had not quite arrived in Pasadena as yet, but the air was not chill and the early evening was a pleasant time. He took off his coat and tie and looked in the refrigerator. There were only two cans of root beer and a six-pack of Pabst. He wanted some milk, but he did not want to go the block and a half to the store to get it. He compromised by opening his suitcase on his bed and taking out the most important items. Then he could put off his duty no longer; he picked up his phone and dialed the Friedkin home.

His call was answered promptly by someone who informed him that Mr. and Mrs. Friedkin were away on a few days' vacation. They would be back tomorrow afternoon. Was it an emergency?

With very little opposition from his conscience Virgil decided that it was not an emergency and said so. He gave his name and said that if convenient, he would call on the Friedkins the following evening. The person at the other end of the line recognized who he was and confirmed the appointment immediately.

Immensely grateful that he did not have to go out again so soon, he splurged a little and phoned an all-night grocery that delivered. He ordered enough to stock his refrigerator once more; then he phoned the station and told the operator that he was back. That completed his essential and required business. Now, for a few hours at least, his life would be his own.

He finished unpacking his suitcase and put it away. Conscious of the symbolism of that act, he stripped and spent a long ten minutes in the shower. He came out refreshed, dried himself off, and put on the deep blue dressing gown that Yumeko had given him. He opened his small bar, put some ice in a glass, and poured a measure of Peter Heering over it. The bitter sweet cherry taste refreshed his palate and gave him a little more sense of well-being. He put Debussy's *La Mer* on his sound system and once more consciously adjusted his thinking to the fact that his recent travel adventure was over. He was at home again and the routine stared him in the face. Once more he was a policeman.

The bell rang and he answered it. He stored the groceries where they belonged, put the half gallon of milk in the corner of the refrigerator where it was coldest, and went back into his living room. He made a small ceremony out of unwrapping the bronze figure he had bought in Katmandu and installing it in the place he had already chosen for it. He stepped back to admire it and felt that he had been able to bring a tiny bit of the far side of the world home with him.

He untied the Tibetan rug and placed it in front of his davenport. It looked extremely well there and added a brilliant exotic note that he was human enough to like. His living quarters were beginning to be a roster of his cases: on the south wall of his living room there was a striking painting of a nude young woman. It was not the chaste, distant type of nude with downcast, averted eyes; the subject looked boldly from the canvas with the full pride of her young womanhood, unashamed of the beauty of her exquisite body.

"Hello, Linda," Tibbs said aloud, and raised his glass to her. That ceremony concluded, he went back into the bedroom and reclaimed the precious jade that he had carefully hidden away. There was never any trouble in the apartment house in which he lived, possibly because a number of police officers lived there, but he had still taken the extra precaution. He restored it to its case and then admired the completed effect. To the music of the *Dialogue of the Wind and the Sea* he opened his mail, threw away three quarters of it unread, and enjoyed the remainder. Then, when his mind was ready for the treat of the evening, he called Yumeko. She was glad to hear from him and her accented voice was as delicious as fresh honey on a hot buttered biscuit.

He made a date to see her and then reluctantly hung up. Her birth had been a tragic accident, but one that he was intensely grateful had occurred. Her father had been a black American soldier, her mother a young Japanese woman. Yumeko had had a miserable childhood in Japan, almost totally rejected because of her means of conception, and her mixed heritage, but she had grown into a person of charm, poise, and beauty. Furthermore, she accepted his attentions and gave her own in return in a way that sometimes made him forget his own composure. Now that he was back, it was perhaps time to do something about that — if she would have him.

He knew that she would and the thought made him strangely, almost intensely happy.

He looked once more at her photograph, surveyed again his somewhat transformed living room, and decided that life was good after all. Then he went immediately to bed and welcomed the deep sleep that came almost at once.

Bob Nakamura got to his feet to greet him when he came into the office. "Welcome back, sport," his partner said. "How's everything?"

"Great," Tibbs answered.

"Quick — did you find Doris Friedkin?"

"Yes; we are now close friends."

"Wow! Virgil, dammit, you did it!" Bob was all eagerness. "Tell me about it — give."

"First let me get my breath," Tibbs answered. "Also I'd better let the lieutenant know that I'm back."

"Relax, everyone knows. You have messages. The lieutenant wants to see you. The captain wants to see you. The Great White Father wants to see you. Your popularity is unbounded."

At that moment the phone rang. Mrs. Stone was on the line. The chief would like to see Virgil as soon as he came in. He promised to be upstairs in five minutes and hung up. Then he turned to Bob. "Bring me up to date on the Kallman murder — fast," he directed.

"Very little that's new," Bob answered. "Billy Owens, the boy who sold his car and then took off, has been located. He hasn't been detained, but we have a close eye on him."

"I've got to talk to him," Tibbs said. "Right away. Before I see the chief, if I can manage it." He picked up his phone and talked to Diane Stone. After a short conversation he waited while she consulted the chief, then she was back on the line.

Reprieved until two in the afternoon, Virgil wasted no

more time. Armed with the address where Billy could be found, he took off in an unmarked official car and once more attuned himself to the freeways and the driving patterns of the Los Angeles area. He found his quarry without difficulty, working in a fast-food franchised stand. Business was nil at the time of his arrival, so he was able to talk with Billy uninterrupted for a good ten minutes. That was all that he needed. The very chastened young man, who had taken a considerable loss on the quick sale of his car and knew it, was no longer inclined to play games. He told the truth and did his best to purge himself of official police disapproval.

Tibbs was not too gentle with him, but he did promise that if Billy would continue to give full cooperation, certain other matters would be overlooked. He secured a sincere promise of no more tricks and then left; this time Billy understood fully the gravity of the situation, and Tibbs had all that he needed. He went back to Pasadena and allowed himself the luxury of a good lunch before returning to the station to face the chief.

Promptly at two he presented himself at the executive suite on the fourth floor and found that a party had been assembled in his honor. Once again his own inclination to play things in a low key came to the fore, but this time he had no choice and he knew it. He walked in, to be greeted warmly by Chief McGowan, who shook hands and invited him to be seated. He exchanged greetings with Captain Wilson, Lieutenant Peron, Sergeant Heatherton, and noted that Bob Nakamura had also slipped into the big office.

Mrs. Stone supplied coffee to everyone, symbolizing that the meeting was to be, at least to a degree, relaxed and informal. "Virgil," the chief said, "we've been waiting very anxiously for your return. You must have had quite an adventure."

"Yes, sir, I did.

"Now, did you find Doris Friedkin?"

Tibbs nodded. "Thanks to very good fortune, I did. I talked with her at length, settled a good many matters, and I can report, sir, that you can consider the case closed."

The relief felt by everyone in the room was apparent; it could almost be seen in the air.

"I made certain commitments, Chief McGowan, that I have to respect. One of them is that certain information I have must not be given out — to anyone."

The chief looked around at the small group. "I'm sure we're all willing to support you in that." He read consent on everyone's face. "Now let's have it."

"Concisely, sir, Miss Friedkin left Pasadena of her own free will and went overseas — to Nepal. There was an irregularity about her passport, but that has been corrected; she now has completely authentic travel documents and I strongly recommend that we let this matter lie."

"It's not in our jurisdiction anyway," Captain Wilson noted.

"Miss Friedkin is well, happy, and has taken up a new life, under a new name, that seems to suit her very well. She had well-considered personal reasons for leaving the country; her only real fault was in not letting anyone know that she was alive and well, and you know how much that cost us. But there's no law that requires her to write home, so, strictly speaking, she was within her rights. Incidentally, when I explained things to her, and what we had gone through here, she was most contrite and asked me to express her very sincere regret; she had had no idea of the trouble she was creating."

"Since she is now found, and since she left of her own will, then the case of Doris Friedkin is closed. You wouldn't care to look into the Tommy Bowman disappearance, now, would you?"

Tibbs shook his head. "On that one, sir, I wouldn't even know where to begin. And too many years have passed."

"I agree. Your time will be better spent, I think, if you can clear up the Nancy Kallman case for us."

"I believe I can do that now, sir. I had an interview this morning that gave me the last information I needed. Also, odd as this may sound, Doris Friedkin was able to help me materially in learning the answer."

Lieutenant Peron was puzzled by that. "But she left here more than a year before the killing took place!"

"That's right," Tibbs answered, "but she still had some things to tell me that I needed to know."

"I'm intensely interested," Heatherton said.

There was a brief interruption as Sergeant Orr joined the party. He had been out on a case and was delayed getting back. The chief brought him up to date and then nodded to Virgil to continue.

While almost complete quiet surrounded him, Tibbs began. "A little more than two months ago Nancy Kallman started out for the West Coast with three of her reasonably close friends — two young men and another girl. It took them a week to get here. They collected no traffic citations on the way — I checked that — and the trip was apparently uneventful. Normally, in circumstances of that kind, I would presume that some sexual activity would be likely, but since the Kallman girl was a virgin when we found her, she certainly was not involved in anything like that. Also, that tends to establish that she didn't go of her own free will down into the Arroyo Seco."

"Agreed," Sergeant Orr contributed.

"After her death was discovered, the car in which she had crossed the country was located and I went to interview the owner, a young man named Billy Owens. He appeared to be entirely in the clear. The car was properly registered to him, and there were no outstanding wants or warrants. Also he told a straightforward story that fitted all of the facts that I had at the time. He and his friends had stopped at Bob's on Colorado Boulevard to get something to eat. While they were there, they met and shared a large booth with some Pasadena kids of their own age. To that whole group Nancy stated that she wanted to stay in Pasadena and not go on to Venice. Whereupon one of the young men in the local party offered to drop her off at the YWCA or some other suitable place for her to stay. Nancy accepted and left the group in his company. Unfortunately, Billy told me that he didn't recall his name. I tried feeding him some names, but he appeared quite conscientious in rejecting them. Quite candidly, he fooled me; his statement up to that point had all made sense and I was inclined to believe him."

"We're all taken in sometimes," Captain Wilson commented.

Virgil continued. "It is an established fact that Billy had been living in Venice for several days when I interviewed him. I considered it highly probable that his story was true, particularly since his other two companions would automatically provide him, and each other, with fairly sound alibis for the most probable time of Nancy's death."

"Have you interviewed the companions?" the chief asked.

"No, sir, I'm coming to that. I instructed Billy Owens to contact them and set up an appointment with him for the next day. I deliberately gave him a good deal of rope because I wanted to be sure of his fullest cooperation later on. Also I already had their names and home addresses from the New Jersey police. Then I took one more precaution and asked Santa Monica to put a tail on him."

"Did he know at the time that Nancy was dead?" Orr asked.

"Yes, he did, and he expressed his regret very sincerely. Now comes the first major inconsistency in this case: I've already indicated that Billy Owens seemed to be entirely in the clear. Also I had checked with New Jersey and they reported back that he had a good reputation as a decent, reliable young man with a solid home background."

"I've known murderers like that," Heatherton interjected, "but normally that would carry weight."

Virgil agreed, and then went on. "Now get this: shortly after I talked with him, and before Santa Monica could act on my request, he apparently panicked; he rushed out and sold his car for half its value at the nearest used car lot, packed up, and split."

"Was the car in good repair?" Orr asked.

"Yes; it was a few years old, but solid. The car lot turned it over in forty-eight hours and got a price well over the Blue Book for it."

"Then obviously he didn't want to have his license spotted; that's the only reason why a kid of that age would part with his car when it was in good shape — particularly in this area."

"He could have been critically short of ready money," Bob Nakamura suggested.

Virgil shook his head. "I looked into that: he took more than enough with him and his father had loaned him some credit cards."

He paused, but there were no further comments. "We now come to a young man called Randy Joplin, whom I interviewed in connection with the disappearance of Doris Friedkin. He claimed to have been her boy friend, and at least suggested that he had been in love with her. He also claimed that her family disapproved of him entirely because of religious considerations."

"That doesn't sound like Herbert Friedkin to me," Peron interjected.

"By his own admission," Tibbs went on, "he was having a very active sex life with a variety of young women. He is definitely good-looking, and he has a lot of money to spend. Interestingly enough, despite his close relationship with Miss Friedkin, he claimed that he was never intimate with her."

"Wait a minute," Captain Wilson interrupted. "We're supposed to be discussing the Kallman case. I'd like to stay on that topic, if you don't mind."

"I'm on that topic, sir; hang in there."

"Go ahead; I'm sorry."

"Mr. Friedkin informed me, confidentially, that his daughter had been a rape victim and named Randy as the man responsible. That's not to go into the record and it stops here. No complaint was filed for the usual reasons, plus the fact that Randy's father is a good and close friend of Friedkin's. He has no knowledge of his son's crime — if he did, in fact, commit one."

"Damn few fathers would be that generous," Bob Naka-mura commented.

"I've got to add something here," Virgil resumed. "Without going into details, I don't wholly believe the rape story. Mr. Friedkin was perfectly sincere in his statement to me, but I'm not satisfied that he was in possession of all of the facts."

"I take it that you have information which he does not," the chief said.

"Yes, I do."

"Of a confidential nature?"

"Yes, sir."

"Then I'll buy your reservations on the assumption that they're well-founded. Go on."

"Back to Randy Joplin. For my interview with him concerning Doris Friedkin, I picked him up at PCC and took him to the Rose Bowl where he could visually see that we were entirely alone and not under surveillance. However, gentlemen, there was something very odd about our conversation: when it began he was very tense and guarded, although he was trying to appear relaxed. But after I made it clear that I wanted to talk to him about the Doris Friedkin case, his sudden relief was strikingly obvious. At once he began to talk freely — too much so, in fact. He literally bragged about his sexual conquests and even remarked that he was probably a damn fool to trust a cop."

"If Herbert Friedkin stated that this boy raped his daughter, then he bears looking into, even though you have your reservations," McGowan said.

"Perhaps he didn't actually rape her, but he could have put the blocks to her mighty hard," Orr suggested.

When it was quiet once again, Virgil continued. "Although I don't like coincidences, after the remarkable change in Randy Joplin's attitude when he discovered that I wanted to talk to him about Doris Friedkin, I began to think about the unknown young man who had volunteered to drop Nancy Kallman off at a suitable place to stay. Randy is both handsome and personable; he makes a very good first impression. He attends PCC, runs with the college crowd there, and is frequently in Bob's — which is a favorite hangout very close by. So it was within the realm of possibility that he could have been the one. Unlikely, perhaps, but not out of reason."

"Since he's an avowed cocksman, the possibility increases a little," Bob offered.

"Randy is very vain," Tibbs went on, "and quite egotistical. He considers himself a man no woman can resist; he made that very clear when he assured me that if Doris Friedkin wouldn't go to bed with him, she wouldn't accept anyone else."

"If you could establish any sort of a connection between Randy and the Owens boy, then you'd really have something," Lieutenant Peron said. "At the moment I like the Owens angle, because there is no logical explanation for his sudden departure immediately after you talked to him."

Virgil nodded. "That's how I saw it, Ron, so I began checking into the matter of phone calls. With the cooperation of the Chief Special Agent of Pacific Telephone, I investigated the possibilities of any calls either way. Unfortunately, the Joplin telephone, which is unlisted, showed no toll charges to Venice, or collect from there. There is no phone installed where Billy was living."

"Too bad," the captain said. "If it had worked out, that would very nearly have capped it."

Tibbs looked at him for a moment. "At that point I at last remembered something that a Miss Peggy Collins had told me, among other things: Doris Freidkin had had her own phone. The joplin family is very well-to-do. I went back to the phone company, apologized for my stupidity, and checked to see if there was a telephone for Randy Joplin at the same address. There was, and on the day of my interview with Billy Owens, there was a collect call shown from a phone booth in Venice. A booth half a block from the place where Billy was living."

"Wow!" Orr exclaimed.

Virgil pretended not to hear. "I got a picture of Randy and went to Bob's restaurant. The manager did not recall anything that was helpful, but one of the waitresses did. She is a very bright young lady, and decidedly attractive. She knew Randy all right, because he had made a strong play for her on several occasions. She had been on duty when the group from the East came in and she had served them and their new Pasadena friends."

"Including Randy?" Peron asked.

"Including Randy. She even remembered Nancy Kallman when I showed her the sketch. She described Nancy as tired, but still a very attractive and appealing girl."

"That's about it," the chief said.

"I have some more. Because she knew Randy so well, and his proclivities, she watched what was going on. At one point, according to her, Randy and one of the young men who had just driven in went out together, apparently to see the car. They were gone about five minutes; then they came in and washed up before they returned to the booth. That gave them plenty of opportunity to confer. So far I haven't established any previous contact between them, and I now know that there wasn't any."

Bob Nakamura took the floor. "It's simple, Randy got a load of the Kallman girl and decided that she was for him. He contrived to get Billy Owens outside under the pretext of looking at what was a very ordinary car and asked him for a clear track. Owens probably told him that it was up to Nancy, but that she didn't put out. To Randy that would be a real challenge."

"According to the waitress," Tibbs continued, "who is working to help her husband through dental college, when the party finally broke up, the Pasadena group left first. Randy lingered and paid the check, something that the others were quite willing to let him do. Then she saw Randy go out with Nancy Kallman and presumed that the girl was likely to be Randy's next conquest. It upset her, which is one reason why she remembers it so well.

"Now, gentlemen, I was at about that point when I left rather suddenly for Nepal and you took over. I thought a good deal about this case while I was traveling and some fresh ideas came to me. I discovered, for one thing, that the cases of the two young women, Doris Friedkin and Nancy Kallman, despite the interval of a year between them, were in many ways interlinked. Some of the same people were involved in them both. After I managed to locate Doris, and we became well acquainted, I discussed the Kallman case with her to a limited degree; she knew many of the people in whom I was interested and a lot about their behavior patterns.

"One thing was highly suggestive to me: she was very definite that Randy was never, even remotely, her boyfriend. They had not been out on a date together, and furthermore, she had never cared for him in any way. According to her, sexual conquest is the one great motivating factor of Randy's life and he will go to almost any lengths to add a particular girl to his scorecard. He tried for her in every reasonable way; when that didn't succeed he began a series of tactics that annoyed her excessively. He sent her suggestive presents which she returned. He repeatedly tried to get her to go to pornographic movies with him. He urged her to try marijuana, knowing that it is one of the few genuine aphrodisiacs. Finally, she actually caught him trying to slip something in a cup of coffee she was having at a college snack bar. At that point, she complained to her father."

"About time," the captain said.

"Further, Doris told me some of the things Randy had done to other girls when he was stalking them. In at least one instance he tried blackmail. He was absolutely obsessed and when he was rebuffed, he almost went out of his mind with frustration."

"None of this is at all funny," Chief McGowan said, "but I am reminded of the famous catalogue aria in *Don Giovanni*."

"The parallel is apt, sir," Tibbs agreed. "As a matter of fact, I had the same thought. To return to the case: when Randy left the restaurant with Nancy, his intentions were definite. Earlier today I talked again with the elusive Billy Owens. When I pointed out to him that he was risking being named an accessory to murder, he wanted 'out' with all his mind and soul. He then told me in detail of his conversation with Randy after he had been asked to step outside — presumably to look at the car.

"Randy had been inflamed with the idea of 'having'

Nancy Kallman; she appealed to him immensely. Billy, according to him, told him that Nancy couldn't be had and advised against his trying. That intensified Randy's determination and Billy, he claims, refused to let him take Nancy with him. At that point Randy went into his good fellow act, promising that he would only try to get acquainted and nothing more. He gave Billy twenty dollars and promised him eighty more if he was eventually successful. Billy overcame his conscience and took the money — an action he now bitterly regrets. He became a little clever and asked Randy how he could contact him; he then suggested strongly that the other girl in the party might be available. Randy supplied him with his own private number.

"Billy read about the death of the girl found in the park sometime later in the paper. Guessing who it might be, because Nancy had not been in touch as she had promised, Billy called Randy and was told to keep his mouth shut if he wanted to live. Shortly after that I appeared and Billy panicked. He had good reason to.

"As I see it, when Randy left the restaurant with Nancy, I doubt if he intended anything other than trying to make her — that was his MO and he wanted to carve another notch in the bedpost. But Nancy was a virgin and dead tired to boot. He didn't take her to the Y or to any other likely hotel. I checked. I suspect that he found some excuse to take her for a drive, possibly she had an address and he offered to show it to her. Then, I believe, he went into operation seduce and hit a stone wall. That inflamed him, his overdeveloped ego, and his strong belief that he could conquer any woman. Perhaps she tried to scream and he grabbed her around the throat. However it was, I nominated Randy to have throttled her, intentionally or not, and to have left her in the park. By that time he was probably thoroughly frightened; an egotist often reacts that way when things go against him — or her. After that, we know what happened.

"That's what I've got so far, but there is no eyewitness I can trace and without a confession, we might have trouble getting a conviction. He could plead that he did not intend to commit murder, and that may very well be true. However, I've also talked with a few of Randy's friends. One of them is a sixteen-year-old girl. Randy seduced her for her first sexual experience, and she will testify to that if it can be in chambers. So we have him cold for statutory rape, if nothing else. That's it."

Sergeant Orr, the interrogation specialist, was the first to break the silence. "His family will provide him with a good lawyer, of course, but I still think he will cop out. He's not the kind who will be able to keep his mouth shut. We'll nail him."

The chief took over the meeting. "Good work, Virgil — as usual. Gentlemen, I believe two very big questions have now been answered. For practical purposes it's all over and, Virgil, you can take a rest. You've earned it."

Tibbs quietly shook his head. "Not yet, sir. Officially it may be wrapped up, but I still have something more to do."

18

FOR THE THIRD TIME Virgil Tibbs sat in the same chair, holding a cup of coffee in his hands, his face deliberately composed and calm. As he waited for the maid to leave the room, he looked once more around him at the superb setting and realized how well it fitted the people to whom it belonged. The Friedkin home reflected the possession of great wealth, but even more it displayed the careful restraint of impeccable taste. It was beyond any possible criticism.

When the door had at last been closed, Virgil looked at his host and hostess. They were obviously anxious, but they were both too well-controlled to display impatience.

"First of all," he began, "I am most happy to be able to bring you some wonderful news: your daughter Doris has been found."

"Is she all right?" The words almost burst from Grace Friedkin's lips.

"Yes, Mrs. Friedkin. Since our paths crossed, I have spent quite a bit of time with her, and we have talked at length. She is very much alive, in apparently excellent health, and I believe that she is also exceptionally happy in what she is doing."

Grace Friedkin's shoulders twitched and she fumbled for a handkerchief. A second convulsion shook her and then she began to cry. The relief from the intolerable tension that had tortured her for more than a year was too great and her body demanded respite. Both her husband and Tibbs understood that completely; Herbert Friedkin himself maintained his own control only with a great effort. "You have accomplished a miracle," he said.

"No, sir — it was my colleagues in the police department, and overseas, who made it possible. They ran the interference and opened the way for me to carry the ball."

"You are far too modest, Mr. Tibbs, particularly when you said, 'when our paths crossed.' That's far too much understatement."

"No, sir, I'm simply being truthful. I have some more news when you are ready to receive it."

Grace Friedkin wiped her eyes and gathered her composure. "I just can't believe it," she said. "How soon will she be home?"

Virgil deliberately sat still and drank his coffee, allowing her time. It was her husband who understood first and put it into words. "She prefers to stay where she is." There was only a touch of audible bitterness in his voice, but his disappointment was obviously heavy.

"I'm confident that she will be back," Virgil said. "In the meantime, I have made certain other arrangements."

"Is she married?" Grace asked.

Before Tibbs could answer, her husband took the floor. "I think we are being inexcusably ungrateful," he declared. "For the first time — and at last — we are getting news about Doris, and we're quibbling about it. Mr. Tibbs, please excuse us, but you will understand."

"Of course, sir."

A moment later he was able to continue. "Doris is now living in the Orient," he told them. "She is working by her choice, in an organization dedicated to helping the destitute and the homeless. I can add that she is making a very significant contribution, and to people who are more than deserving of it. You have long been distinguished for philanthropy; now your daughter is carrying on this tradition. You have very good reason to be proud of her."

He stopped once more to let the information sink in.

"Now I have something else to tell you which will, I think, give you much additional cause for happiness." He looked at them both carefully and read their visible feelings before he went any further. "You have a grandson. He is a beautiful child, and appears perfect in every way."

Grace Friedkin gasped slightly. "So she is married!"

Herbert Friedkin glanced at Tibbs and understood. "That doesn't necessarily follow," he pointed out. "You remember what happened."

Virgil picked up that thread before it could unwind any more. "I don't believe it was a result of that," he said.

His hostess looked at him. "You don't mean . . ." she began.

Once more her husband came to the rescue. "Doris is an adult young woman, qualified to make her own decisions. As far as I know, she is quite normal. The mores of today are not those of the early Puritans. I think we have to accept that."

"Do you know anything about the father's . . . religion?" Grace asked.

"No, Mrs. Friedkin, I don't. That is one subject Doris didn't want to discuss and I didn't press her. She did tell me, quite specifically, that it was no one you knew or had ever met. She also added that it had not been a casual thing, but something in which she had been emotionally very deeply involved. A little later she did say that she came out of it and that it is now definitely finished."

"Is the child Caucasian?" Friedkin asked.

"Yes, sir, it definitely is."

He looked at his host who was suddenly mute with embarrassment. His face was flushed and he was struggling to find words. There were none, he realized that, and had the good sense to let the matter drop there.

"Has she enough clothes and things?" Grace Friedkin asked.

"Yes, as much as she wants or requires. She is standing on her own feet, and I believe that she is taking some pride in it."

"She comes by that honestly," Friedkin declared. "I'm hearing more good news tonight than at any time in my life. Please go on, Mr. Tibbs."

Virgil did. "Doris has asked me to tell you both that she now realizes how wrong she was in not communicating with you; she asked me to submit her complete contrition, and her love. In plain language, she was afraid. And she is asking for your forgiveness."

"You can reach her, of course."

"Yes, sir — quite easily."

"Then please tell her that our forgiveness is complete. Our relief, and joy, at this moment more than make up for everything."

"That's more than generous, sir. Frankly, I told her directly that she had brought you both great suffering and she would have to do a great deal to make it up to you. I also let her know that she had given our department an immense job on which we spent hundreds of man-hours of work."

"When is she coming home?" Grace asked again.

"Perhaps before too long. But only for a visit; she doesn't want to stay. She is very deeply committed to what she is doing and she wants to continue."

"Good for her," Friedkin said. "Now that I've had time to digest the news, I want very much to see my grandson."

Virgil set down his coffee cup. "You have just spoken the magic words," he said. "Doris has been terribly concerned, and frightened, over your reaction to her child. I made certain promises to her, some of them dependent on your feelings concerning your grandson."

Tibbs reached into his pocket and extracted a photograph. "This is quite recent of her, and the baby. You will notice that she has changed the color of her hair, which I don't think will disturb you."

Herbert Friedkin moved swiftly to his wife's side and together they shared the photograph. They studied it for a long time before either of them spoke, then Mrs. Friedkin said, "She does look quite well."

"It's a beautiful child, just as you said," her husband added. He looked up. "Have you anything else?"

Virgil nodded. "I have a letter for you both from her." He produced it and handed it over. "After you have read it, if you will give me your reply, I'll see that it reaches her as soon as possible."

Herbert Friedkin took the letter and then put it carefully down. "We will share this together after you have gone," he said. "We will want to read it many times over. Tell me, is there anything else you care to add? Anything at all would be monumentally important to us both."

"You will probably find a great deal in the letter," Tibbs responded. "I haven't read it, so I don't know how much. You are right; she is not married and when I last saw her, there was no one in prospect. She is presently known by another name which she chose herself, for reasons you will understand. If you will allow me, I'd like to add that I was captivated by her. You have a wonderful daughter and despite what she did, she loves you both very much. She said that many times over."

Herbert Friedkin stood up. "Mr. Tibbs, I repeat that you have accomplished a miracle, and I have no way of expressing our gratitude to you. It would please me very much if you would join our circle of close and valued friends. You mentioned a young lady; please bring her to dinner so that we may enjoy her company too."

Virgil rose, said his good nights to his hostess, and then with Friedkin started toward the door of the room. As he walked into the entrance hallway of the mansion, the striking Buddha was still sitting in its niche, its remarkable eyes looking directly at whoever stood before it. Virgil paused — his mind recalling too vividly the immense eyes of Buddha on the great stupa in Nepal.

"Mr. Tibbs."

He turned and faced his host.

"Where Doris is now — you mentioned a relief organization. In your opinion, do you think that a contribution from me would be appropriate at this time?"

"Let me check that out."

"A good idea." He noted once again Virgil's admiration of the Buddha and made a swift decision. "The statue is yours," he declared. "I insist on it, and it's not subject to discussion. I know the regulations, but I'll have a word with Chief McGowan."

Tibbs looked at him. "I'm most honored, sir, but I absolutely refuse."

"We'll talk about it later, then."

Virgil walked a few more steps toward the door and then turned. "I'm glad that I was able to bring you good news," he said.

"You certainly did. May I call you Virgil?"

"Please."

"Then call me Herbert. Virgil, you have given me back my daughter, and a grandson as well. I can't express my gratitude."

"There's no need, Herbert — it was a pleasure."

"For a brief while," Friedkin said, "I was terribly fearful that the young woman . . . who was found in the park . . . was my daughter."

"I fully understand," Tibbs answered him. "It must have been ghastly for you, under the circumstances. Because, of course, she was."

The industrialist looked at him. "Why do you say that? Doris . . ." He stopped when he saw Virgil's quiet, slightly tired, but notably intelligent face.

"Perhaps you recall our conversation, Herbert, when we talked about your former secretary, Mary Stepanik."

"Of course."

"You knew that she left your employ and went East because of her pregnancy, to have her child there. You were a great help to her at the time. But I couldn't help noticing that when I came to see you about her, you asked after her fully, but never mentioned her child. That suggested to me that you already knew what had happened to her.

"Secondly, you told me that you knew Nancy Kallman's father only slightly, but right after that you added that he was seeking a divorce from his wife because she refused him almost all sexual contact with her. You see the inconsistency: you would have to know a man very well indeed before he would disclose a matter that intimate and personal to you."

Herbert Friedkin looked as though he wanted to speak, but he said nothing.

"There were some other points," Tibbs continued conversationally. "After I had told you quite a bit about Mary Stepanik, to use her maiden name, you asked me quite abruptly if I needed the name of the father. Since I already had most of the other facts, you were obviously probing to see if I was aware of your position in that regard. Also, Herbert, when I first mentioned the murdered girl to you, you didn't ask me if she had been identified. You already knew. I'm quite certain that Nancy's mother phoned you the news, although I didn't attempt to trace the call."

"Is there anything else?" Friedkin asked.

"Yes, if you'd like. I have suggested that you already knew who Nancy Kallman was. Obviously you had never met her, but when I did tell you her identity, you sat still for several seconds with your eyes tightly closed. I recall that you said, 'Poor Mary!' but it struck me at the time that your emotion went considerably beyond normal concern for a former employee whom you hadn't seen or heard from for twenty years

"You are a sensitive man, Herbert, and you could not conceal your grief, even though you already knew that your daughter Nancy was dead. Of course this is a comment only between us. We have the man who killed her, so there is no need to probe officially any further. Off the record, please accept my understanding, and my deepest sympathy. I hope that your new grandson will help to make it up to you."

Herbert Friedkin did not respond to that. He shook hands and wished his guest goodnight. Virgil acknowledged the hospitality he had received, said the appropriate things, and saw the door close. Then he walked down the long concrete footpath to the place where he had parked his car.

THE PERENNIAL LIBRARY MYSTERY SERIES

Ted Allbeury

THE OTHER SIDE OF SILENCE   P 669, $2.84
"In the best le Carré tradition . . . an ingenious and readable book."
           —*New York Times Book Review*

PALOMINO BLONDE   P 670, $2.84
"Fast-moving, splendidly technocratic intercontinental espionage tale
. . . you'll love it."   —*The Times* (London)

SNOWBALL   P 671, $2.84
"A novel of byzantine intrigue. . . ."—*New York Times Book Review*

Delano Ames

CORPSE DIPLOMATIQUE   P 637, $2.84
"Sprightly and intelligent."
           —*New York Herald Tribune Book Review*

FOR OLD CRIME'S SAKE   P 629, $2.84

MURDER, MAESTRO, PLEASE   P 630, $2.84
"If there is a more engaging couple in modern fiction than Jane and
Dagobert Brown, we have not met them."   —*Scotsman*

SHE SHALL HAVE MURDER   P 638, $2.84
"Combines the merit of both the English and American schools in the
new mystery. It's as breezy as the best of the American ones, and has
the sophistication and wit of any top-notch Britisher."
           —*New York Herald Tribune Book Review*

E. C. Bentley

TRENT'S LAST CASE   P 440, $2.50
"One of the three best detective stories ever written."
           —Agatha Christie

TRENT'S OWN CASE   P 516, $2.25
"I won't waste time saying that the plot is sound and the detection
satisfying. Trent has not altered a scrap and reappears with all his old
humor and charm."   —Dorothy L. Sayers

Andrew Bergman

THE BIG KISS-OFF OF 1944　　　　　　　P 673, $2.84

"It is without doubt the nearest thing to genuine Chandler I've ever come across. . . . Tough, witty—very witty—and a beautiful eye for period detail. . . ."　　　　　　　　　　　　　　　　　　—Jack Higgins

HOLLYWOOD AND LEVINE　　　　　　　P 674, $2.84

"Fast-paced private-eye fiction."　　　　—San Francisco Chronicle

Gavin Black

A DRAGON FOR CHRISTMAS　　　　　　P 473, $1.95

"Potent excitement!"　　　　　　　—New York Herald Tribune

THE EYES AROUND ME　　　　　　　　P 485, $1.95

"I stayed up until all hours last night reading The Eyes Around Me, which is something I do not do very often, but I was so intrigued by the ingeniousness of Mr. Black's plotting and the witty way in which he spins his mystery. I can only say that I enjoyed the book enormously."

　　　　　　　　　　　　　　　　　　—F. van Wyck Mason

YOU WANT TO DIE, JOHNNY?　　　　　P 472, $1.95

"Gavin Black doesn't just develop a pressure plot in suspense, he adds uninfected wit, character, charm, and sharp knowledge of the Far East to make rereading as keen as the first race-through."　　—Book Week

Nicholas Blake

THE CORPSE IN THE SNOWMAN　　　　P 427, $1.95

"If there is a distinction between the novel and the detective story (which we do not admit), then this book deserves a high place in both categories."　　　　　　　　　　　　　　　　　　—New York Times

END OF CHAPTER　　　　　　　　　　P 397, $1.95

". . . admirably solid . . . an adroit formal detective puzzle backed up by firm characterization and a knowing picture of London publishing."

　　　　　　　　　　　　　　　　　　—New York Times

HEAD OF A TRAVELER　　　　　　　　P 398, $2.25

"Another grade A detective story of the right old jigsaw persuasion."

　　　　　　　　　　　—New York Herald Tribune Book Review

MINUTE FOR MURDER　　　　　　　　P 419, $1.95

"An outstanding mystery novel. Mr. Blake's writing is a delight in itself."　　　　　　　　　　　　　　　　　　—New York Times

THE MORNING AFTER DEATH　　　　　P 520, $1.95

"One of Blake's best."　　　　　　　　　　　—Rex Warner

John & Emery Bonett

A BANNER FOR PEGASUS   P 554, $2.40

"A gem! Beautifully plotted and set. . . . Not only is the murder adroit and deserved, and the detection competent, but the love story is charming."   —Jacques Barzun and Wendell Hertig Taylor

DEAD LION   P 563, $2.40

"A clever plot, authentic background and interesting characters highly recommended this one."   —*New Republic*

THE SOUND OF MURDER   P 642, $2.84

The suspects are many, the clues few, but the gentle Inspector ferrets out the truth and pursues the case to its bitter and shocking end.

Christianna Brand

GREEN FOR DANGER   P 551, $2.50

"You have to reach for the greatest of Great Names (Christie, Carr, Queen . . .) to find Brand's rivals in the devious subtleties of the trade."   —Anthony Boucher

TOUR DE FORCE   P 572, $2.40

"Complete with traps for the over-ingenious, a double-reverse surprise ending and a key clue planted so fairly and obviously that you completely overlook it. If that's your idea of perfect entertainment, then seize at once upon *Tour de Force*."   —Anthony Boucher, *New York Times*

James Byrom

OR BE HE DEAD   P 585, $2.84

"A very original tale . . . Well written and steadily entertaining."   —Jacques Barzun and Wendell Hertig Taylor, *A Catalogue of Crime*

Henry Calvin

IT'S DIFFERENT ABROAD   P 640, $2.84

"What is remarkable and delightful, Mr. Calvin imparts a flavor of satire to what he renovates and compels us to take straight."   —Jacques Barzun

Marjorie Carleton

VANISHED   P 559, $2.40

"Exceptional . . . a minor triumph."   —Jacques Barzun and Wendell Hertig Taylor, *A Catalogue of Crime*

George Harmon Coxe

MURDER WITH PICTURES   P 527, $2.25
"[Coxe] has hit the bull's-eye with his first shot."

—*New York Times*

Edmund Crispin

BURIED FOR PLEASURE   P 506, $2.50
"Absolute and unalloyed delight."

—Anthony Boucher, *New York Times*

Lionel Davidson

THE MENORAH MEN   P 592, $2.84
"Of his fellow thriller writers, only John Le Carré shows the same
instinct for the viscera."   —*Chicago Tribune*

NIGHT OF WENCESLAS   P 595, $2.84
"A most ingenious thriller, so enriched with style, wit, and a sense of
serious comedy that it all but transcends its kind."

—*The New Yorker*

THE ROSE OF TIBET   P 593, $2.84
"I hadn't realized how much I missed the genuine Adventure story
. . . until I read *The Rose of Tibet*."   —Graham Greene

D. M. Devine

MY BROTHER'S KILLER   P 558, $2.40
"A most enjoyable crime story which I enjoyed reading down to the last
moment."   —Agatha Christie

Kenneth Fearing

THE BIG CLOCK   P 500, $1.95
"It will be some time before chill-hungry clients meet again so rare a
compound of irony, satire, and icy-fingered narrative. *The Big Clock* is
. . . a psychothriller you won't put down."   —*Weekly Book Review*

Andrew Garve

THE ASHES OF LODA   P 430, $1.50
"Garve . . . embellishes a fine fast adventure story with a more credible
picture of the U.S.S.R. than is offered in most thrillers."

—*New York Times Book Review*

THE CUCKOO LINE AFFAIR   P 451, $1.95
". . . an agreeable and ingenious piece of work."   —*The New Yorker*

Andrew Garve (cont'd)

A HERO FOR LEANDA P 429, $1.50
"One can trust Mr. Garve to put a fresh twist to any situation, and the ending is really a lovely surprise." —*Manchester Guardian*

MURDER THROUGH THE LOOKING GLASS P 449, $1.95
". . . refreshingly out-of-the-way and enjoyable . . . highly recommended to all comers." —*Saturday Review*

NO TEARS FOR HILDA P 441, $1.95
"It starts fine and finishes finer. I got behind on breathing watching Max get not only his man but his woman, too." —Rex Stout

THE RIDDLE OF SAMSON P 450, $1.95
"The story is an excellent one, the people are quite likable, and the writing is superior." —*Springfield Republican*

Michael Gilbert

BLOOD AND JUDGMENT P 446, $1.95
"Gilbert readers need scarcely be told that the characters all come alive at first sight, and that his surpassing talent for narration enhances any plot. . . . Don't miss." —*San Francisco Chronicle*

THE BODY OF A GIRL P 459, $1.95
"Does what a good mystery should do: open up into all kinds of ramifications, with untold menace behind the action. At the end, there is a bang-up climax, and it is a pleasure to see how skilfully Gilbert wraps everything up." —*New York Times Book Review*

FEAR TO TREAD P 458, $1.95
"Merits serious consideration as a work of art." —*New York Times*

Joe Gores

HAMMETT P 631, $2.84
"Joe Gores at his very best. Terse, powerful writing—with the master, Dashiell Hammett, as the protagonist in a novel I think he would have been proud to call his own." —Robert Ludlum

C. W. Grafton

BEYOND A REASONABLE DOUBT P 519, $1.95
"A very ingenious tale of murder . . . a brilliant and gripping narrative."
—Jacques Barzun and Wendell Hertig Taylor

THE RAT BEGAN TO GNAW THE ROPE   P 639, $2.84
"Fast, humorous story with flashes of brilliance."

—*The New Yorker*

Edward Grierson

THE SECOND MAN   P 528, $2.25
"One of the best trial-testimony books to have come along in quite a
while."   —*The New Yorker*

Bruce Hamilton

TOO MUCH OF WATER   P 635, $2.84
"A superb sea mystery. . . . The prose is excellent."
—Jacques Barzun and Wendell Hertig Taylor, *A Catalogue of Crime*

Cyril Hare

DEATH IS NO SPORTSMAN   P 555, $2.40
"You will be thrilled because it succeeds in placing an ingenious story
in a new and refreshing setting. . . . The identity of the murderer is really
a surprise."   —*Daily Mirror*

DEATH WALKS THE WOODS   P 556, $2.40
"Here is a fine formal detective story, with a technically brilliant solution
demanding the attention of all connoisseurs of construction."
—Anthony Boucher, *New York Times Book Review*

AN ENGLISH MURDER   P 455, $2.50
"By a long shot, the best crime story I have read for a long time.
Everything is traditional, but originality does not suffer. The setting is
perfect. Full marks to Mr. Hare."   —*Irish Press*

SUICIDE EXCEPTED   P 636, $2.84
"Adroit in its manipulation . . . and distinguished by a plot-twister which
I'll wager Christie wishes she'd thought of."   —*New York Times*

TENANT FOR DEATH   P 570, $2.84
"The way in which an air of probability is combined both with clear,
terse narrative and with a good deal of subtle suburban atmosphere,
proves the extreme skill of the writer."   —*The Spectator*

TRAGEDY AT LAW   P 522, $2.25
"An extremely urbane and well-written detective story."

—*New York Times*

UNTIMELY DEATH   P 514, $2.25
"The English detective story at its quiet best, meticulously underplayed, rich in perceivings of the droll human animal and ready at the last with a neat surprise which has been there all the while had we but wits to see it."   —*New York Herald Tribune Book Review*

THE WIND BLOWS DEATH   P 589, $2.84
"A plot compounded of musical knowledge, a Dickens allusion, and a subtle point in law is related with delightfully unobtrusive wit, warmth, and style."   —*New York Times*

WITH A BARE BODKIN   P 523, $2.25
"One of the best detective stories published for a long time."
                                    —*The Spectator*

Robert Harling

THE ENORMOUS SHADOW   P 545, $2.50
"In some ways the best spy story of the modern period. . . . The writing is terse and vivid . . . the ending full of action . . . altogether first-rate."
—Jacques Barzun and Wendell Hertig Taylor, *A Catalogue of Crime*

Matthew Head

THE CABINDA AFFAIR   P 541, $2.25
"An absorbing whodunit and a distinguished novel of atmosphere."
                                    —Anthony Boucher, *New York Times*

THE CONGO VENUS   P 597, $2.84
"Terrific. The dialogue is just plain wonderful."   —*Boston Globe*

MURDER AT THE FLEA CLUB   P 542, $2.50
"The true delight is in Head's style, its limpid ease combined with humor and an awesome precision of phrase."   —*San Francisco Chronicle*

M. V. Heberden

ENGAGED TO MURDER   P 533, $2.25
"Smooth plotting."   —*New York Times*

James Hilton

WAS IT MURDER?   P 501, $1.95
"The story is well planned and well written."   —*New York Times*

S. B. Hough

DEAR DAUGHTER DEAD   P 661, $2.84
"A highly intelligent and sophisticated story of police detection . . . not
to be missed on any account."   —Francis Iles, *The Guardian*

SWEET SISTER SEDUCED   P 662, $2.84
In the course of a nightlong conversation between the Inspector and the
suspect, the complex emotions of a very strange marriage are revealed.

P. M. Hubbard

HIGH TIDE   P 571, $2.40
"A smooth elaboration of mounting horror and danger."
                                               —*Library Journal*

Elspeth Huxley

THE AFRICAN POISON MURDERS   P 540, $2.25
"Obscure venom, manical mutilations, deadly bush fire, thrilling climax
compose major opus.... Top-flight."
                              —*Saturday Review of Literature*

MURDER ON SAFARI   P 587, $2.84
"Right now we'd call Mrs. Huxley a dangerous rival to Agatha Christie."   —*Books*

Francis Iles

BEFORE THE FACT   P 517, $2.50
"Not many 'serious' novelists have produced character studies to compare with Iles's internally terrifying portrait of the murderer in *Before
the Fact,* his masterpiece and a work truly deserving the appellation of
unique and beyond price."   —Howard Haycraft

MALICE AFORETHOUGHT   P 532, $1.95
"It is a long time since I have read anything so good as *Malice Aforethought,* with its cynical humour, acute criminology, plausible detail and
rapid movement. It makes you hug yourself with pleasure."
                              —H. C. Harwood, *Saturday Review*

Michael Innes

APPLEBY ON ARARAT   P 648, $2.84
"Superbly plotted and humorously written."   —*The New Yorker*

APPLEBY'S END   P 649, $2.84
"Most amusing."   —*Boston Globe*

THE CASE OF THE JOURNEYING BOY   P 632, $3.12
"I could see no faults in it. There is no one to compare with him."
                                        —*Illustrated London News*

DEATH ON A QUIET DAY   P 677, $2.84
"Delightfully witty."   —*Chicago Sunday Tribune*

DEATH BY WATER   P 574, $2.40
"The amount of ironic social criticism and deft characterization of scenes
and people would serve another author for six books."
                    —Jacques Barzun and Wendell Hertig Taylor

HARE SITTING UP   P 590, $2.84
"There is hardly anyone (in mysteries or mainstream) more exquisitely
literate, allusive and Jamesian—and hardly anyone with a firmer sense
of melodramatic plot or a more vigorous gift of storytelling."
                              —Anthony Boucher, *New York Times*

THE LONG FAREWELL   P 575, $2.40
"A model of the deft, classic detective story, told in the most wittily
diverting prose."   —*New York Times*

THE MAN FROM THE SEA   P 591, $2.84
"The pace is brisk, the adventures exciting and excitingly told, and above
all he keeps to the very end the interesting ambiguity of the man from
the sea."   —*New Statesman*

ONE MAN SHOW   P 672, $2.84
"Exciting, amusingly written . . . very good enjoyment it is."
                                        —*The Spectator*

THE SECRET VANGUARD   P 584, $2.84
"Innes . . . has mastered the art of swift, exciting and well-organized
narrative."   —*New York Times*

THE WEIGHT OF THE EVIDENCE   P 633, $2.84
"First-class puzzle, deftly solved. University background interesting and
amusing."   —*Saturday Review of Literature*

Mary Kelly

THE SPOILT KILL   P 565, $2.40
"Mary Kelly is a new Dorothy Sayers. . . . [An] exciting new novel."
                                        —*Evening News*

Lange Lewis

THE BIRTHDAY MURDER   P 518, $1.95

"Almost perfect in its playlike purity and delightful prose."
                              —Jacques Barzun and Wendell Hertig Taylor

Allan MacKinnon

HOUSE OF DARKNESS   P 582, $2.84

"His best . . . a perfect compendium."
  —Jacques Barzun and Wendell Hertig Taylor, *A Catalogue of Crime*

Frank Parrish

FIRE IN THE BARLEY   P 651, $2.84

"A remarkable and brilliant first novel. . . . entrancing."
                                                    —*The Spectator*

SNARE IN THE DARK   P 650, $2.84

The wily English poacher Dan Mallett is framed for murder and has to
confront unknown enemies to clear himself.

STING OF THE HONEYBEE   P 652, $2.84

"Terrorism and murder visit a sleepy English village in this witty, offbeat
thriller."   —*Chicago Sun-Times*

Austin Ripley

MINUTE MYSTERIES   P 387, $2.50

More than one hundred of the world's shortest detective stories. Only
one possible solution to each case!

Thomas Sterling

THE EVIL OF THE DAY   P 529, $2.50

"Prose as witty and subtle as it is sharp and clear. . .characters unconven-
tionally conceived and richly bodied forth . . . . In short, a novel to be
treasured."   —Anthony Boucher, *New York Times*

Julian Symons

THE BELTING INHERITANCE   P 468, $1.95

"A superb whodunit in the best tradition of the detective story."
                              —August Derleth, *Madison Capital Times*

BOGUE'S FORTUNE   P 481, $1.95

"There's a touch of the old sardonic humour, and more than a touch of
style."   —*The Spectator*

Julian Symons (cont'd)

THE COLOR OF MURDER   P 461, $1.95
"A singularly unostentatious and memorably brilliant detective story."
—*New York Herald Tribune Book Review*

Dorothy Stockbridge Tillet
(John Stephen Strange)

THE MAN WHO KILLED FORTESCUE   P 536, $2.25
"Better than average."   —*Saturday Review of Literature*

Simon Troy

THE ROAD TO RHUINE   P 583, $2.84
"Unusual and agreeably told."   —*San Francisco Chronicle*

SWIFT TO ITS CLOSE   P 546, $2.40
"A nicely literate British mystery . . . the atmosphere and the plot are
exceptionally well wrought, the dialogue excellent."   —*Best Sellers*

Henry Wade

THE DUKE OF YORK'S STEPS   P 588, $2.84
"A classic of the golden age."
—Jacques Barzun and Wendell Hertig Taylor, *A Catalogue of Crime*

A DYING FALL   P 543, $2.50
"One of those expert British suspense jobs . . . it crackles with undercur-
rents of blackmail, violent passion and murder. Topnotch in its class."
—*Time*

THE HANGING CAPTAIN   P 548, $2.50
"This is a detective story for connoisseurs, for those who value clear
thinking and good writing above mere ingenuity and easy thrills."
—*The Times* (London) *Literary Supplement*

Hillary Waugh

LAST SEEN WEARING . . .   P 552, $2.40
"A brilliant tour de force."   —Julian Symons

THE MISSING MAN   P 553, $2.40
"The quiet detailed police work of Chief Fred C. Fellows, Stockford,
Conn., is at its best in *The Missing Man* . . . one of the Chief's toughest
cases and one of the best handled."

—Anthony Boucher, *New York Times Book Review*

Henry Kitchell Webster

WHO IS THE NEXT?   P 539, $2.25

"A double murder, private-plane piloting, a neat impersonation, and a delicate courtship are adroitly combined by a writer who knows how to use the language."   —Jacques Barzun and Wendell Hertig Taylor

John Welcome

GO FOR BROKE   P 663, $2.84

A rich financier chases Richard Graham half 'round Europe in a desperate attempt to prevent the truth getting out.

RUN FOR COVER   P 664, $2.84

"I can think of few writers in the international intrigue game with such a gift for fast and vivid storytelling."

—*New York Times Book Review*

STOP AT NOTHING   P 665, $2.84

"Mr. Welcome is lively, vivid and highly readable."

—*New York Times Book Review*

Anna Mary Wells

MURDERER'S CHOICE   P 534, $2.50

"Good writing, ample action, and excellent character work."

—*Saturday Review of Literature*

A TALENT FOR MURDER   P 535, $2.25

"The discovery of the villain is a decided shock."   —*Books*

Charles Williams

DEAD CALM   P 655, $2.84

"A brilliant tour de force of inventive plotting, fine manipulation of a small cast and breathtaking sequences of spectacular navigation."

—*New York Times Book Review*

THE SAILCLOTH SHROUD   P 654, $2.84

"A fine novel of excitement, spirited, fresh and satisfying."

—*New York Times*

THE WRONG VENUS   P 656, $2.84

Swindler Lawrence Colby and the lovely Martine create a story of romance, larceny, and very blunt homicide.

Edward Young

THE FIFTH PASSENGER   P 544, $2.25
"Clever and adroit . . . excellent thriller. . . ."   —*Library Journal*

If you enjoyed this book you'll want to know about
THE PERENNIAL LIBRARY MYSTERY SERIES
Buy them at your local bookstore or use this coupon for ordering:

Qty	P number	Price

postage and handling charge $1.00
_____ book(s) @ $0.25

TOTAL

Prices contained in this coupon are Harper & Row invoice prices only. They are subject to change without notice, and in no way reflect the prices at which these books may be sold by other suppliers.

HARPER & ROW, Mail Order Dept. #PMS, 10 East 53rd St., New York, N.Y. 10022.

Please send me the books I have checked above. I am enclosing $_____ which includes a postage and handling charge of $1.00 for the first book and 25¢ for each additional book. Send check or money order. No cash or C.O.D.s please

Name_____

Address_____ _____

City_____ State_____ Zip_____

Please allow 4 weeks for delivery. USA only. This offer expires 3-31-86. Please add applicable sales tax.